SHE'S THE ONE

WHO GETS IN FIGHTS

S. R. CRONIN

Cover design by Deranged Doctor Design
Editing by Goddess Fish

This book is a work of fiction and, with the exception of historical information, the events, characters and institutions in it are imaginary.

This is book is dedicated to Anthony Korahais of Flowing Zen with thanks for not only teaching me how to be healthier and happier but also for putting me in touch with the warrior within me.

And to those women with whom I practiced qigong over the years, with thanks for showing me how all ages, types, sizes, and shapes of women can find their inner strength. As I wrote this, I imagined all of us out there together, throwing rocks and tackling invaders as we joined forces to defend our realm.

Warning: You Are About to Enter Ilari

Welcome to the thirteenth century in a universe almost identical to your own. The one major difference here is the existence of *Ilari.*

Ilari (el ARE ee) is a small hidden coalition of principalities in far eastern Europe. It has never been conquered thanks to its natural protection and the magic of its people. The lack of outside influence means that much will be new to you. But fear not, you have tools to help.

A map of *Ilari* is located at the front and back of this book. The back also has a description of the twelve nichnas (tiny principalities) that comprise *Ilari*.

Ilarians do not use any variation of the Roman calendar, as Rome never invaded their realm. Each chapter starts with a picture of the Ilarian calendar. The darkened area shows when that chapter takes place.

Ilarians use nine-day anks and forty-five-day eighths of the year. Each eighth begins with one of their eight seasonal holidays. Details are at the back of the book.

They have some unique words with no English translation. Those words are also given to you at the back of the book.

On the last page, you will find a list of the characters you are about to meet.

All of this information is also on the website *Seven Troublesome Sisters* at https://troublesome7sisters.xyz/ and can be downloaded and printed.

Ilarians of the 1200s have contact with the outside even though legend says interaction with others used to be rare. Ilarian scholars know facts about world history and have some idea of current events beyond their borders. What they know sounds like what you know because the world outside of *Ilari* is like ours.

However, the world inside is filled with surprises.

Enjoy your visit!

The Map of Ilari

The Year of Immense Concern

~ 1 ~

The One Thing I Do Well

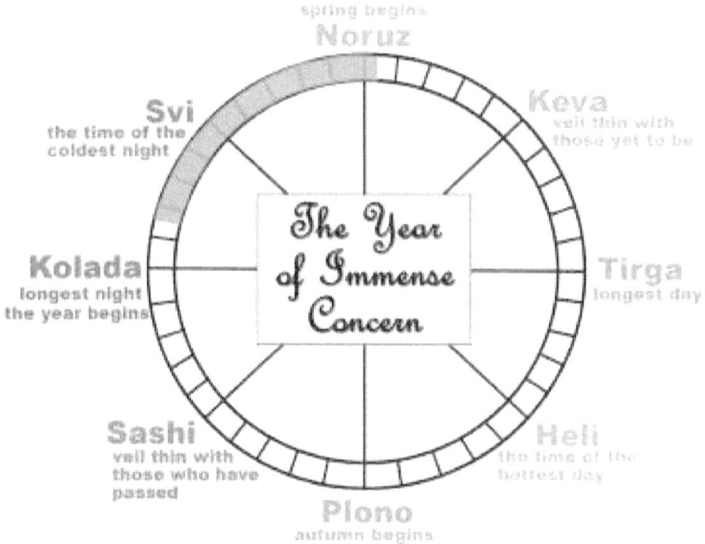

"What's your name?"

I pressed the point of my wooden stick gently into the softest part of his neck when he asked the question.

"Do you concede?" I responded.

"Of course I do. Were these real swords I'd be dead and we both know it. You fight well."

Yes, I knew that, too.

My opponent, a tall skinny lad with light brown hair, lacked the skill to bring out my best, but I didn't say so. He'd agreed to spar with me; it was more than many males did. And this young man from somewhere in Bisu had told me I fought well, *not* that I fought well for a girl. That earned him an answer.

"Sulphur."

"Huh?"

"My name. It's Sulphur."

He laughed and I pressed the stick back into his flesh.

"Hey, I meant no offense. But that is one odd name."

I shrugged. "I come from one odd family. Seven daughters."

"Wait. I've heard of you people. Your dad studies rocks?"

"That's us. We farm, too."

"And you fight. Are all your sisters like you?"

Not even close.

"No. None are like me."

"Then we've something in common. I've three brothers and none are like me either."

I stepped back, freeing him to move. As I dusted myself off, I surveyed the damage. I'd torn my dress in two places and covered one side with mud. My mother would not be happy to see another ruined frock.

"Thanks for the chance to practice," I said. "If I run into you again, maybe …"

"Sure. Any time." He laughed. "I don't mind getting beat by a girl if I can learn from her."

After I got on my horse and rode away, I realized I hadn't asked him his name. Well, Bisu wasn't far from my home. Perhaps I'd see him again.

As one of the oldest three daughters, a few anks ago I'd been gussied up in a gown that appeared to be made from spun gold. The seamstress said she'd hoped to match the color of my hair. I'd shocked everyone by chopping it short, but she insisted it remained my best feature. The dress must have cost a fortune and it was varmin uncomfortable. But because I and my two older sisters had all finished our advanced studies without finding a husband, my distressed mother thought it best to send us to the Kolada ball at the palace in Pilk.

She put Ryalgar, our oldest, in a rich red get-up that got the job done. An actual prince of Pilk took a shine to my academic sister and by the end of the evening a courtship began. My mother's eyes shown with joy when she heard the news.

Coral, my next sister, had been packaged in a soft pink confection that I think even she hated, and she'd landed with some oaf she despised. Me, I'd been as polite as I could be for as long as I could, then I'd taken a brisk walk around the grounds alone until it got late enough for me to retire to my quarters and get out of that dress.

Now, clothes were a problem again.

I'd torn more than my share of them and my mother's frustration at the state of my last ripped dress worried me. I'd already claimed to have been chased by a bull in Bisu, to have slipped and fallen into a creek bed in Gruen, and to have climbed a tree to rescue a neighbor's cat. I'd run out of plausible excuses. I needed special clothes to train in.

I'd never been good with a needle and thread, but I had two sisters who could sew anything out of almost nothing. One was away at school, so I asked the other for help. Coral made two pairs of strong trousers and a couple of long tunics with split sides from scraps she found. Modest yet functional, and they fit in my saddlebags so I could change in the barn.

****

As Svi neared, the dropping temperatures forced me to cut back on my workouts. Instead, I helped my father around the farm. Dad seldom asked his daughters to do heavy chores but I knew he appreciated it when we did. He didn't often ask his daughters questions, either, but as the wind blew through crevices in the barn on this cold afternoon, he made an exception.

"Why do you want to fight?" he asked as I set a broken wagon axle on his worktable.

When I was young, Dad indulged me by teaching me how to handle weapons and even sparred with me on occasion. He'd stopped as I grew into a woman, of course, but he'd probably heard about my begging men to help me with my training. I guess I had to be grateful he hadn't discussed it with my mother, at least not enough so that she tried to intervene.

"It's bad enough when a man has to fight," he said, picking up the wooden mallet he used for pounding joining cuffs together. He bent down, his grey hair falling forward, and slammed the mallet against the cuff a few times before he continued. "It's a grisly, sad business. Life dealt you a lucky card not having to raise a weapon to harm another. Why do you want to throw that card away?"

I hadn't thought of it that way.

"I've had to fight all my life, Dad. It comes naturally to me." I hadn't meant to say that, but perhaps he needed to know what went on when he was gone.

"No you haven't. Why would you say such a thing?"

I knew my answer would hurt him, so I tried to soften my response.

"You gave us a better life by teaching all over the realm. Mom had help in the kitchen and you had farmhands for the heavy work. We had, we still have, many things other families don't. I appreciate them."

He looked at me in surprise, but I went on. "You know Ryalgar stepped in and took charge of the farming things while you taught. Even when she was young, she kept things going here. And Coral, well, she became Mom's right hand, soothing whatever kid needed it."

"I recognize that. Big families ask a lot of their older children." He tapped the mallet against his other palm, giving his hands something to do.

"Yeah, well, while they were busy, someone had to keep the farmhands' sons from trying to do things they shouldn't with Celestine. And the neighbor boys from picking on Iolite. Seven girls? There were plenty who tried to push us around, Dad, and you never heard about it. By the time I turned eight, I was your biggest and strongest child, so I pushed them back. For you. I got you to teach me more every time you came home, so I wouldn't get hurt. Somewhere along the way, I learned to enjoy protecting others."

He gave me a look I'd never seen before, a look holding both sorrow and disbelief.

"Please understand; I don't want to hurt people. I want to keep those I care about safe. It's the one thing I do well."

The various expressions on his face coalesced into one, and to his credit appreciation won out.

"I should have paid more attention. … your mother never mentioned such troubles to me. I'm sorry, Sulphur. I had no idea."

"Don't apologize, Dad. Mom didn't always know about it, and we managed fine. I like who I am. I just don't want to pretend I'm some helpless woman, okay?"

"I understand." He chuckled. "You are *not* helpless."

It was the opening I'd been waiting for. There would never be a better time to ask.

"Then would you support my joining the army? It means the world to me."

"Oh Sulphur, please no. That is such a hard life for a woman. And I don't know how your mother would feel about …"

I interrupted him with a laugh. "Dad, you know exactly how she'll feel about it. Come on. My whole life she's told us 'it's just as easy to fall in love with a prince.' The truth is, I'm in no hurry to fall in love with anyone, and no princes are standing in line to fall in love with me."

I'd lost his attention. His thoughts had gone elsewhere.

"Maybe I *can* help. I know someone who'd work with you if I asked him to. He once mastered these, um, unusual fighting techniques." He paused. "You really want this?"

"It's everything I want."

"Okay then. If you're going to be a Svadlu, I want you to be a good one."

"And I want to be a good one too. I'll learn anything your friend will teach me."

Days later, Dad came through. His contact lived at a nearby farm and invited me to visit the next morning.

Winds from the north blew hard as I rode, reminding me the winter storms hadn't finished for the year. When I arrived, a tiny elderly man with withered skin met me at the side of the road bundled in blankets. He waved me down the path to his barn.

We spent the morning in the big empty building, with my horse at one end and a lone horse of his at the other. The two horses stared at each other while the man gave me instructions in a high squeaky voice that I strained to hear over the jangling of windchimes that hung inside the barn windows.

I followed his directions as best I could, squatting down then jumping up then balancing on one leg as I raised the other high behind me and stretched my arms over my head. The variety of exercises had no clear connection to fighting, but the workout he foisted on me was thorough, so I accepted his invitation to come back the next day.

As I prepared to leave, I asked him about his contacts in the Svadlu, and he told me he had none. He'd learned his techniques as a young man working as a mercenary in another land.

"Your father says you want to join the army bad," he said "Those who trained me would see such a strong desire as a weakness."

Hmm. Not many of those types in the Svadlu.

"Do you think my desire is a fault?" I asked.

He laughed, a high little laugh that sounded eerily like all the wind chimes he'd made from tiny bits of glass.

"No one gets anywhere interesting without some wanting. You seem like a nice girl, though. Be sure you're headed somewhere you want to go."

Strange man.

By the time I left, the wind had died down but the chimes still tinkled as loudly as when I'd arrived.

Strange place.

After a few mornings, I felt aches and pains in parts of my body where I'd never felt them. I'd experienced similar soreness before when I'd worked to get stronger. Apparently, I had places I didn't know I needed to strengthen.

The man promised my father he'd see me first thing each morning for as many days as I wished through the rest of the winter. I showed up almost every day for the next four anks and eventually his increasingly complex regimen of balancing and stretching felt less odd. By the time spring came, I heard his tinkling wind chimes in my dreams.

Then, I added his jumble of moves to my normal workout. Whatever challenges lie ahead, I liked the idea of being strong everywhere.

~ 2 ~

It's Your Turn

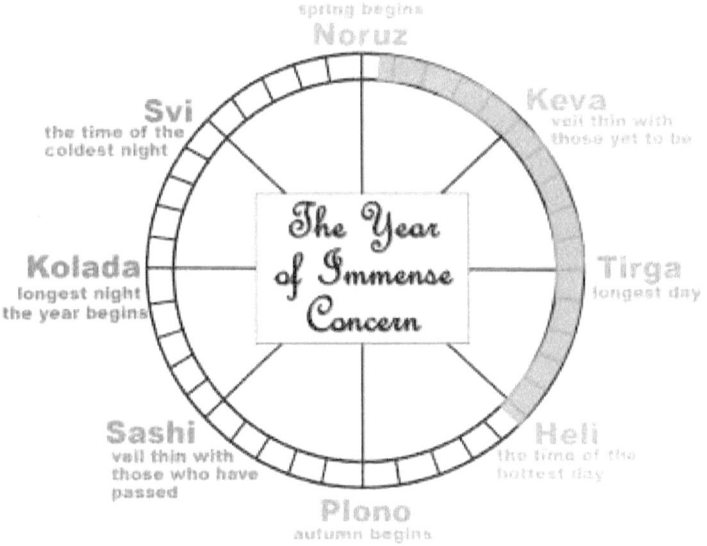

spring begins
Noruz

Keva
veil thin with
those yet to be

Svi
the time of the
coldest night

The Year
of Immense
Concern

Kolada
longest night
the year begins

Tirga
longest day

Sashi
veil thin with
those who have
passed

Heli
the time of the
hottest day

Plono
autumn begins

I'm sure most of Vinx assumed I lacked aspirations. Ryalgar had followed in the footsteps of my scholarly father and impressed everyone with her knowledge. Coral had returned home to teach while she waited for her prince to come. I'd heard every child in the school loved her.

But me? I had no obvious interests or hobbies. I didn't apprentice to learn a serious skill, as a few women did, or find some silly job in the market or at a tavern where I could flirt with men, like most single women.

No, I did chores on my parents' farm and tried to be a helpful big sister to the four girls who came after me, at least whenever

7

they came home from school and were around. Other than that, I couldn't be found. Where *had* I been all morning?

In early spring, after the last of the snow melted and the mud dried, I told my parents I wished to visit friends I'd made while studying. Then I rode to Pilk to learn more about joining the Svadlu. I knew they had a booth at the largest market there, often staffed by Svadlu officers who'd answer questions. I had a lot of them.

They accepted women, but what were the standards? Were they the same as for the men? Being a Svadlu provided status and a fair amount of pay, so they never wanted for recruits. How many people who tried to join were accepted?

The next day I found the booth. Officers wore cloaks of saffron yellow, but this man boasted a scarlet cape covered in regalia, identifying him as a Mozdol. My nervousness surprised me as I approached him.

"Hello, lass," he greeted me with warmth. "Let me guess. You've got a younger brother who wants to join us but he's too nervous to come talk to me himself. Am I right?" He seemed pleased. With what? That he induced nervousness in potential recruits?

"Uh, no. Sir. I was hoping to get some information on me joining."

"You?"

He looked at me more closely. Of course I wore a dress, not my fighting clothes, so I didn't much look the part, but he squinted at me anyway.

"You're tall. Well-muscled for a woman and you look to be in good shape. Have you ever held a sword?"

"I've been sparring since I was a child."

That impressed him.

"And I'll do whatever you need to me to. Answer questions about weapons, engage in fights, perform tests of strength, whatever you need." I spoke too fast in my eagerness.

"Slow down," he chuckled. "All that's good, but actually, none of it matters compared to what I'm going to tell you next."

He hesitated as if he wasn't sure how to explain this vital fact to someone as ignorant as me.

"You're a farmgirl, right?" He looked at my clothes again.

"Yes, sir."

"Well, the Svadlu are more of a city operation. We do things differently than on the farm."

"What do you mean?"

"I mean being a member of the Svadlu is a fairly good deal. Lots of young people want in."

"I know. That's why I've worked so hard."

"And that's good, but most successful recruits get in because they have a sponsor. You know, someone already in the Svadlu who vouches for them. Um, especially if you're, well, you know, a woman. Then it helps a great deal if one of us says you're up to it."

"But I can prove I'm up to it!"

"I suspect you can." The look he gave me held respect, but he stayed firm. "A sponsor makes the difference. Why don't you ask around? Surely your family knows someone who can help you."

He looked up. Several people stood behind me now, all hoping to talk to him. "If you'll excuse me …"

I rode back to Vinx dejected. I already knew my family had no contacts in the Svadlu and I had no idea of who I could turn to find some. Why did I have to know someone in order to get in? What stupid kind of way was that to run an army?

****

As spring grew warmer, I realized something had gone awry with Ryalgar's prince. She stopped seeing him and cried often, though in her pride she tried to cover her tears. My mother retreated into a stony depression. Then Ryalgar shocked us all by deciding to leave society and go hide in the forest with the Velka.

The Velka consisted of mostly old women who dealt with herbs and made potions. Superstitious types attributed all sorts of powers to them and some even claimed the Velka had once been capable of hiding our realm from invaders. I paid little attention to such rumors. Some folks enjoy being scared by magic, while others want charms to exist to rescue them from one problem or another.

One of Ryalgar's best qualities was her intelligence, so I had trouble believing she really thought the Velka could do much. Rather, I thought she just wanted to get somewhere new. It was her choice to make, of course, and I wouldn't have cared about it, except she formed one of the two barriers between me and society's expectations. As long as she was a spinster, no one looked too hard at me.

Yet, she'd made up her mind. On the holiday of Keva, we all rode with her to the forest's edge and said our good-byes, then watched her disappear into the trees to become one of them. To become not one of us. After that, in the eyes of many, I only had one unmarried older sister.

However, Coral loved teaching Vinx's young children, so I hoped it would be years before a man tempted her away. But one already had; I just didn't know it.

Coral found a prince of her own during the winter, and in her kind way she had kept quiet about her good fortune out of consideration for Ryalgar. Once that problem disappeared, out came the story. Near Tirga she told us about him and of how she carried his child. My parents began to plan a hasty wedding.

I knew all eyes would look to me next.

"It's your turn, Sulphur."

"Come on, even you can find a boyfriend."

"When should we start planning for your wedding?"

What was I going to do?

I had no idea. I had hoped to be in the Svadlu well before Coral married. Now with her pregnant and me facing this insane requirement of finding a sponsor, I could think of no way I could get in fast enough.

Not until I asked Coral about this great catch of hers.

"His name is Davor. He's so handsome." She giggled.

The handsome thing didn't impress me much, but I tried to smile appreciatively. In fact, I worried about her choice. Coral's hiding her relationship for half a year to spare my oldest sister's feelings meant none of us had the time to vet this man properly. A family needed to ensure the intended was worthy. And her unexpected pregnancy made matrimonial plans hard to stop. Only a little over two eights remained until the wedding.

"What nichna is he from? He's not a prince here in Vinx, or I'd have heard of him." In fact, I knew the names of all the princes in the entire realm and there wasn't a Davor among them. I wondered if "Prince" Davor had misled sweet Coral.

"I thought Mom told you. He's not a prince of *any* of the twelve nichnas; he's a Mozdol. When his troop skirmished with a band of thieves, he led them so bravely they held his Mozdolo on the next holiday. Being a Mozdol *is* supposed to be the legal equivalent of a prince..." She trailed off, looking for my approval.

"It is." This was the best thing I'd heard yet. I nodded in appreciation. "It's better, I think, because the title has to be earned. So, does he still serve in the Svadlu?" I kept my voice nonchalant.

"Oh yes. He says the military is his life. He's only eight years older than me but he already has a high rank. I think you'll like him."

Coral didn't understand. I liked him already.

"And he's from Lev!" she said.

"What?"

That part was unfortunate. Lev sat in the rolling hills at the heart of Ilari's prized wine region. Its grapes were worth far more than the simple grains we grew in Vinx, and the Levish flaunted their stylish ways. Many in Vinx objected to their frequent snobbery. Perhaps he was the sort of man who'd consider himself too good to be a sponsor for the likes of me.

Well, at least our household was better off than most farms. Thanks to my father's various teaching positions, our spacious house was well-appointed by Vinx standards. I could hope the handsome Davor wouldn't be too full of himself to find us, to find me, acceptable.

A few days after Heli, the mysterious man who'd managed to impregnate my sister despite the Velka's best herbs finally came to call at our farm.

I knew I was tall for a woman, with big muscles and big breasts, so I was used to men looking at me with a combination of interest and confusion. My blonde hair, cut short for convenience, bewildered them too.

When Davor met me, he gave me the same baffled look I'd become used to, then told Coral he couldn't believe we were sisters. Though her fine red hair and soft, almost chubby curves were all her own, the truth was each of us seven girls were cut from different cloths.

Coral hadn't lied about him. He *was* handsome, with a head full of thick dark hair and a charming smile. He was personable as well. He complimented my mother and all my sisters and then he tried to engage in conversation with every one of us. I knew plenty of men who wouldn't make such an effort with women.

The more I warmed to him, and he to me, the more I realized my hopes were reasonable. Davor wasn't going to be some brother-in-law from Lev I'd have to tolerate. He was going to be the single best chance I'd ever have for achieving my dream in life. And, my sister was happily pregnant with his child. Could it get any better?

"So, Sulphur, what are your plans?" he asked me as Coral placed after-meal sweets on the table. I tried not to smile too much.

"I'm off to visit my oldest sister, Ryalgar, in a few anks."

"Oh yes. She the one who lives in the forest with the Velka, right?"

He didn't sound condescending about the Velka, like many military types. Another point for him.

"She joined them only two eighths ago. I'm sure Coral told you the relationship with the man she cared for fell apart. I guess she thought being a witch in the forest was her next best option."

I noticed my mother's expression had gone cold. For some reason, Mom disliked the Velka, and any mention of Ryalgar's decision made her visibly tense.

"It'll be my first time to visit her, and I'll be bringing her back to our house."

"I didn't realize the women were allowed to leave like that."

Coral chimed in. "Of course they are. They just don't want to very often. I went to see her a few anks ago and it's so much nicer than I expected. She seems happy." Coral glanced at our mom. Mom said nothing. "And …. the reason she's coming here is for our wedding." Coral glowed at the thought, or maybe it was just the flush of being with child. Davor turned back to me.

"And what do you plan to do after this wedding?"

"Um. I have some ideas. Maybe I can discuss them with you in more detail later?"

Mom had gotten up to check on something in the kitchen, but I noticed my dad's expression. He'd been quiet all evening, not warming to Davor like the rest of us, but he perked up at my mention of having plans. I wondered if he'd heard about this sponsor thing and guessed how I wanted Davor to be of use to me.

I decided to broach the subject of joining the Svadlu with Davor the next morning after breakfast and include my dad in the conversation. I rose early, excited to put my plan in action. I pulled on my clothes as fast as I could and almost ran into the kitchen, expecting to see our guest and my family gathering around the table. But Coral was nowhere to be seen, and my father was already out in the fields working.

"Where's Davor?"

"He left at dawn," my mother answered as she set more food on the table. "I sent him off with apples and pastries because he had to be in Pilk by late morning. What a nice man. It's a shame he couldn't stay longer. Are you hungry?"

~ 3 ~

Acting on Instinct

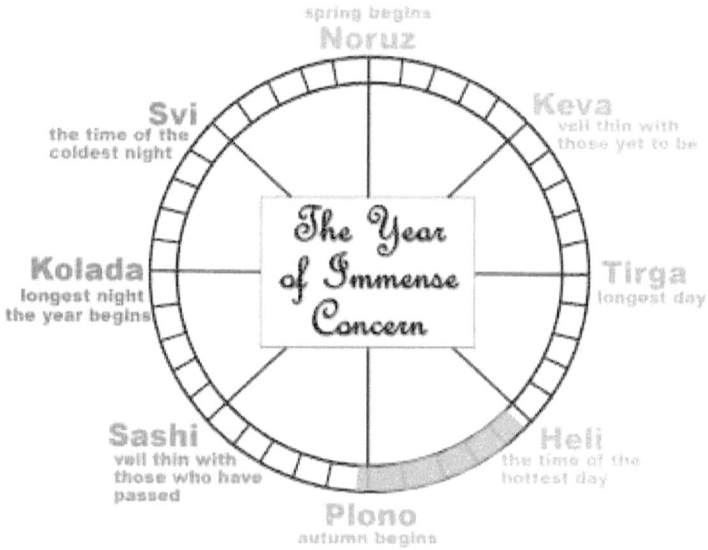

I hoped Davor would return soon, but he didn't. Weren't there arrangements to be made for the wedding? For their life together afterward? Didn't he want to spend time with his betrothed?

When I asked Coral about his absence, she turned serious and changed the subject.

"You must know about this military threat that looms over Ilari."

I did. For nearly a year now, rumors had circulated about a horde of invaders coming from the mountains to the east. Word was they fought from horseback, swarming into places and taking over before the surprised victims could gather their weapons.

Some said they only wanted tribute, taking a small amount of farmed goods to supplement the bleak diet provided by their own cold mountains. Others said they demanded a near slavery that no realm should tolerate. Some reported these invaders burned everything to the ground, indiscriminately killing the helpless and harmless along with the soldiers.

The lack of consistent information had turned them into a frightening monster of mythical proportions. Yet, the reports all agreed on one point. They moved further westward every winter and soon we'd be in their path.

"Yes. I know of the Mongol threat. Ilari could face a tough challenge this coming winter or next."

"The Svadlu especially," she said. "They already take this quite seriously."

"As well they should."

I considered this threat to be an added incentive for joining soon. If I got trained and put into a fighting unit, I'd have a chance to help Ilari.

"Davor is a key part of this effort."

"Really?"

"Yes. He's been tasked with training the soldiers to meet this challenge. It's why he can't leave Pilk now, with so much happening."

Well, this did make sense. I had no idea my hopeful sponsor bore such a responsibility.

"When will you see him again?"

I noticed the sadness on Coral's face. Indeed, being the wife of a soldier was no easy thing.

"Probably not until the wedding."

"I'm so sorry to hear that." I meant it for her, of course. This should have been a happier time in her life but to be honest, I was sad for me as well, knowing I had nearly an eighth to wait before I could ask this stranger the question on which my entire life hinged.

Then, I saw the advantages of asking for an important favor around such an auspicious time. Doubtless Davor would be at his happiest and eager to please his new wife's family. Maybe it was lucky I hadn't had the opportunity to ask sooner. I couldn't imagine a groom saying no to such a reasonable request from a new sister-in-law.

First, though, I had to go fetch Ryalgar from her new home and bring her back to our farmhouse so she could attend Coral's wedding. I thought of the Velka as a sad group of older women who hid from life and had little, huddling together in the trees as they made potions and lotions to sell at the many markets throughout Ilari.

So, I was surprised when the small donkey I'd been given to ride through the thick vegetation entered a large clearing. In the center sat a well-constructed and unusually attractive massive stone lodge. My sister lived here? Perhaps I'd underestimated her decision.

She greeted me with a happy glow. During a feast held in a huge room filled with candlelight, she brushed aside invitations for social gatherings later in the evening so she could spend time with me. We hadn't hung around much growing up, so I was flattered.

After dinner, when we retired to Ryalgar's room, I got to know her new best friend, Joli, a sturdy woman with dark hair cut above her shoulders. She came from the forests of Zur and had Ryalgar's odd talent for moving objects without touching them. When my hair fell repeatedly in my face, I blamed Ryalgar and turned to her, annoyed, but Joli laughed and confessed she'd been joking around with me.

"I'm not nearly as good as Joli is. At least not yet," Ryalgar said. I admit the "not yet" part got my attention. I'd seen Ryalgar deflect smoke away from her as we grew up and always thought of her skill as a barely useful quirk. At a more advanced level, though, this ability could be helpful in a fight. Did Ryalgar have any idea? She probably didn't.

"Everyone here develops whatever talents they have," she added and the Velka became more interesting than I'd once thought.

The next day, I had the rather odd experience of meeting my grandmother. Odd because I believed she died soon after I was born, but my parents had lied about her. She'd run away to the Velka instead, and I guess calling her dead was easier for them.

"You've got your own path," she said as we shared lunch. "You're a unique kind of human, Sulphur, and I've always cheered you on." It felt strange knowing an unseen older relative had followed the ups and downs of my life, but the woman was so supportive of my goals it was hard to object. The one piece of grandmotherly advice she gave me was to stop hiding my ambitions to be a warrior.

"Your time has come. Ilari needs you. Don't be shy."

Funny, no one else had *ever* accused me of being shy. But I was, sometimes, inside. Perhaps this estranged grandmother understood me better than others.

****

Once I had Ryalgar safely back at the farm, I tried to stay as far as possible from all the harried wedding preparations. I wanted this celebration to go well for Coral and for my family, of course, but my own situation left me too nervous to be as helpful as I should have been.

Given I'd had anks to think about it, I'd obsessed over exactly when to ask Davor for this favor. I'd decided that, despite my anxiousness, when he first arrived was not a good time. He needed to focus on Coral and get up to speed on the wedding plans. Then his own family and friends would be arriving and he needed to pay attention to them, making sure they got settled in and comfortable.

However, if I waited until the day after the marriage, he might surprise me and leave again before I spoke to him. I didn't want to make the same mistake twice.

That left his wedding day. It wasn't a bad choice. He'd be in the best of moods then and would surely welcome an added chance to forge a positive relationship with a new in-law. It was as perfect as I could hope for.

****

Although Plono is the first day of autumn, the weather usually stays warm until it has passed. Coral's wedding day was no exception. It held the heat of summer, and as we got ready in the morning we dabbed at our faces and squirmed in the discomfort of our fancy clothes. I hoped for an afternoon breeze.

We rode as a group to the place my parents had rented, and I stayed near the back, making small talk with my twin sisters. Only a year and a half younger than I, they'd recently finished their advanced studies and neither had a potential husband, at least not one they'd told anyone about.

I sat with them throughout the ceremony. I'd always considered Vinx's customary exchange of vows to be quick, but Coral and Davor's went on forever. Perhaps it was my nervousness, or perhaps it was just the heat.

Out of respect for Coral, I'd decided to not only wait until the ceremony ended but also to wait until the dinner finished. Nobody likes to be interrupted when they eat.

Olivine usually had little to say but as we enjoyed the traditional wedding pies stuffed with game and grains, her bright eyes shown as she talked of her paintings. This sister had a passion for something too, even if her something differed from mine.

After the meal, Celestine got up from our table to perform a song for the newlyweds. Her long fingers flew over her psaltery and her honey-tinged voice brought tears to the eyes of many.

"She wrote that song for Coral and Davor," Olivine said, reminding me that Celestine hid an uncommon amount of talent under her fascination with clothes and friends. Between the two of them, the twins managed to keep me calm and distracted.

Then I waited while the bride and groom observed the little traditions people love. I didn't want to take away from a single moment that mattered to Coral because she deserved all the happiness this day could bring. The problem was that by the time the customary fluff ended, everyone had consumed a good bit of wine and ale, including me and the groom.

I didn't want to just barge up to their table, so I watched him as the sun began to set. When he finally wandered away, I jumped up and I ran after him. I knew he probably sought the outhouse, but I didn't realize how much that would reduce his patience.

"Davor! Can I have a word?" I sounded confident, which was good because I shook inside.

"A quick one," he laughed. "I have to piss something awful."

The heat had encouraged drinking more ale than normal, and I should have suggested we talk after he relieved himself, but I worried he'd forget about me.

"I have a favor to ask of you." I charged ahead, ignoring the slur in his words telling me I wasn't getting him at his best.

"Sorry," he laughed. He hitched his pants, giving his crotch a pull. "I don't sleep with my wife's sisters."

I'd heard this crude sort of joke often enough, but even drunk I didn't expect it from him. I'm sure my face flushed, and my embarrassment pushed me on.

"I want you to sponsor me. Please. To join the Svadlu."

"What? You? Me? Are you nuts?" The liquor didn't enhance his tact. "Women don't belong in the army. I don't know why they let them in. It never comes to any good when they do."

In retrospect, I shouldn't have argued with him. But in my defense, I had been drinking, too. More than usual, hoping the extra ale would calm my nerves as well as cool me down.

"I've trained hard. I'm a good fighter, and I know what I'd be signing on for. I'd do you proud. I promise."

I stepped in between him and the path to the outhouse as I spoke. That was my worst decision, but again, I wasn't thinking clearly. He stepped forward to push me to one side and get on to his destination, perhaps more desperate to reach it than I realized.

It should have been fine. His push was gentle and no harm would have come from it, but after all that time practicing, I responded to his shove without thinking. So many repetitions had made it instinctual. I shoved back.

He hit the ground, and wisps of dust flew up all around him as he landed. With a gasp of pain, his bladder let loose. I stood speechless as he pissed his pants and the ground all around him.

"You filthy freak!" He snarled at me as he lay in the dirt, his lower half soaked in his own urine. "Look what you made me do and in my wedding clothes."

"I'll find you more clothes," I offered. "I can make this right. I promise. Give me a few minutes. Then, can we talk about this?"

"No, we cannot talk about *this*. Ever. Your answer isn't no, it's a prucking cartload full of goat scump no. Don't ever bring it up again."

He stood up to his full height, pissed pants and all, and stared at me. "Go get one of my chums to come to the outhouse to help me. Now. And if you ever mention this to anyone else, I swear I'll find a way to have someone cut your throat. Do you understand?"

I understood. I'd just blown the biggest opportunity of my life, and it didn't look like there was any way to undo it.

"Now get away from me!" he said as turned and headed to the outhouse he no longer needed.

~ 4 ~

Always a Way

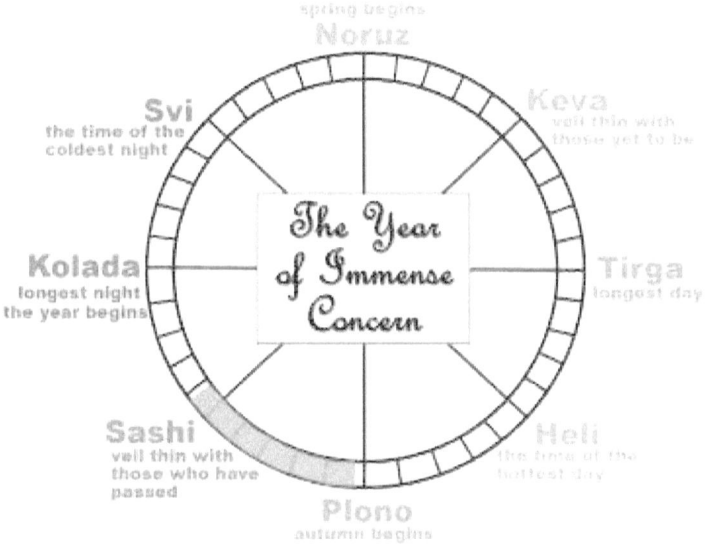

I barely spoke to anyone for the next two anks, and the worst of it was no one noticed. Getting Coral moved into her new house absorbed my mother's attention while my dad focused on getting in the crop of feed oats before the weather began to turn.

When Ryalgar left a few days after the ceremony, they looked for me to escort her back to the forest. Olivine handled it when no one could find me to do it.

All four of my younger sisters busied themselves adjusting to the new family order and wondering what would happen next. Our youngest two returned to school two days after the wedding, while the twins settled back into the lives they created as unmarried young women with artistic pursuits. I guessed they both had lovers they'd kept hidden to spare my feelings in much the same way Coral had kept her relationship with Davor quiet until Ryalgar left.

If I could do nothing else, I had to stop this nonsense. Unlike Ryalgar, I had no desire to marry, and I didn't think I ever would. Marriage didn't seem compatible with the life of a soldier, I found most domestic chores boring beyond belief, and I had no desire to raise a child. So, my younger sisters needed to get on with their lives, and I had to find a way to make a graceful exit from a world that didn't appear to have a place for a woman like me.

The not-having-a-place-for-me thing stung, to be honest, and after an ank or two it became all I could focus on. As the days shortened, the feeling grew until it crowded out everything else. I didn't eat, I couldn't sleep, and I considered ending my life. I'm not proud of the fact, but it was easy enough to conclude the whole family would be better off without the problem of what to do with Sulphur.

But I couldn't do it. I couldn't even get myself to focus on a way of doing it. Oddly enough, I had Ryalgar and the Mongols to thank for it.

When I'd been in the forest, Ryalgar and I discussed these thieves from the east. I'd confided in her about my dreams of joining the Svadlu and discovered she knew more about the dangers our realm faced than I'd have guessed. She didn't want to hide in the forest while others raided our homeland, and she sought her own way to help protect Ilari.

She and I agreed our realm would need all the fighters it could get. So, the idea of having potential soldiers, good soldiers, die by their own hand before the battle began made no sense to me, even amid my despondency. For all that I wanted to force everyone, especially Davor, to feel guilty about my lack of choices, I also didn't want my life to end stupidly. I wanted my life to end in glory, dying for those I loved. Or perhaps not dying at all, at least not for a long while

So I held on tight to the idea that Ilari might need me, despite everything, and that bit of light got me thru the darkest of those times.

****

22

The day after my father finished putting the hay from the feed oats into storage, he headed off to teach a class for two anks at one of the schools in Pilk. I knew he'd want to discuss my future when he returned, and I had to get away from the farm before that happened. Everything that had transpired between Davor and me -- Davor's crude joke, the urine everywhere – left me too embarrassed to tell my father. Even the memory of it made me cringe.

Maybe this would have gone differently if I'd talked to my dad about a sponsorship first. Did Dad know about it? Even if not, did he have friends who could have sponsored me instead? The little man with the windchimes didn't have contacts in the Svadlu, but perhaps other people Dad knew did.

But I hadn't gone that route and now, with someone as important as Davor as an avowed enemy, I worried no sponsor could make my life in the Svadlu bearable. If I did get in, would Davor manage to get my throat slit just so he wouldn't have to look at me? It seemed possible.

I had to get away. But where?

I had no close friends in Vinx, only the boys who'd tolerated me growing up, letting me spend time with them because it was easier than shooing me away. I'd lost touch with my friends from school, who I'd never been that close to anyway.

I considered visiting Ryalgar but worried she or my grandmother might pressure me to stay in the forest if they figured out how hopeless I felt. Impressive as the Velka were, my place wasn't there.

So. I couldn't go into the forest. Or stay here. What choice did that leave?

The only other place I *could* go was to the house of the man who hated me. I packed what I needed for several days and set off, so I could spend time with his new wife.

If you'd have asked anyone which sister was needier, Coral or me, I'm sure they'd have picked Coral. She cried more often and took things more personally. But they'd have been wrong, at least during the two anks I spent at her new house.

Right after the wedding Davor returned to Pilk and his role in the Svadlu, so I was there, supposedly, to help Coral settle in. She was nearly two eights of a year away from giving birth, and she'd gotten much larger. Her bulk made simple tasks difficult and, without a husband there, I could chop and carry wood and fetch water.

She, on the other hand, could calm me down. In a firm but reasonable way, she argued that I had many options left to explore. Wealthy people hired others to protect them and their lands. Businesses, schools, and travelers sometimes needed those who could fight well and were not associated with the Svadlu. Father's contacts could be useful for more than training. Perhaps he could help me find a position to my liking. Once I had such, there'd be less pressure on me to marry, too.

I didn't think she understood how those options were second class to being a real Svadlu, but because I knew she wanted to cheer me up, I thanked her and told her I'd look into her ideas.

Then one night, after I drank more wine than I intended, she managed to cajole me into telling her the entire awful story of my piss-filled encounter with Davor on his way to relieve himself. As we sat in front of a dying fire, she got me to laugh at what happened, and somehow the laughter helped heal what all the agonizing had not. Throughout my retelling, Coral managed to point out how it all had been so unfortunate, but could still be fixed.

She expected Davor back in a few days, probably before Sashi, the next holiday. Husbands and wives made every effort to celebrate the eight holidays together and while she hadn't received any word from him, she couldn't imagine he wouldn't at least ride over for a day and a night.

As Sashi neared, I kept my bags packed and my horse ready to ride at the first sign of him in the distance. She and I agreed it would be better if I was gone by the time he dismounted.

But the holiday came and went and he never appeared and never sent word. I could see the worry on her face. There were many possible explanations but none of them were good.

Finally, two days after Sashi, we saw a horseman in the distance.

"Go," she said. "Whoever it is, I'll be fine. It's better if you're gone."

I agreed, but as I threw my belongings onto my horse, I worried.

"I'll send Olivine over to check on you in a day or two. If she finds out the rider wasn't him, or that he came and left again, then I'll come back and help you some more."

"I'd like that."

She walked over to me and my horse and put one hand on his neck and the other on my arm. "Sulphur, listen to me. I wish we'd talked before you approached Davor, but there's no undoing that. So, I'll try to find a way to get him to sponsor you, because I know it's what you want most. Don't give up on this. There's always a way."

Me, the one sister who had never needed soothing from her in all these years, started to cry at those words as I rode away.

I came back to the farm in better spirits, although I held no hope that Coral could make good on her promise. I returned to my routine of chores and workouts and tried not to think too much about the future. Dad hadn't returned yet, but I felt ready to face him when he did.

A few days later, as I chopped wood in front of the house, he rode up still dressed in the soft grey wools and leathers often worn by teachers, and never worn by farmers. I knew he'd want to change his clothes right away.

He must have noticed the wistful look on my face though as he dismounted because he waved for me to follow him to the barn as he tended to his horse. There my story came tumbling out for the second time. Perhaps I found it easier to tell my father the scholar than my father the farmer.

"Did you know about this sponsorship thing?"

"Sort of. I mean I had the impression it helped an applicant, but wasn't a requirement. I didn't mention it to you because I didn't know where you'd get a sponsor."

"So you don't know anyone who could help me?"

"No, but now that we know how important it is, I'll ask around. Maybe someone I know knows someone." He looked dubious and I wondered if he only said it because he sensed how close to despair I'd come.

Then, one clear, cool autumn morning a few days later, three Svadlu arrived at our farm and I discovered times had changed. My worries had become completely unfounded.

~ 5 ~

Lifting Rocks

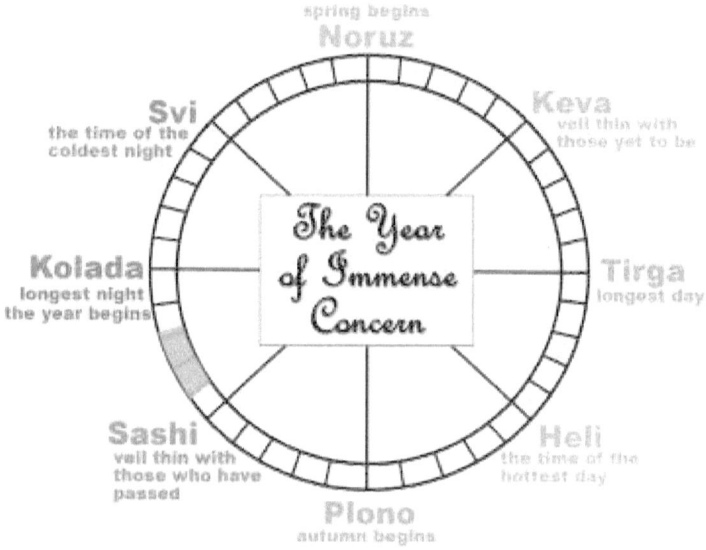

My father repaired the railing on the front porch as the three men rode up, two of them wearing the bright yellow cloaks of the officers. He spoke to them before he brought them inside.

My mother was out for the day, but both twins were home. On a day so mild, Olivine sketched in the backyard and I heard Celestine humming in her room as she composed a song. I envied them and their seemly pursuits. Art and music were acceptable and even admirable activities for educated women. Their lives were so much easier than mine.

We all gathered in the main room as my father and the Svadlu came in. I swear Olivine and Celestine looked hopeful, as if they expected the men brought an invitation to a royal ball. I wanted to remind my sisters I'd been to one and it had been quite a disappointment.

As I watched the men, my father glanced my way. Did the soldiers' visit have something to do with me? When my father met my eyes before he spoke, I knew it did.

"Did you girls know the Svadlu have recently decided to *double* their numbers before winter comes?"

"I heard something about that in the market," Celestine said in a tone that conveyed she hadn't been expected to be asked about anything so boring. She rolled her eyes. "The Mongols."

"It's a serious threat," my father rebuked her. "These men have come seeking candidates to join the army. Those who wouldn't normally consider such a move are being encouraged to do so, for the sake of our realm."

"I've never known the Svadlu to go door to door recruiting," I said. "People struggle to get in, not the other way around."

"You're right," one of them answered, appreciative of my acknowledging the Svadlu's status. "But these are unusual times, and we face an unprecedented problem. We targeted your farm today because we were told there was a daughter here with fighting skills."

His eyes took in Olivine's slight build, the passion in her green eyes, and the artwork in her hands. His gaze moved on to Celestine, who'd been the family beauty since birth. Her grooming and dress were both exquisite, particularly for a farm girl in the middle of the day.

He looked at me. "Would you be able to come with us?"

"Are you going somewhere I wish to go?" I couldn't help grinning at him.

"If you hesitate, we've been asked to give you a message from your sister's new husband." The man cleared his throat and recited in the singsong tone of a messenger. "Given the circumstances of Ilari's great need for competent fighters, I hereby request that you, Sulphur, choose to apply for admission to the Svadlu. You may consider me as your sponsor."

The man resumed his normal tone of voice. "Davor is one of the best we've got, so you've got a Heli of a powerful fighter in your corner. To be honest, few would turn such a request from him down."

I couldn't begin to imagine how Coral had managed this, but I knew this abrupt turn-around had to be her doing. I'd be grateful to her for the rest of my life.

"How long do I have to pack up my things?"

Another of the soldiers answered. "We're going to four more farms in the area, all reputed to have contenders for recruitment. We'll be back for you shortly after noon, perhaps with other recruits. Will that give you enough time?"

I turned to my father with questions in my eyes.

"Go on," he said. "Get ready. I'll explain everything to your mother when she gets back."

A larger than expected group arrived in the early afternoon. There were eight Svadlu now and five apparent recruits in various stages of bewilderment. A young woman, two younger men, and two older men all looked at me as if I could supply some explanation for why they'd agreed to do this. Perhaps they thought I had answers because I had the only confident smile.

As we rode, one of the younger men hung back to speak with me. He was thin with light brown hair and he looked familiar.

"We met when you practiced fighting with some Bisuites last winter," he said.

"You're from Bisu?"

"Yup, near the border with Vinx. You're easy to remember, we don't get many girls who fight. You get talked about some."

"At least a few of the things they say are good, I hope."

He laughed. "You're reputed to be fierce, and I can vouch for that. I'm Rooslin. I remember your name is Sulphur."

"Nice to meet you. Again. So, is joining the Svadlu something you aspired to before today?"

He shook his head and I noticed he had a gentle smile. I liked that. "No, but under the circumstances this looked like my best alternative."

He shrugged and said no more, so I didn't ask.

The fourteen of us had to cover most of the width of Vinx and then go half of the length of Gruen before we arrived in Pilk. After Sashi the days grow short, so it was nearly dark by the time we reached the Svadlu encampment. Even the dusk couldn't obscure the construction going on nearby.

Many of the borders inside of Ilari are informal. Everyone knows where they are, and people and goods flow freely between friendly nichnas. Other boundaries are defined by nature; usually by rivers or one of our sets of cliffs. A few, found in areas of old animosity, are kept by fences or walls.

The farming nichna of Gruen sits southwest of Vinx. Being near the Wide River, it's blessed with richer soil and more rainfall, so its farmers grow more desirable crops than our simple grains. We have a friendly relationship with the Gruenites and an open border. The same applies to Gruen's other border with Pilk, or at least it had until now.

I studied the wall being erected between Pilk and Gruen. The Svadlu were building this? It was as high and as thick as any wall I'd seen.

"Welcome to the Svadlu building crew," a slight but fit woman several years older than I said as I dismounted. She wore a woman's-sized version of the saffron cloak as she gestured to me and the five others.

"You six belong to me. Get some food." She pointed in one direction. "Then get some bedding." She pointed in another. "Breakfast is at dawn, I'll find you then. Be ready to work. We've got a lot of rocks to move."

"But I signed on to fight."

There was no humor in her laugh.

"You signed on for whatever we need you to do, sweetie. Tomorrow, we need you to move rocks. The next day? We'll probably need you to move more rocks. Now, I'd hurry if I was you. They often run out of food here at dinnertime."

I decided to meet this unexpected turn of events with all the good cheer I could. If I were the only new Svadlu being forced into hard labor, I'd have suspected Davor was behind it. But it wasn't personal; recruits from across the realm had been brought here to work on the wall. It was more like incredibly poor timing on my part.

I was lucky to be in good shape and able to exceed the quotas they gave me. The other woman and one of the two older men struggled more than the others, so if I had any energy left at the end of my shift I did what I could to help them.

"They're probably doing this to weed out the weaker ones," Rooslin said to me after a couple of days, when he noticed me helping the others.

"You think I should let them fail?" I didn't like his message.

"No, I happen to agree with you. Potential soldiers should be judged by more than how many rocks they can lift in a day." He picked up a large one and began to help me. "Let's buy these others enough time to prove their worth in other ways, if they can."

After that, it was easy to keep everyone in our group above their quotas.

The other woman reminded me a little of Ryalgar; well educated but unused to using her body. With our help she was less exhausted and after few days she began experimenting with ideas. Soon she had all five of us prying up the ends of the rocks with metal rods she'd found somewhere, then she organized a sort of hand-off system that was easier. After a couple more days we noticed other teams imitating our techniques.

The older man with the bad back was a friend of one of the cooks, so soon our little team had ample supper portions being saved for us, sometimes with extra treats reserved for the officers, like dried fruit or sweet dessert wine. Our morale improved.

Tamara, our leader, must have been impressed because her tone softened with each day as she watched us work.

"I hate to mess with success," she said one morning a few anks later, "but I've been told to break up this little group."

She wore her dark blonde hair in a single long braid that hung all the way down her back and I'd noticed she often played with it when she talked, particularly when she delivered news she knew we wouldn't like. She played with her braid now.

"Why?" Rooslin was upset. "You don't like that we're doing well?"

"I like it very much. But my next job is to get each of you to the right place." She pointed to the woman who had streamlined our work. "You. You're never going to make much of a fighter. What were you thinking when you joined?"

The woman hung her head. "I wanted to help defend Ilari."

"And so you will," Tamara said. "But not with us. I'm sending you to engineering. They can use a brain like yours."

The woman gave a happy little shrug. I suspected she'd be welcomed by the engineers and far happier with them.

Tamara turned to the man with the bad back. "And what were *you* thinking? You don't belong with us." His shoulders sagged. "Never mind. Everyone has their reasons for joining. Lucky for you, your friend over there says you cook better than he does and we need cooks. Report to the kitchen. You can help save Ilari by keeping our soldiers fed."

He stood up tall. "Yes, madam."

She turned to the other two men in our group. "You've lifted more than your share of rocks. It's time to let newer people take over. You're off to training. Go learn to be good Svadlu. I'll see you around."

They made little gestures with their hands and arms that were popular signs of victory, and she laughed. Then she turned to Rooslin and me.

"Well. I didn't expect to find two of you."

"Two of what?" Rooslin asked.

"Two people I want to take back to headquarters with me. You two don't need to go to training. Under the circumstances, you've been fast-tracked. You're Svadlu already. Get your horses. Let's go.

~ 6 ~

Meeting My Sponsor

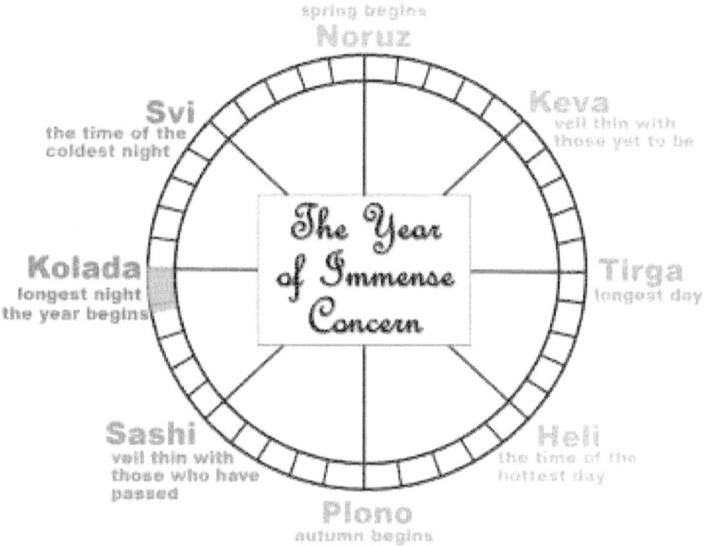

spring begins
Noruz

Keva
veil thin with
those yet to be

Svi
the time of the
coldest night

The Year
of Immense
Concern

Kolada
longest night
the year begins

Tirga
longest day

Sashi
veil thin with
those who have
passed

Heli
the time of the
hottest day

Plono
autumn begins

Two rivers run out of the high mountains to our north and define the shape of Ilari. The Wide River forms the western border of the realm before it takes a big, slow turn and becomes even wider, forming our flood-prone southern border as well.

The narrow Canyon River rushes through a rocky gorge along our northeast, forming the realm's border along all our driest nichnas. That leaves the marshy lowlands of the east as the only easy way to enter Ilari.

A third river, the Little River, divides the realm. It starts in a series of springs in mountainous Tolo and meanders its way through the realm to flow through Pilk, our most populated nichna. Most of Pilk's ten thousand people live along this river in houses clustered closer than homes in other parts of Ilari.

I'd been to Pilk often as a child, and did my advanced studies there as I grew into adulthood. I'd never been inside the Svadlu headquarters, although I'd walked by and admired it many times. I didn't expect such beautiful construction inside and such well-tended courtyards hidden from public view.

I understood now that a Svadlu did more than keep the peace. A Svadlu swept walkways, trimmed shrubbery, and repaired roofs, doing whatever was necessary to maintain the army and its home. Somewhere along the way, I'd glamourized a life that was, of necessity, often mundane.

So, was I happy to be here anyway, possibly about to be assigned to gardening chores? You bet your sweet arse I was. Even doing dishes or carrying rocks, I'd be doing it as a Svadlu and no one could take that honor away from me now.

The next days were the best of my life. I got the chance to spar with different weapons, and to show what all my hard work had taught me. I knew I was quick and strong, and for once, when others noticed it too, they didn't regard me as a freak. Instead, they saw me as talented. I was about to be assigned to a squad and given real duties.

Then someone pointed out that Kolada approached. Possum scump.

Ilari celebrates eight holidays: the two equinoxes, the two solstices, and the four points in between, with drinking, feasting, dancing, and a good deal of sex. Young unmarried tidzys of both genders are granted almost unlimited freedom for a few nights, as they experiment and seek out a mate. Meanwhile, couples, married or otherwise, go to extra lengths to be together.

The holidays had been a problem for me since I left childhood. I was too strong to attract many boys, and those who liked me seemed to want things I didn't. I took fighting seriously; I had no urge to mix it with tenderness. The males I ended up with seldom gave me pleasure.

I tried the alternative. Although girls weren't supposed to pair off with other girls everyone knew it happened. Once again, my strength and style worked against me. I seemed to attract girls who wanted a boy, not me, and these girls seldom gave me pleasure either.

I supposed sex *could* be a lot of fun; most others sure seemed to get a kick out of it. But honestly, I didn't understand all the fuss. I'd have been fine if the holidays never happened.

Worse yet, I had no idea what the rules were in my new profession. There had to be nine Svadlu men for every woman. Most grown men in Ilari were wed, but the army had a larger proportion of single men. Would they expect me to .... scump, I hoped not. What about the other women?

Just when things were going so well.

Maybe I could feign an illness through the celebration. I wondered if Tamara could help. She could at least give me some information.

Tamara laughed when I tried to bring the subject up. I'd learned to respect this tough woman from the mountains of Tolo and to appreciate her bluntness.

"Are you worried because you *do* want to have sex, or you don't?" she asked.

"Don't."

"Fair enough. The Svadlu come in all kinds, and you're not the only one to feel the way you do. Look, we're not tidzys anymore. Many of us have partners, and those who don't are adult enough to know their own minds. Sure, some of the single Svadlu link up on the holidays and it goes all ways, as you'd guess. Others make their lack of interest known. Expectations are that you should feel free to ask. Don't be offended if refused. Or if asked. Or if not asked. You get the idea."

She noticed the skepticism on my face. "Okay, not everyone manages to adhere to these high ideals at all times, but we try. The two biggest rules are no means no and yes means be careful and don't get stupid about it."

She saw the tension in my shoulders and my clenched hands.

"It's okay, Sulphur. Really. Here, you don't have to be anything but a good warrior. That's what matters."

Prucking duck scump. She meant it. Was I going to cry again? I sure hoped not.

****

34

Three days before Kolada, my oldest sister rescued me from my holiday concerns. I don't think she did it on purpose; I suspect she had her own worries. She took the unusual step of sending a Velka right into the Svadlu headquarters to request I be allowed to assist my father in escorting my pregnant sister into the forest. Apparently Coral would give birth there in safety, at the request of her Mozdol husband. The Velka assumed I'd be permitted to have a few days to complete this task.

Although plenty of my fellow fighters knew Davor sponsored me, I'd yet to see him from a distance, much less exchange any words with him. That was fine with me. I guessed he didn't like our arrangement, and the longer he took to confirm that the better.

After the Velka delivered her message to both me and Tamara, she left. I'm not sure what Tamara did about it, but by noon Davor had found me.

He walked in while I practiced with a sword. I tensed at the sight of him and nearly made an incredibly amateur mistake. I caught myself. No, I would not let this man reduce what I was.

I went after my opponent with renewed vigor, and I saw his eyes widen.

"Trying to impress your sponsor, huh?" he hissed.

"You bet your arse," I said. He laughed and gave me a better fight. I tried to remember his face, so I could return the favor if I ever had the chance.

When we'd finished, Davor called out from the other side of the room. "I heard you were good!" When I didn't answer, he came closer.

"Look, Sulphur. I did your sister a favor, and I know you know that. Don't worry. Although I don't intend to help you, if you keep your nose clean and do your best, I'll stay out of your way."

That sounded like the best arrangement I could hope for. "Thank you." I think I managed to say it without a trace of fear, resentment, or relief.

"You should know I agree with Ryalgar on this request. Coral could use more of an escort. Go get her and my unborn son to safety and then take a couple of days with your sisters as my thank you. When you've had your fill of time together, get back here and get to work."

The next morning I intercepted my dad and Coral, who traveled at a turtle's pace across Vinx. The three of us visited about little things as we rode, and it brought back my better memories of being a child. When we fell into silence, though, an unwanted recollection crept in.

It was a holiday. Warm out, so maybe Heli or Plono. I was nearly eight, and the whole family was there, seven little girls barely six years apart. Ryalgar, Coral, and I held on to each other's hands with me in the middle, looking out for both of them. A drunk stumbled into our path, nearly tripping my mother and the twins.

"Get the pruck out of my way, you stupid pruska," he said. Funny, after all these years, I can still hear the man's voice. I let go of my sisters' hands and stepped towards Mom, ready even then to intervene if she needed help.

"And take your little pruskas with you," he added, as I stepped forward. "Pruskas, every varmin one!"

At that age, I didn't know what a pruska was, but I knew enough to realize it was an uncommonly strong insult. Several of the older boys had called me one not long before, and the shocked reaction of others had given me clues.

My mother turned to my father, obviously expecting him to defend his family's honor from the slur slung at us by this drunken rantallion. So many times my father had been absent when we needed him, but at this moment, he was not. He was there. I stood down, leaving the defense of the family to him where it rightly belonged.

And I was devastated. He reached out, helped the man up, and wished him a good day. A good day!

I stared at Dad, not wanting to believe what I'd seen.

My mother was furious, and it was one of the few times I felt I understood the woman. Dad muttered something to her about how she ought to be more reasonable, and the two of them didn't speak again for a long time. So long that I wondered if they ever would.

I've never said anything about the incident to my father. What does a daughter say? But the next time an older boy called *me* a pruska, I beat the living scump out of him until his entire face was bloody. Two other boys pulled me off, begging me to calm down before I went too far.

I've never allowed myself to lose it like that again, not in practice, not in any kind of skirmish. I know better.

But you know what? Not one boy ever called me a pruska again.

I forced the ill-timed memory from my head as we arrived at the forest's edge. I'd long since accepted that my well-meaning father was no warrior, and over the years I'd I tried to love him for the man he was. I bid him farewell and took over the job of getting my pregnant sister to safety.

Coral and I mounted the donkeys brought by our Velka escort, and the journey changed. These small animals picked their way through the underbrush well, but expected riders to duck their heads to avoid injury from low branches. We focused on our safety as we rode, enjoying the rich earthy smell of the newly fallen leaves cushioning our path.

I could hear sounds from the lodge before I could see the clearing. Some sort of performance or sporting event occurred as people cheered. When we emerged from the thick of the trees, I saw one of the last things I expected.

Dozens of women watched my quiet sister Olivine practicing with a bow. As far as I knew, Olivine had no great skill in this arena, but here she was, with Ryalgar standing behind her, as she fired arrows into the trees with more speed than I thought possible.

I turned to Coral.

"Did you know Olivine would be here?"

"Yes, but I thought she'd be gone by the time we arrived. They planned this visit at my wedding. I didn't know about an exhibition with her bow. I wonder if that's why she stayed on a few extra days?"

"This makes no sense at all." And it didn't to me, because I had already become so steeped in the ideals of the Svadlu. Coral had no such biases. "Why is she doing this?" I asked.

"I think they're working on a way to defend Vinx," Coral whispered.

"Why?"

It was one of the few times in my life when my sister Coral looked at me like she couldn't believe I'd asked such a stupid question.

The Year of
Extreme
Distress

~ 7 ~

My First Skirmish

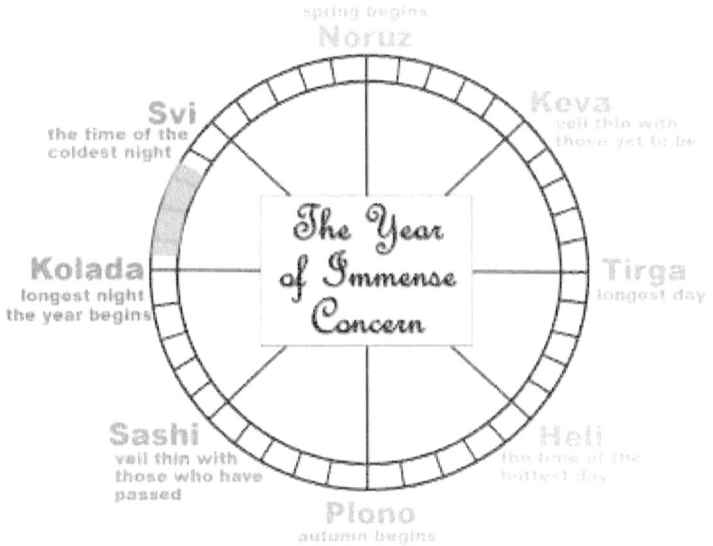

I know families who support the Svadlu. Their sons and occasionally their daughters join and serve with distinction, and they provide financial and emotional support by funding purses given out for specific bravery or by lodging soldiers on their lands.

My family wasn't like that. Our strongest ties were to the learning community and, for reasons I didn't understand, Ilari's most educated felt little affinity for those who kept our society safe. Even knowing this, I didn't expect the hostility I encountered from my three sisters once the four of us settled into Ryalgar's oversized room, each of us finding a corner to put our bedding.

They weren't hostile to *me*; I think they all supported my career and were happy I'd gotten to join. They were, however, far more distrusting of the Svadlu's intentions and their abilities than I expected.

I never doubted the power of our fighters or their integrity. I'd admired them for as long as I could remember. Now, my three sisters insisted the Svadlu were not only incapable of defending us against the Mongols, but that they also planned to betray half the realm in an ill-fated attempt to save the other. It was preposterous.

But they persisted. Ryalgar explained how hard it would be to defend the exposed outer nichnas where we'd grown up. She'd spent anks researching everything known about these invaders and felt certain the Mongols' powers of fighting on horseback were unsurpassed. They'd overrun lands far more prepared than ours. I had to admit, Ryalgar could research a topic like no one I'd ever met.

And Coral appeared to have done more with Davor than make a baby. Conversations were had, and the plan to offer up the eastern half of the realm if the battle went poorly had been in the offing since before her pregnancy. Coral wasn't one to lie, or even to misunderstand the intentions of another. She read people prucking well.

My sisters' solution? They wanted to train the farmers and herders and even the women of the forest to fight. It was the most ridiculous idea I'd ever heard.

"If you're right, why not just train more Svadlu?" I demanded. "We'll triple our numbers if we have to. Even poorly trained fighters are better than those with no training at all! And they're surely better than anything you and the Velka can do."

"Remember my friend Joli?" Ryalgar responded. I'd met Joli on my earlier visit when she'd gotten my attention by making my hair fall into my eyes. Her skill impressed me. More than once I'd seen Ryalgar do similar things like rolling needles within her reach, but I'd never seen her move something as large as a clump of hair.

"Joli and I belong to a group of women with unusual talents. Why would we hide in the forest, doing nothing, while our country is raided?

Well, she had a point. The Velka weren't fighters in the normal sense but maybe the Svadlu could use abnormal help to fend off these invaders. Did any of the places overrun by these thieves have anything like the Velka?

"Sometimes a thousand mosquitoes can do what a lion cannot," Coral said.

"Yeah, well, most of your mosquitoes are going to end up dead," I replied.

"All of them will if we don't do something," Ryalgar countered.

"Then you're going to need real soldiers to teach your farmers and herders some skills. The Svadlu won't support such a plan. Heli, they might kick me out for even talking about this. I suppose I could find ways to do it on my own time, and maybe find others to help me…"

That's when I realized my loyalty to my family outweighed my allegiance to the Svadlu. I would sneak around and defy my superiors to keep my sisters safe. I couldn't help it. Looking out for them was what I did.

I promised Ryalgar that as soon as I left the forest I'd try to find others to help me secretly train farmers to fight. I never got that far. I received my first posting instead.

****

I didn't get the easiest assignment. Everyone in the Svadlu wanted to serve as protection detail for royalty and visitors of prominence from other realms. Mozdols and officers could do nothing but this if they wished; however recruits like me had to prove themselves before they got such a plum opportunity.

The most common first posting sent a soldier off to break up a small fight between nichnas with long-standing grievances. We all knew where these happened. The Zurians pushed at any neighbor not lucky enough to have a river or cliff separating them from Zur. The Edsers got prickly whenever anyone in K'ba wandered across the border by accident or out of curiosity. The Faroojers, who barely got by in the marshlands of the Wide River's big turn, were distrusted by their well-off neighbors on both sides. Trouble occurred along the old wall separating Faroo from the rest of the realm whenever the river flooded.

The Svadlu took an oath to protect all citizens of Ilari, and their reputation made it easy for them to end these skirmishes.

Usually the problem evaporated as the military arrived. This would have made a great first assignment for me, but it wasn't the one I drew, either.

Another common first assignment involved arresting thieves and outlaws. Our approach depended on the hooligan's home. We captured Ilarians and returned them to their own nichna for justice. More often, though, the problems came from foreigners sneaking in to pilfer some of our wealth. The Svadlu dealt with these brigands without mercy, making this a more dangerous duty, especially for a first timer. Bloodshed sometimes occurred. I'd have been apprehensive if this was my first assignment, but it wasn't.

I drew the rarest type of duty, and the most dangerous. My superiors called upon me to defend one of Ilari's borders.

The northern edge of Ilari rises rapidly into a high mountain range. The nichna of Tolo occupies this border, where Ilarians pass into the high mountains as needed for travel and trade. Early this morning word reached the Svadlu that troublemakers from further up the mountains had overrun a small village in Tolo. At first I worried these invaders were the dreaded Mongols unexpectedly entering our realm, but reports said otherwise. A small band from the north had commandeered the town, demanding food, bounty, and more from the residents.

Tolo has the most extreme winter weather of any nichna and is sparsely populated, with only a couple of thousand Tolovians who mostly mine ores and act as if the rest of Ilari barely exists and hardly matters. No one wanted to charge up into the mountains in winter to defend ungrateful Tolovians from their newly aggressive neighbors.

My commander, Tamara, was Tolovian and her Mozdol superior placed her in charge of the force being sent. As I watched her get ready for our departure, I understood this was no nuisance to her. She would be defending those she loved.

In the end, forty-five of us left at mid-day, heading into a snowstorm fully armed and bundled in furs. Rooslin and I began the ride side by side.

"Does it make you nervous going into battle for the first time with almost nothing but other untested new people?" he asked.

"What do you mean? The Svadlu would never do that. I'm sure this group contains a good mix of skills."

He laughed. "I love how trusting you are. You've never heard the phrase 'If it doesn't sound pleasant, send the new people?'"

No, I hadn't.

"I recognize a lot of these faces from our rock-moving days," he explained. "But ask around. Maybe I'm wrong."

I trotted ahead and made my way up to ten riders, introducing myself and asking each one a few polite questions. Most chatted with me as they answered but even those who didn't fancy talking gave me the information.

"How many of the ten are first timers?" Rooslin asked after I rejoined him.

"Ten."

Neither of us said more about it as we rode upward along the western banks of the Little River.

The snow stopped after a couple of hours, leaving us riding through a sunny and bitterly cold afternoon. We were lucky the winds remained scarce. Near the end of our ride, Tamara split us into three groups, each with an officer as its leader. She sent Rooslin to ride with others, but kept me in her troop, and motioned for me to ride beside her.

"Are you sure?" I felt the position belonged to one with more seniority.

"I am." Then, as an afterthought. "You're the only person in this group I've seen fight. I want you at my side."

I suppose her remark made me proud, and more determined to do right by her. Otherwise, perhaps I wouldn't have done what I did.

The sun dipped behind the hills to our southwest by the time we arrived at the village, but the sky would remain light for at least another hour. Tamara stopped us on the outskirts, behind a clump of fir trees near the river's edge.

"My group will ride in alone and attempt to find out what these people want. Perhaps this can be handled without bloodshed. Always best. The man at the back of my team will blow once on the horn if he wants group two to follow us into town. Sometimes a bigger show of force is all that is needed to move a conversation along." She turned to the leader of group two. "You. Enter but do not engage unless we are already fighting. If we aren't, just stand behind us and look fierce. You understand?"

He nodded. She turned to the leader of group three. "And you. Cross the creek after we enter town. It's not that deep here. Circle behind the village. Two sounds from our horn means attack them from behind with all you've got, but be careful not to hurt the villagers. You won't hear our horn blow twice unless we're in trouble."

This, my first exposure to military strategy, fascinated me.

I rode in at Tamara's side, both scared and proud. We smelled smoke as we rode, and as we got closer we could see twenty or thirty men feasting at tables. Terrified townspeople waited on them. It was easy to understand why.

Ten or so villagers were tied together in a circle around a pole surrounded by kindling. Two burly men with flushed faces stood at either side, each holding impressive flaming torches. Ropes wove through the clothes and hair of the hostages, binding them into an inseparable ring. The few children in the group cried, and an older woman tried to calm the youngest child.

The men who feasted turned toward us as we rode in.

"Ah, the famed Svadlu finally arrive. These poor villagers have been waiting for you all day," one man laughed. "What a shame. We were nearly done with them, too. Now we have to stop our fun and fight you."

"Madam," a villager shouted to Tamara. "I'm the mayor." He pointed to the unfortunate people tied together around the pole. "That's my family."

I heard Tamara mutter an extremely vulgar word.

"Or maybe we *don't* have to fight you," the man enjoying the feast said. "Perhaps, you'd like to wait on us instead." He slapped his knee, delighted with this new plan. "Get me some ale," he ordered Tamara as she sat on her horse. She didn't move.

"Now," he said. He motioned to one of the sweat-covered torch holders, who lowered his crackling flames closer to the kindling.

As the fire got dangerously close to the twigs, Tamara jumped off her horse, and I jumped with her. I knew from the tautness in her body that she was about to fight, and from the direction of her leap that she'd attack the man who spoke to her.

She lunged towards him with her knife drawn and I lunged towards the closest man holding a torch. I'm told I put my sword through his heart in a single motion as I leapt. I don't remember it. I only remember reaching to seize his torch before it hit the ground, then noticing another had grabbed it for me and was dowsing it with water.

I moved towards the second man as he eyed me with apprehension. He pointed his torch closer to the kindling.

"Don't come any closer," he said.

What to do? I knew I could kill him too, but perhaps not before he started a fire. Could the recruits behind me manage to free the hostages from the flames fast enough once a fire started? I hated to bet anyone's life on that.

I could lunge for his torch instead but he'd likely kill me as I did.

I couldn't see behind me, and I dared not take my eyes off the man to turn my head. The inexperienced soldiers who had my back remained quieter than I would have liked. I heard fighting over at the table of the feasters, and I guessed those confident in battle had jumped in to aid Tamara. I was probably on my own.

I circled to the man's left side as he inched his right hand, and the torch it held, closer to the kindling.

When I reached his left side, I gave a defeated shrug and lay my sword down.

"Smart gir...." He never finished his word. I sprang at him like a wildcat, using some of those odd muscles the old man with the wind chimes had put me in touch with. His surprised backward movement as I leapt helped me force him down on top of his own flaming torch. He screamed in pain as his body squelched the fire. I have no idea if he died then, or later.

The recruits behind me sprang into action once it was safe, freeing the people tied together around the pole, and dispersing the kindling. I was grateful. To be honest, I felt incapable of anything. I just stood there and watched them.

"Sulphur? You okay?"

The sharp words came from Tamara. I turned to her, filled with guilt.

"Sorry. I meant to be helping the others. I'm just, I'm having trouble moving."

"You put these two down?" She pointing to the bloody corpse of the first torch holder and the partially charred body of the other.

"Yes. I think I did both."

"You think. Have you ever killed anyone before?"

"No, madam."

"You saved this village, you idiot. Now sit down and put a blanket around yourself. That's an order."

~ 8 ~

A Direct Result

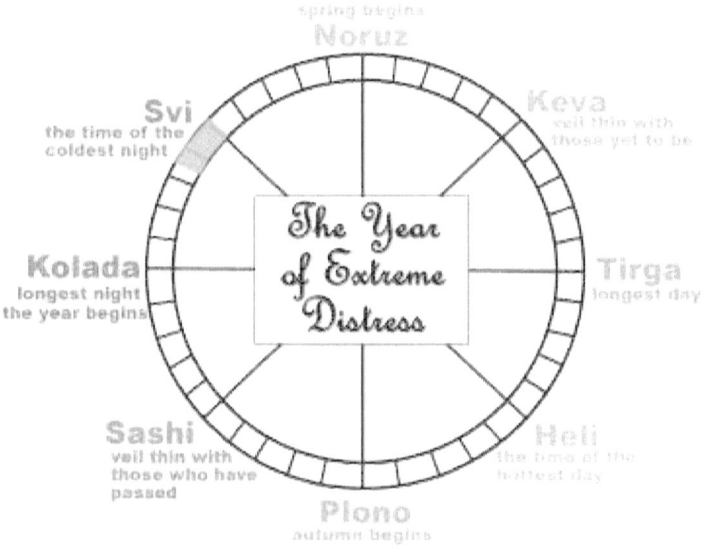

We spent the night in the village, and the next morning we bundled up the bodies of the three of ours who'd been killed after they joined Tamara in the fight. The attackers lost twice as many, plus of course the two torch holders I'd killed.

About half of their remaining group fled into the dark before we could capture them. I later learned that after we left, the villagers tied those we did capture to the same pole the mayor's family were bound to and burned them alive. To this day I'm glad I didn't have to see it.

As I rode out of Tolo, I couldn't get warm. I shivered in my saddle, seeing again the surprise in the first torch holder's eyes as I leapt off my horse. I watched him move in slow motion, like he was immersed in molasses, as I came towards him. I watched the point of my sword approach his chest. It got closer to him every time I replayed the scene, but I'd yet to see the tip of it pierce his skin. That part of my memory didn't exist.

I now had no doubt I could and would do what needed to be done in battle. But, for the first time in my life, new worries gnawed at me. My father's question made sense. Why would anyone *want* to do this? Worse yet, why did *I* want to? And, was I sure I did?

The ride back to Pilk took forever and yet ended in no time at all. Funny how an interval can sometimes go both fast and slow. For though I felt frozen as an icicle on my horse, the time was too short for me to solve my dilemma. Did I want to be a fighter? I'll never know what I would have decided if I'd been given more time to think, because I wasn't.

Early the next day, two Svadlu came to my quarters and demanded I go with them. Puzzled, I walked between them as they indicated. Others averted their eyes as we marched along the cobblestone street until we arrived at Svadlu headquarters. The men took me to a small room in the rear of the building. A plain chair faced a panel of men in full uniform, their scarlet cloaks showing their rank as Mozdols. I presumed the slight man with thinning hair seated in the center was their commander. He told me to sit and it seemed wise to obey.

They began to question me about the incident.

Why had Tamara led the group in as she did? Why did I kill the first man? What did I think about Tamara's actions? Had I given thought to the safety of the others? How did Tamara react to what I had done? What had gone through my head as I circled behind the second man with a torch?

Their brusque manner never became hostile as I did my best to tell them what had happened. My answers to many of their questions were the same. I hadn't given anything much thought; I'd acted on instinct hoping to save lives. My brain had barely been involved in the process.

After they'd asked me everything two or three times, and I answered as well as I could, they dismissed me with no further explanation. I walked back to the barracks on my own, even more confused than I'd been in the morning.

Then I figured out what must be happening. These Mozdols were Davor's friends. I'd given him a reason to remove me from the Svadlu, and he'd set things in motion to do so.

How could I have been so stupid? If I'd sat on my horse and done nothing, like everyone else, maybe it would have all worked out fine. Perhaps I could have stayed in the army. Even if I wasn't sure I wanted to remain a soldier, I didn't want my time in the Svadlu to end like this.

Before dinner, Tamara came to see me.

"I heard you were grilled today. How'd it go for you?"

"I don't know, to be honest. They asked me a lot of questions, so I must be in a lot of trouble."

"What?" She looked at me surprised. "Sulphur. They didn't question you because of what *you* did. I'm the one who let anger overtake my judgment, jumping off a horse and attacking a man because he insulted me. You're the one who kept the incident from turning into a fiasco involving the charred bodies of the mayor's family. You didn't understand I was in trouble?"

No, I hadn't understood at all. I supposed Tamara's actions were a little rash, but they didn't strike me as unreasonable under the circumstances. I think I'd have done much the same. Maybe that was the problem.

"I'm sorry to hear it. What's going to happen to you?"

She gave me a sad shrug. "If I'm lucky, I'll be demoted."

I didn't want Tamara to lose her command. I liked reporting to her. Could I help?

When I asked, she grinned a little as she asked "Did you say good things about me?"

I had to laugh. "Yes, but only because I meant them."

"That's the best reason of all." She pursed her lips together as she thought. "Don't worry about your future," she said. "You'll be fine."

She'd have been right under most circumstances, but she had no idea how much Davor disliked me.

49

The next morning a messenger summoned me to Davor's quarters. The messenger wouldn't answer my questions as we walked, so I followed him in silence, my dread growing with each step.

I forced my pride aside and considered how my discharge could be for the best. For even though I liked fighting, and winning, I now knew I had no taste for killing. Watching one sword in my mind as it approached another's chest in slow motion was enough. I didn't want to end more lives and get ten or twenty more such images to haunt me.

I'd find other, less dangerous, uses for my skills. Plenty of opportunities of the sort I'd discussed with Coral existed, although I hadn't wanted to admit it to her then. Private guards were always needed, and they seldom if ever had reason to draw blood.

Then I had a better idea. Perhaps Ryalgar and her Velka would hire me as a trainer until the Mongol threat passed. Then I could stay out of battles, *and* I wouldn't have to sneak around to help my sisters. All my problems would be solved, or at least most of them. For a while.

Davor motioned me into his office and waved his hand at the messenger by way of dismissal.

"This particular interaction, by custom, is done in private. You understand."

I nodded. My feet and calves had gone numb. "Yes. I appreciate that."

"Good. This action is a direct result of your behavior while on duty in Tolo. I want to assure you it has nothing to do with my assessment of you. You understand that, I hope."

"Sure." I didn't believe him, but I saw no point in arguing about it.

"You should also know being female has complicated the issue in your case. Many wanted to handle it differently because of your gender."

"I don't see why that should matter?"

He laughed. "Well, it does. This hasn't happened with a female before. Actually, I guess it did about two hundred years ago, but who remembers that, huh?"

I just stared at him. I didn't know what to say.

"Others said, hey, you fight like a man, you get treated like a man. I have to admit, they have a point."

I nodded.

"So the real questions on everyone's mind seems to be what you want to be called. Mozdolita? Mozdolrina? Mozdolessa? No one remembers what they did two hundred years ago, so we don't really have a precedent for the name."

My mouth kicked in before my mind did. "Why can't I be a Mozdol like anyone else?"

Then the purpose of the question sunk in. I wasn't being kicked out. They wanted to honor me.

"Because a Mozdol is a prince," he said with the patience he would have shown a small child. "You're a girl. A girl can't be a prince."

"Why can't Mozdol be the word for all honorary royalty?"

"I knew you'd complicate it by saying something like that." His irritation with me grew. "Some suggested the same thing, but most Mozdols opposed the idea. If *you're* a Mozdol, it makes being a Mozdol less impressive. Is that what you want?"

"I don't want to make anyone less. I just want to make me more."

"Fine. I'll tell them you want to be a Mozdol. There may be enough gratitude for the way you kept that mess in Tolo from turning into a disaster for you to get your wish."

I didn't comment.

"Mozdolo ceremonies are always held here in Pilk, on a holiday. Yours will be at Noruz, and I'll be honored there as well. I'll be sitting at your side." He looked me in the eye. "Don't get any ideas about this meaning I'm happy to have you as a Svadlu. I'm not. What I *am* happy for is the nice bit of coin this will bring me."

"I understand."

"Perfect. If you continue to stay out of my way and cause me no further problems, I'll cause you none either. Do we still have an agreement?"

"We do."

That night, as I lay in my bunk, too many thoughts whirled through my head.

Why had I been so naïve, and so preoccupied with my own problems, that I failed to appreciate Tamara's situation? What would happen to her? Could I have said more to exonerate her?

How did I feel about being offered an honor granted to few? Granted to almost no women? Had the last one really been two hundred years ago?

How many Mozdols were there, anyway? They seemed to run the army, but no one explained to the new people how it worked. Who was their leader? Was he the man in charge of my interrogation? I needed to find out.

Would there be things I'd be obligated to do? Probably.

Was it fair that because of a single event I'd get respect and some wealth no matter what else I did? Probably not.

Of course, I could decline the honor. I didn't know if anyone had ever done so, but if they had, the Svadlu kept it quiet.

I could even resign tomorrow. I could go train farmers to fight for Ryalgar. I could give up fighting altogether and never raise a sword again.

But I already knew I wasn't going to do any of that.

I wanted to fight for what was right. I wanted to be commended for my bravery. I wanted to be a Mozdol.

And, I had no intention of letting anyone refer to me as any kind of princess. Ever. Silly name. Powerless role.

No, I'd be a prince and pruck my mother's insistence I go marry one instead.

~ 9 ~

Drinking Buddies

Two days later another uncommunicative messenger summoned me to Davor's office. I once again worried as I walked, but the events of the past two days gave me comfort. I'd received quiet congratulations from several saffron-cloaked officers and from a few Mozdols, and gotten remarks from my fellow combatants about my unusual speed and bravery. Their words combined to reassure me.

I also received admonitions to remain quiet for now about becoming a Mozdol. The honor required the approval of the ruling prince of my own nichna, a reasonable consideration given the

53

ceremony made me, in essence, an honorary member of his family.

The approval was usually a formality barely blinked at, but in my case Vinx's ruling prince wished to speak with me before signing off on it. I didn't doubt my youth and gender triggered his concerns, but I didn't take it personally. Giorgi, our ruling prince, had only ascended to the throne this past year and his youth and inexperience left him eager to do the right thing.

I'd learned in my studies that many monarchies outside our realm waited until their elderly ruler actually died before passing leadership to his oldest male child, whether said child had proven he could produce an heir or not. This left the new ruler without access to the wisdom of the elder, and created confusion about succession if he didn't produce an heir. Such inefficient rules baffled me, but one had to learn tolerance for the oddities of others.

At any rate, Vinx's young prince ruled by virtue of being the oldest male child and of having impregnated his betrothed at an early age, making him the proud father of a male heir of his own. Everyone in Vinx knew his new role frightened him and most of us thought his father, and probably his mother, too, largely ran the nichna while he got his feet on the ground.

I thought I'd have no problem reassuring him and his parents that I'd bring honor to Vinx.

Nonetheless, I worried about what Davor wanted. Two mysterious summons in three days.

A woman waited with him in his office. Based on her practical clothing, I took her to be a Velka.

"This woman brings a message for us both," Davor said. He looked pleased with the world. "Thank you for rushing over here. She wanted to wait for you to share it."

He motioned to the woman to begin. She spoke in the trained sing-song voice of the messenger, her cadence making it clear the words were not her own.

"Let it be known that on the fifth day of the fifth ank of Kolada, two days before the Holiday of Svi, the woman Coral did give birth to a healthy baby boy which she has chosen to name Davot. He feeds and grows well and she is healthy and recovering from the rigors of childbirth."

The woman smiled at both of us.

To Davor she said "Congratulations. You are a father."

To me she said "Congratulations. You have a nephew."

A nephew? A little boy in our family? Oh, I looked forward to meeting him.

With that she gave Davor a slight curtsy, and he motioned to her to pause, as he fumbled in his pockets to find a few coins to press into her palm. "A little extra for your trouble," he said.

He waited until she was out of the door, then reached under his table and produced a jug. The cork popped out with ease; I suspected this jug was opened often. He grinned as he poured us each a healthy portion, and I could smell the strong liquor from where I stood. He handed me my mug and raised his.

"To my son, Davot."

I didn't know what etiquette demanded of the situation, but I was sure I shouldn't refuse to drink, despite the early hour. So I raised my mug.

"To my sister Coral!" He raised an eyebrow at my addition. Perhaps this wasn't how it was usually done, but it seemed reasonable to me. Coral had, after all, done all the work.

Then he shrugged and added, "To mother and child." We both drank our fiery liquid down in a gulp, like the good soldiers we were.

I turned to go, but he stopped me.

"Sulphur, wait. I have something I wish to say to you."

I paused in the doorway.

"I'm not a fool," he said.

If ever there was a time to be silent, this was it.

"I understand our relationship has changed today," he added. "We share blood now, and we always will. I'm coming into fatherhood later than most men, and have no reason to think I'm going to be particularly good at it. I can ill afford to complicate matters with grievances with you or anyone in my son's family. Please. Let us forget our unfortunate start and focus on our mutual thanks for the new life we've been blessed with."

It was quite a flowery speech, especially for him, and it impressed me. I guessed he spent some time composing it.

"Wise words," I said.

"Good." His sigh of relief was audible. "One of your better qualities is your lack of desire to hang onto petty squabbles the way most women do."

I held my tongue again. I had little tolerance for blanket slurs against my gender, or for that matter against any group, but this wasn't the time to try to educate my brother-in-law.

"Normally your direct commander would walk you through this Mozdol thing, but she's been relieved of her duties while her actions are being investigated. Do you have any questions? Can I be helpful?"

"I'm sorry to hear about Tamara. I do want to know more about how this works. What happens after the ceremony?"

He nodded. "I forget how little you know. Being a Mozdol has its own culture, its own expectations. With your background on a wheat farm, you've been exposed to little of it."

He reached back under the desk and poured us both a second drink.

"Have a seat. Let me tell you about being a Mozdol."

So I sat and took the mug, fearing I'd be drunk by noon.

Davor proceeded to tell me stories of his own experiences and of other Mozdols, too. Sure, there was a lot of self-aggrandizing involved, but he sprinkled in useful information.

I learned there was a head Mozdol appointed by the ruling prince of Pilk and approved by a vote of the other eleven ruling princes. Kazimir from Kir was the current one. While many welcomed a chief commander from anywhere but Pilk as a refreshing change of pace, Kazimir's inflexibility had gained him detractors. He hadn't been present at my interrogation.

Three other top Mozdols, also called commanders, helped Kazimir run the Svadlu. Davor thought the second-in-command, an older Mozdol with thinning hair from Pilk named Irakli, had chaired my questioning.

I learned there were eighteen active Mozdols altogether; I'd make nineteen. Each had several officers reporting to him; I'd be assigned my officers later. Twenty-two retired Mozdols scattered around the realm kept their honors and privileges but no longer served. I had that to look forward to someday.

Before I left Davor's office, he told me my status had changed to "light duty" until after the ceremony.

"It's typical for someone in your shoes. Can't have the honoree hurt in a skirmish beforehand. So, until the end of this eighth, you'll have minor guard duties around Pilk, nothing more. Take a day for your own needs whenever you wish between now and then."

He laughed as he reached to poured us both another half mug.

"You'll probably need to take one tomorrow."

Two days later, a messenger delivered a summons for me to meet with the ruling prince of Vinx. The prince held court in one of the many suitably appointed receiving rooms lent to other rulers by the Royals of Pilk. I expected Prince Giorgi to have a large entourage with him, and perhaps some of his family, but I found only him and a guard sitting in a large room waiting for me.

"Please. Sit and join me," He motioned to the one empty seat. "I'd like the chance to get to know you."

So I sat, and we talked. Luckily, the strongest drink served was a suitably watered-down light afternoon wine.

Giorgi was a pleasant young man, probably younger than me. He asked enough questions to confirm his desire to make the right decision. I got the idea he didn't enjoy deciding things on his own, and he probably wouldn't have chosen "ruling sovereign" as his occupation if he'd been given a choice.

I got more comfortable as we spoke, so I finally mentioned what had bothered me since I arrived.

"I mean no offense your highness, but I'm surprised you didn't bring more of your family, given your newness to these responsibilities."

He laughed, unoffended.

"That was for your sake. My parents are wonderful, but can be set in their ways. My mother resents that you won't take a feminine title for this honor. She feels you insult all womanhood with your request to be a Mozdol. I wanted to speak to you alone, to see if it was true."

"I mean no insult to anyone."

"I don't think you do. You're a proud warrior but not much of the princess type, and I mean no offense by that either. The title Mozdol suits you. I'll recommend we approve your commendation without asking you to change the honorific." Giorgi smiled. "It may be my first clash, but I'm confident I can win this one."

"Thank you." What a pleasant surprise.

"I do have a favor to ask in return."

Of course. The royal politics I'd been warned of would have to be involved in such a concession.

"What can I do for you, Your Highness?"

"You can look out for Vinx. You probably think you already do that, but I need more from you. We only have one other living Mozdol from our nichna, and he retired a year ago. I took the throne without having the customary voice, ears, and eyes in the command chain of the Svadlu. No other nichna, except Scrud of course, suffers from such a lack. You'll now become that for me, for all Vinxites."

"I didn't realize Mozdols served their home nichnas in such a way. I'm honored to be of service, of course."

He gave a slow sigh, telling me his next message would be less pleasant. "Sulphur, this responsibility comes at a difficult time. For me and you."

"You're referring to the preparations for the Mongols?"

"I am. There's no agreement as to the best way to defend our realm. Many of the Svadlu want to evacuate everyone from the eastern edges and pull back to defend only the land easiest to protect. It's a strategic approach I understand, at least intellectually. Not surprisingly, though, the Vinx royal family is officially abhorred by the idea. We've received a lot of support from the other ruling families, particularly the influential rulers of Pilk. We want our ideas to prevail. It's your job to make sure they do."

My job? Bat scump. My sisters talked about this plan when we met in the forest, and I'd argued that the Svadlu would never consider such a thing. Now, my ruling prince said they were. Soon, I'd sit in on strategy meetings the likes of which Sulphur the recruit would never have been privy to.

So far I hadn't told my sponsor Davor how my sisters were hatching plans to defend Vinx in case the Svadlu wouldn't. It hadn't seemed like appropriate information to share with him, given my limited knowledge and our strained relationship.

But all that had shifted. He and I were drinking buddies now. Would giving him this information cause my sisters problems? I didn't think so. The Svadlu should be delighted to learn they had would-be helpers. But I wasn't sure.

As for Prince Giorgi, who expected me to be his source of information, he was on the opposite side of the question. He shared my belief that civilians had no business taking up arms, and the Svadlu ought to defend all of the realm. Did I owe *him* an explanation of what my sisters were considering? Why? In a world that went his way, my sisters' efforts would be unnecessary but harmless. Why complicate things?

"Are you okay?" The worry in my face must have concerned him.

"I'm fine, merely disturbed by these two opposed approaches to defending the realm. I'll keep my ears open for you, of course, and we'll speak often, Your Highness, as you wish."

He stood and gave me a slight tilt of the head, and I understood I was being dismissed as a near equal. As almost another prince.

****

I wondered how Davor and other Mozdols would feel about getting help from civilians like my sisters. If they welcomed the idea, whether to placate the masses or to sway the outcome of the battle, then I could get them talking to Ryalgar. They could work together. That would be best.

But wait.

If I did that, then the ruling family of Vinx could decide my loyalties lay elsewhere because anything that shored up the Svadlu's plans also hurt the interests of Vinx. I was supposed to be helping the royalty of Vinx prevail.

Steaming piles of scump. I hated this sort of nonsense.

Who was I loyal to?

I'd sworn an oath to defend Ilari and this oath seemed to be my first responsibility. So, which course of action best served all of us, not the Svadlu or the Royals, or my family, or anyone else. Would giving up the outer nichnas, with or without Ryalgar's involvement, be best for the whole realm? Or would Ilari be better off if we defended the entire realm with all the strength we could muster?

There was no way to know, of course, but I believed our best chance had to be a well-trained army, not a witches' plot or farmers armed with pitchforks. That meant I needed to see that the strategy purposed by the Royals prevailed.

That included not mentioning Ryalgar's schemes to anyone. Not at this point.

After Noruz, I'd do my best to talk Ryalgar out of her ideas. The harshness of winter had surely prevented her from doing much, but with spring coming she'd set her plans in motion. If I couldn't persuade her to stand down, I'd be stuck sneaking off to help her teach the farmers battle skills. What choice would I have? I didn't want these people fighting in the first place, but if they did end up doing it, I wanted them to do it well.

Pruck, this was going to get complicated. I had to hope I could talk Ryalgar out of her plans.

~ 10 ~

Granting One Wish

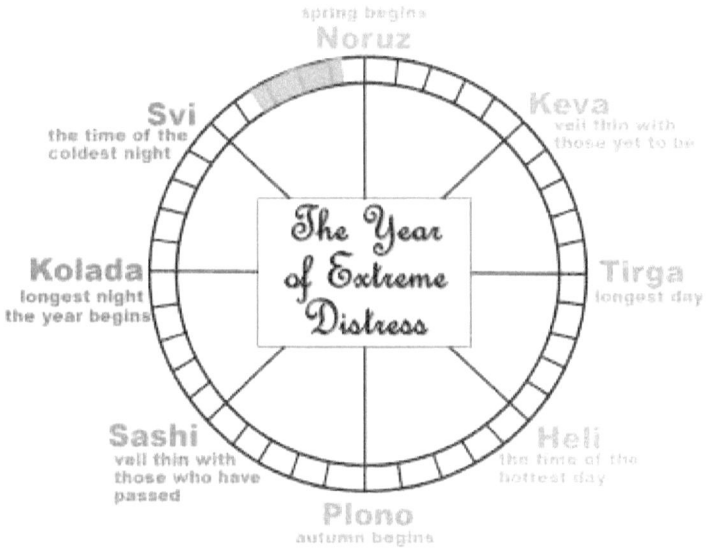

I didn't see Tamara after the day I was questioned, which was odd. I wanted to find her and learn what she knew of her fate, but Rooslin found me first. He'd been in the infirmary since we returned, being treating for damage to his shoulder. When I'd gone to visit him, he'd been sleeping and I hadn't made it back since.

Then there he was, wearing his arm in a sling as he entered the large mess hall shared by the enlisted men and women.

"Are you okay?" We each asked the question as he walked toward me and we both had to laugh.

"I'm fine," he said. "They released me this morning, saying I've torn some connectors holding my shoulder in place, but will heal with time and light duty. But you? Everyone's talking about you. What happened?"

I shrugged and realized I'd been doing a lot of shrugging since I'd returned from Tolo.

"I may never know. I acted without thinking, I can't remember details, and suddenly I'm a big hero."

"How do you feel about that?"

Funny, no one else had asked me that question.

"It seems unfair, to be honest. Tamara is in trouble for her rashness, and I'm being praised for mine."

"So?"

"Confused. Guilty. Conflicted. Grateful. Proud. Worried about Tamara."

"Me too," he said.

"Which one?"

"Most of them, but especially worried about Tamara. Want to come with me to look for her?"

"Sure."

We headed over to the quarters set aside for the few female officers. As a male, Rooslin wasn't allowed in and, because of my low rank, I wasn't either but I thought my new celebrity status might buy me some flexibility. He waited outside the fence while I peeked inside. I saw another officer in their dining area and asked her about Tamara.

"You're Sulphur?"

"Yes." I couldn't tell from her tone whether being Sulphur was a good thing or a bad thing.

"Well, come on in. Word is you'll be living here soon enough, at least until you get your own place."

"I've been told to be quiet about ...."

"Yeah, yeah," she said. "Officers talk. The first woman Mozdol in two hundred years? That must have been one Heli of a sword fight you got into up in Tolo."

"It wasn't. I'm as baffled as anyone."

"Good." She liked my answer. "One never knows what they'll choose to reward, but hardly ever does a female come out on the winning side of it, so I'm happy to see one of us beat the odds."

She squinted at me, as if she was deciding to tell me more. "Issa over there," she pointed to a lone woman finishing breakfast at a small table on the other side of the room. "Issa has killed over ten men with her sword. Vicious brigands every one. Do you think she deserves to be a Mozdol?"

"Based on what you told me, she deserves it more than me. Do you think I should turn the honor down?"

"Pruck no!" She practically yelled it. "One of the older Mozdols has had it in for Issa from the start. She's never going to be one of them, and you won't help her or anyone else by refusing this. You'd probably just make it harder for the next woman when she comes along, in a hundred years or so …"

Issa had been ignoring us while we talked, but at this last comment she stood up to leave.

"You talk too much," she said to the woman who'd been speaking to me. She turned to me.

"Tamara is a Heli of a fine officer. They're holding her in confinement over at headquarters, and they won't let any of us see her. You want to do something to show you're worthy of being a Mozdol? Take your newly important arse over there and see if you can get in. If you do, let her know we're doing all we can to speak up for her."

"I'll do that." Now that I knew where Tamara was, I'd have gone without this officer's push.

As I turned to leave, Issa added "If one of the men had jumped off his horse like Tamara did, brandishing a knife after being insulted? They'd erect a prucking statue of him."

Rooslin and I walked the short distance to the headquarters while I explained the situation. I wished I'd asked Issa the reason she'd been given for being not allowed to see Tamara.

"I guess I'll try to bluster my way in," I said.

Rooslin gave me a friendly punch on the arm. "Yeah. Act like a guy." He laughed at my surprised look. "Oh come on. We're not all oblivious to male behavior. I believe those women officers about the randomness. Your being honored must serve someone's greater agenda or it wouldn't be happening. I'm not naïve."

I guess he wasn't, but maybe I was.

"Serving someone's agenda? That never occurred to me." It made me a little sad. "Who could my appointment help? Except for Davor, but I can't believe he's pushing this. He's tolerating it because he benefits."

"I agree," Rooslin said. "It's bigger than him. So who?"

"Wait, I met the new ruling prince of Vinx yesterday. He has to approve my appointment because it technically makes me part of his family."

"How'd you two get on?"

"Well, I think. He mentioned Vinx currently had no other Mozdol, and a Mozdol is a nichna's connection to the Svadlu."

"That's got to be it then. Important people don't want Vinx to claim they had no representation during these upcoming decisions about the Mongols. You must have been the first Vinxite to come along with a reason to be honored."

"Enough of one they'd give the honor to a woman?"

Rooslin winced. "I don't mean to be cynical, but your being female could have been a plus. I mean, first Vinx gets this unusually young ruler. Not the most decisive guy in the realm. Then you come along providing the necessary representation for Vinx as an inexperienced female with few connections and almost no knowledge of how the system works. Vinx is represented but has no clout."

"Chicken scump. I wish I had your talent for seeing a devious scheme behind every rainbow."

"It would serve you well in your new role." We both laughed. "But you've got me instead, you know. I'll be glad to point out every possible dastardly hidden plot behind what happens, if you'd like."

"I wonder if I could make you my assistant?"

"Are you joking?"

I wasn't. If any of what Rooslin guessed was true, his paranoid imagination was just what I needed.

When we got to headquarters, I walked up to the man in charge. "I need to speak with Tamara, my former commanding officer."

He looked at me. "Regarding what?"

Rooslin answered. "She has questions about her upcoming promotion. To Mozdol." He put all the emphasis he could on the last word then turned to me and added in a loud stage whisper "It's okay, everybody knows about it by now."

"Who's he?" the man in charge asked me.

"My assistant."

"I see. I'll go get the woman for you."

They seated her in a small room, let Rooslin and me enter, then closed the door behind us.

Tamara looked awful. She had a black eye and bruises on her face and arms, and she shivered like she'd been cold for days. She sniffed until Rooslin handed her his handkerchief.

"What in the Goddess's name have they done to you?"

"It's okay. Yesterday they roughed me up a little, trying to get me to reveal any truths I'd withheld about my actions. There weren't any. Otherwise, you know, it's just been time alone in a small cold dark room with no idea of what's happening. Nothing serious."

I appreciated her attempt at humor but it wasn't funny.

"We've got to get you out of here," I said.

"I know. Good thing you can, in a couple of anks. I'll be okay for that long."

"What are you talking about?

"You don't know? Then why do they keep telling me you can get me released by asking for it during your Mozdolo."

"Me? I don't have that kind of power."

Rooslin shoved his chair back, standing up in anger. "Those puss-filled rantillions. Of course they'd think of something like this."

Tamara and I both stared at him.

"What are you talking about?" I asked.

"I'm guessing no one mentioned you get one request at your Mozdolo? It's a customary gift from the realm, and it can be anything the Svadlu can grant."

I'd never heard of such a thing, but then again I apparently hadn't heard of most of what went on.

"Davor should have told you," Tamara said. "No, I should have told you, and I would have if they hadn't locked me away. It's true. You can request my freedom at your Mozdolo."

"Can I request they restore your command?"

"I think that counts as two requests. You only get one." She turned to Rooslin. "Why are you cussing? I'd be out of luck without this inane custom."

"No, you wouldn't be in prison in the first place if it didn't exist," he said. "Look. Everyone knows you and Sulphur get along. Of course she'd use this to free you, and more so if they send you out to see her a little beat-up. I'm sure they knew you had nothing to hide, Tamara, and no reason to lay a hand on you except to upset us."

"But why bother hurting Tamara?" I asked.

"Oh, in the name of Heli, you *do* need my assistance, don't you? Think of this. They've waited a year to find a Mozdol from Vinx, maybe in part because of this crazy custom. Who knows what another person might ask for? But in your case, Tamara's plight guarantees you won't make some more difficult or unwanted request."

For once, I understood what he was saying better than he did. I could free Tamara, or I could insist the Svadlu defend Vinx in the upcoming invasion. Maybe they'd find some technicality around the latter request. Can't ask for anything involving military strategy; it's written in the details. But the ensuing uproar would be problem enough.

So when Tamara leapt off her horse, and I leapt off mine, we handed these mysterious commanding Mozdols a perfect solution to the Vinx problem.

Now what was I going to do about it?

I told Tamara I'd find out more. After Rooslin and I left her with all the reassurances we could think of, I went to see my new drinking buddy, Davor.

"You again," he said when I walked in. "I'm fresh out of grog, honey."

"Good. Is it true the Svadlu will grant me one wish at my Mozdolo?"

He laughed. "I wouldn't have worded it like that, but yes, I forgot to mention the Mozdolo gift. Pick anything you like, although they'll make a counterproposal if they think it unreasonable, which they almost always do. I wanted steak once an ank for life; they make sure I get beef of some sort, at least any ank when I'm in Pilk. It's not all it's cracked up to be." He looked at his empty jug. "I should have asked for never-ending refills of my hooch."

"Can I get Tamara released from prison? She doesn't even know why she's being held."

He looked at me but didn't answer.

"Is she being held just so I'll release her?"

He raised an eyebrow. "You might be smarter than they think."

This time I didn't answer.

"How would you like to help me with a more difficult question?" he said. "A few days ago, some Svadlu came upon a group of civilians doing military exercises. Would you agree that's odd?"

"In normal times, yes, but people have been scared by all this Mongol talk."

"Would you find it odd if I told you your father was leading the group?"

"What? My dad? That's worse than odd. I can't think of a less combative person in the entire realm."

"I'd be inclined to agree, having met the man a few times, but my soldiers confirm it was him."

"That's ridiculous. Please, let me go talk to my dad and find out what's going on."

"Well, I would, but I have someone better to go talk to him."

"Better than his own daughter?"

Davor found my comment amusing.

"No, I'm sending his daughter, but it will be one who isn't a Svadlu and is more likely to be told the truth."

Right. Coral was Davor's wife even though the two of them lived separately. He could insist she do this. And, he was right about her. She'd get my father to talk in the unlikely event he had something to hide. Only I suspected Ryalgar's plans were the only thing my father had concealed, and Coral already knew all about those.

"I'm meeting my wife and my new son, tomorrow. I'm sure Coral will do as I ask. If you like, I'll let you know what I learn."

"Please do."

****

Now I really needed to talk to Ryalgar. I'd already planned to try to dissuade her from beginning her defense plans with the arrival of spring. Having learned I had the power of one request, I wanted to use it to petition the Svadlu to side with the Royals and defend the eastern nichnas. Such a request, if granted, would make all Ryalgar's efforts unnecessary. She had to know.

But I had no guarantee they wouldn't substitute beef for steak in my case, too. Whatever the beef looked like, it might not justify taking a chance with Tamara's future. Yet how could I value one life over the safety of the realm? Then again, why would the Svadlu continue to hold Tamara for no reason once my Mozdolo was over?

And how had Dad gotten caught doing something involving Ryalgar's plans? It meant she'd already begun setting her ideas in motion and I'd moved too slowly. Sheep scump.

The next morning I sought out the Velka in the market to send word to Ryalgar that I needed to speak with her as soon as possible.

That afternoon a messenger arrived for me. I hoped he'd confirm a meeting between me and Ryalgar, and soon. But no, the message came from Davor. He had to speak with me at once.

~ 11 ~

Quite an Achievement

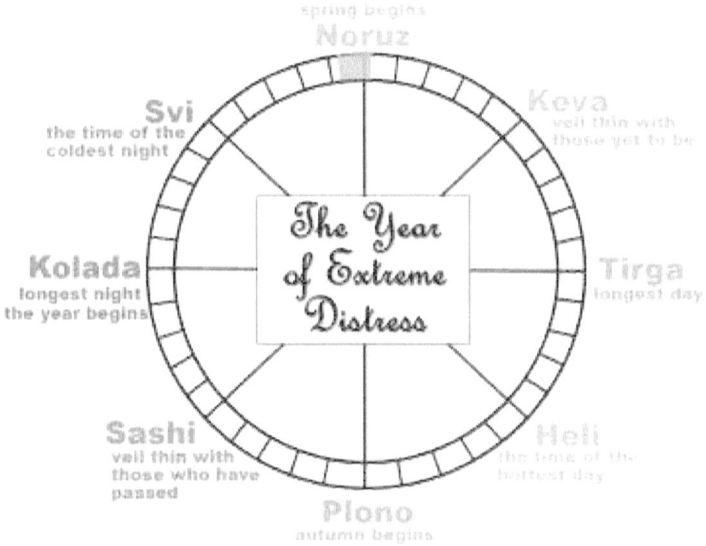

"I'm spending a lot of time with you lately," Davor said with an eye roll as I entered. His face couldn't seem to decide if he was amused or annoyed.

He gestured to his second chair, which I was getting to know well. "Have a seat," he said. I noticed the jug remained out of sight.

"Did you know my youngest brother is an arrogant little prick? I hope he'll outgrow it, but until then, I can't do much about it. So, I'm working hard at not holding your family against you."

This didn't sound good.

"Did you know your oldest sister has been devising her own plans to defend Ilari from the Mongols?"

I nodded as I sat. "When I saw her last, when I brought Coral into the forest to have the baby, she talked about finding ways to defend Vinx if we wouldn't."

"And you didn't think to mention this to me or anyone else in the Svadlu?"

I took a deep breath and looked Davor in the eye. Whether he liked it or not, I would soon be nearly his equal. I knew I had to start acting like it. Besides, I'd done nothing wrong.

"If I reported everything I heard anyone talk about doing, you'd have me locked up as a nuisance. Last time I saw Ryalgar she had no idea of how to go about such a thing; she was simply concerned about Vinx. She worries a lot. It hardly seemed noteworthy."

He nodded. "Well, her ideas grew and now she's got your dad involved and a lot of other farmers too. The whole thing has become embarrassing for us."

Embarrassing? He was worried about the Svadlu's image?

"What exactly do you expect the people of Vinx to do if the Svadlu won't defend their lands?" I asked.

"I expect them to evacuate when we tell them to and hide and stay hidden as instructed."

"While their houses and farmlands are burned? Would the people of Lev do that? Would your family? Would you?" I knew my tone was no longer respectful and I didn't care."

"Careful soldier. You're not a Mozdol yet."

I stopped and looked at the floor, giving my temper time to cool.

"Yet. I understand your passion. Your sister Coral shares it, and she's persuaded me to talk to Ryalgar in person, to hear her side of this." He shrugged. "I'll meet with her and Coral the night before Noruz, the night before your Mozdolo. If our discussion goes well, if we can reach some understanding, then I'll invite your sisters to attend your ceremony. Would you like that?"

"I would. Whatever they're planning, they are my family. I hope to invite my parents as well, as soon as the ruling prince of Vinx signs off on my advancement."

"He hasn't yet? What's the hold-up?"

"I'm told it will be any day now."

"Good. Meanwhile, let's keep each other informed." The bite in his words reminded me I hadn't lived up to his standards of providing pertinent information to one's sponsor.

He stood. I was dismissed, with no drink being offered.

The days leading up to my Mozdolo were the strangest of my life.

Here was my country, preparing for war, while I performed ceremonial duties that needed no skill and barely took up half my time. Tamara remained in prison; Rooslin checked on her almost every day. She suffered from the miserable conditions, but hadn't been otherwise harmed.

I seldom went with him, fearing the more I saw of her the less I could make a clear-headed choice. I knew she, Rooslin, and most others expected me to ask the Svadlu to release her. I seemed to be the only person who wasn't sure about what I'd do. In fact, I agonized over it.

Two days before Noruz, a messenger arrived from Giorgi to inform me that the royal family of Vinx had approved my appointment. Given the delay, I guessed the young ruler got more of a fight from his mother than he expected. He'd won the argument, though; the document proclaimed I would be made a Mozdol.

Once I learned of the approval, I considered my new obligations to Giorgi and Vinx. I wished to start this relationship off well so I found a messenger employed by Vinx, and thus presumably loyal to Giorgi, and composed a hasty letter to him detailing everything. I told him of my dilemma about freeing Tamara, and asked for his advice on whether I should push for Vinx's defense instead. As I wrote, I intended to honor his wishes either way. After all, I was, or would soon be, his Mozdol.

I also told him of Davor's planned meeting with my oldest sister, and Davor's concerns that my family's actions made the Svadlu look bad. I wished to be as forthcoming as possible. In my nervousness, I sealed the letter with far more wax than necessary, then I begged the messenger to ride fast and to deliver any reply with equal haste.

The delay of Giorgi's approval meant I barely had time to invite my parents to attend my Mozdolo. I rushed a message off to them as well and paid the extra coins for fast delivery. Given my dad's lack of fondness for the military and my mother's more traditional aspirations for me, I had no idea how they would feel about the honor being bestowed on their daughter.

After I got their response, I still didn't know. They only said they now prepared for their journey to Pilk in haste and would see me the night before Noruz. For all I knew my dad was unimpressed and my mother was horrified. But they'd be here.

We met in the late afternoon at an upscale tavern for an early dinner. Noruz revelers, dressed in their finest clothes, filled every table and most of the standing space. I stood in the doorway, studying my family for any sign of what they thought about my accomplishment. I got no clue.

My two youngest sisters neared the end of their higher education at schools near Pilk, and of course my parents wished to visit with them, too. Well, at least with one of them. Iolite, my sister who suffers from a chronic illness, had both parents doting over her. From across the room, I could tell they inquired about her health. The other sister, Gypsum, was nowhere to be seen, but Gypsum often missed family events, so her absence didn't surprise me.

Iolite saw me first and her strange purple eyes lit up. She's smaller than most, as are all who suffer from her disease, so as a child she'd needed more looking after than the others. I'd always been happy to help her and we'd grown close that way.

"Sulphur, I'm so proud of you!" She yelled it across the room in her high voice and, to my embarrassment, half the people in the room turned to me.

"Congratulations," a few of the more drunk ones yelled out.

Other's followed suit.

"What's the occasion?"

"You inherit a fortune?"

"You finish school with honors?"

"You're going to marry a prince?"

At this last question, my mother's eyes finally met mine. She was a tall woman, like me, and she stood up to her full height and smiled at me, and then at the room full of people. It wasn't a warm smile, but more one of acceptance. Maybe even one of accepting defeat with grace.

"No," my mother said in her most commanding tone. "My daughter is going to be a prince. Tomorrow."

"Huh?"

"Ain't possible."

"Wait, I heard about her. The lady that killed all those people up in Tolo. It's true. They're making her a prince." This particular drunk was quite excited to discover he knew something no one else did.

"Yes." I needed to speak up. "I thank you all for your good cheer. Please go on with your celebrations. There will be a round of ale on me after I have some time to greet my family."

I sat down amidst their cheers and whistles, for the free ale if not for me. My dad whispered, "How many people *did* you kill in Tolo?" It was the first thing he said to me.

"Two." I spat out the word. I wanted to tell him it haunted me still. I wanted him to know I'd considered quitting the Svadlu. But not here, not now, and not after that greeting. Before I told him any of those things, I wanted him to hug me and tell me he was proud of me, not look at me like he barely knew me.

My mother touched my arm.

"While this isn't something we'd ever have predicted, Sulphur, your dad and I recognize this honor as quite an achievement." The look she gave my dad said *don't we, dear?* "We're here to honor you, our daughter."

"Of course we are," my dad said. His eyes met mine for the first time, and I saw the same acceptance in them I'd seen in my mother's smile. So that was how it was going to be. They'd tolerate the path I'd taken.

Holidays made for slow service and noisy taverns, so none of us found the dinner pleasant. Dad had less patience for crowds than most, and any commotion agitated Iolite, so part way through our meal Dad suggested he and Iolite go for a walk. Mom and I stayed to finish eating.

She and I seldom talked much, but that evening my mind drooped with worries, so I told her Ryalgar and Coral were in town.

"What! Why didn't they let us know?"

"They didn't let me know either, I only heard about it through Davor. He's having a secret meeting with them tonight, and they weren't supposed to tell anyone. He said he'd invite them to my Mozdolo, and they'd surprise you tomorrow."

My mother's eyes lit up as I spoke. "Do you think Davor and Coral might move in together like real married people?"

That was what mattered to her?

"No, Mom. The meeting is about military strategy, not their marriage."

"That makes no sense. Neither Ryalgar nor Coral knows the first thing about battles. If anyone …"

She never got to finish her sentence because a man ran into the tavern yelling. "Run! The Mongols are here. The invasion has started!"

What?

Outside the door, I could hear the beginnings of panic.

"Get out!" "Hide." "Take Cover." "Flee!"

I stepped in front of my mother, lest these beasts enter the building.

"I'm sure they're *not* outside this tavern," my mother said. "Come on. Let's go out and look."

She headed for the door so I followed her. What else could I do? Outside, frightened people yelled for help while others pleaded for safety. A few looted newly abandoned merchants' stands. The only thing missing from the chaotic scene was an actual Mongol.

"Where are they?" I demanded of a foot soldier passing by.

"In Pilk center, madam," he told me. "They're outside the offices of the Ruling Prince of Pilk."

My mother grabbed my arm. "Your dad told me he'd walk with Iolite over to Pilk Center."

Oh pruck. "Don't worry, they'll take cover. We can't help them, Mom. Let's get you back to the inn. Now."

She wasn't happy about it, but she came with me. I took the time to get her settled in, and to ensure no invaders had been seen anywhere near her place of lodging. Then I went to report for duty.

Crowds milled around the Svadlu headquarters even at this late hour. Understandable, given the circumstances. Considering my restriction to light duty, how could I best help? I searched for someone in command, but instead I found the messenger I'd hired yesterday to deliver my letter to Giorgi. He'd come to headquarters to find me, to deliver Giorgi's response.

When I reached for an envelope, he shook his head. "It's verbal. Giorgi is here in Pilk now, and he didn't have time to write this message down."

"Then let's go outside. Don't declare the dispatch, I don't want any attention. Just tell it to me like we're talking."

He nodded, but he had trouble complying and had to start over twice. I finally got that Giorgi delayed his reply to me to await the outcome of Davor's meeting with Ryalgar and to learn of the Royal's response to what Davor found out.

"Giorgi is deeply saddened to learn that your sister pleaded with the Svadlu to abandon Vinx and its surrounding nichnas. She claims she can defend them better than the army can. An astounding claim. More remarkably, they agreed to her plan and persuaded the other royals from the eastern half of the realm to support this outlandish scheme. Vinx has no realistic recourse but to join its neighbors."

"What?" I yelled it at the poor messenger, who gave me a helpless look and began to use his singsong voice.

"I send this in haste to answer your immediate questions. Do not waste your one request by asking the Svadlu to behave any other way. They will not, so save your friend. Then continue to do your job in all things. Vinx needs you to be a respected Mozdol now more than ever. Do not endanger your title. We will talk in person soon, dear brother. Uh, dear sibling. Remain of good cheer. Vinx will find a way."

With that, the messenger moved his hand across his face, using the customary gesture to imply he took off the mask of the message's author and resumed his own face.

After my outburst, I understood why messengers needed to put some distance between themselves and what they said.

******

A Mozdolo should be one of the greatest days of one's life. Mine was one of my worst.

Although only ten Mongols arrived in Pilk the day before, and they left the realm by nightfall, people remained agitated. Only Giorgi attended my ceremony; the others in his family sent regrets, citing safety concerns. Few Svadlu came, and only three Mozdols attended. The head man, Kazimir, didn't bother.

Irakli, the second in command and the one who had presided over my questioning, did the honors with an apologetic half-smile. As he held out the fabulous scarlet cape that conferred my new status upon me, he whispered "Take it now but give it back after the ceremony. It's a spare man's cape, we'll have to get one made to fit you later."

I didn't get the chance to respond because Davor picked that moment to walk in, or rather to stumble in, with another woman on his arm. No one seemed surprised to see her, which made me realize they weren't. I hurt for my sister Coral.

My parents never came. Later I got their message that Iolite had a severe spell the night before so they left to return her to school. They couldn't delay until midday? Ryalgar and Coral never showed up, either. I didn't know if Davor told them about it or drank so much he'd forgot.

Before my Mozdolo, I decided my first loyalty lay with Ilari but on the day I became a prince of the realm, I didn't know what loyalty to Ilari meant anymore. Was my allegiance supposed to go to the Svadlu's cowardly strategy? To my sisters' ridiculous plan? What other options did I have? Even if my loyalty rightfully belonged to Vinx, I best served my nichna by being a good Mozdol and playing along. It was a role that suited me poorly.

The Svadlu delivered the only good outcome of the day when they agreed to my appeal to free Tamara as my Mozdolo gift.

"Showing mercy to a comrade is a noble request," Irakli said. He made no effort to hide his delight that I'd played the part they'd designed for me.

I caught Rooslin's eye, and his wink told me he agreed. At least I had him and his suspicious mind on my side.

The next morning, I didn't even have that.

~ 12 ~

Not Naïve

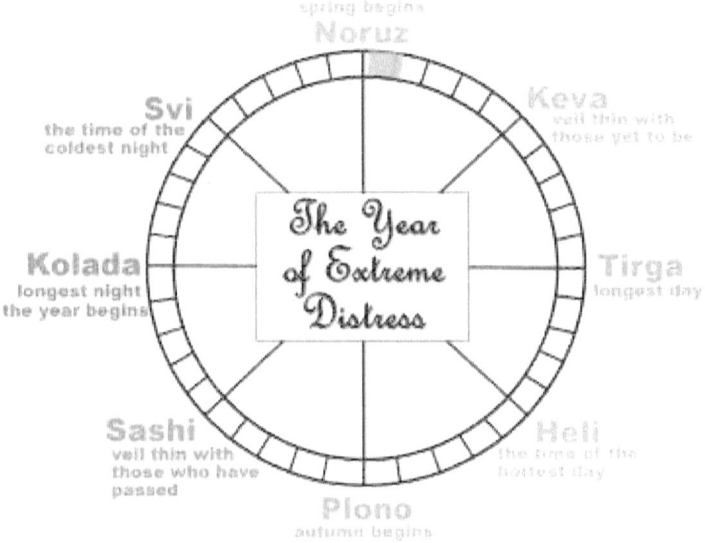

spring begins
Noruz

Svi
the time of the
coldest night

Keva
veil thin with
those yet to be

The Year
of Extreme
Distress

Kolada
longest night
the year begins

Tirga
longest day

Sashi
veil thin with
those who have
passed

Heli
the time of the
hottest day

Piono
autumn begins

"You're going where? Why? Your shoulder hasn't even finished healing?"

The day after my Mozdolo, Rooslin got word to saddle up and join a group headed to Faroo. It made no sense.

"We're looking for a band of thieves who crossed the Wide River a while back and have been hiding in Faroo preying on small groups. This morning the doctors told me my arm is fully functional. I know it's not, but when I argued with them, they suggested my only problem involved a lack of courage. What could I do?"

He slammed items into his saddlebag as he spoke, favoring his good arm as he worked.

"Are they trying to get you killed? Because of me?" Yesterday left me peeved but this made me furious.

He laughed in his unamused way. "Perhaps I overdid it convincing you to be more suspicious. Even *I* don't think anyone wants me dead. But it's possible someone decided I encouraged you to ask too many questions and should be less available to you for a while."

"How long do you think you'll be gone?" I wanted my closest ally back soon. When Rooslin whispered his wisdom in my ear, I felt stronger.

The way he cocked his head to one side told me I wouldn't like the answer. "This mission won't go fast; these thieves have been hard to catch. But I'm traveling with five others, all with plenty of experience. Honestly, I don't think I'll be in danger. I'll stay in the background and be careful."

"Please do."

He stopped packing to look at me. "Tamara should be released today; I think she'll be sent to the enlisted women's quarters. That's a tough adjustment for her. Give her my best, and tell her the three of us will be out drinking ale together in a few anks."

He gave me half a hug with his good arm then mounted his horse as gracefully as he could with his injury. As he rode off, I wondered what prucking idiot sent an injured man into a fight.

I intended to find out.

First, I went back to my quarters. I'd been told to pack my meager belongings and move to the building housing our few female officers. Most Mozdols had their own place, but I'd yet to get the Mozdol stipend, much less to collect one or more of the purses Mozdols often received. Yet, Davor deemed it unseemly for me to bunk with the enlisted women. I didn't look forward to moving in with Issa, who'd killed ten outlaws, and with her friends, who considered me undeserving.

Alone in the room full of small beds, I took my time packing. Rooslin was right; it would be good if I could be here when Tamara arrived. So I pulled out my few garments, shook the wrinkles out of each, and then refolded every one into a perfect square. The process served no purpose other than to be slow and to soothe me. After yesterday's disappointment, I needed some soothing.

I looked up when I heard someone enter, hoping it was Tamara. Instead I saw one of the last people I expected to see.

"You *are* here!" my sister Olivine said, her coppery hair glinting in the sunlight as her small frame half-filled the doorway.

"Of course I'm here. This is where I live and work. Why are *you* here?"

As far as I knew, Olivine still split her time between living with my parents in Vinx and pursuing her life as a painter in the artsy nichna of K'ba. My mother thought Olivine had a secret artist boyfriend there as well, and she probably did.

"I came to exhibit my work at a special Noruz showing. It didn't go so well." She fidgeted with her fingers as she spoke, leading me to think it had gone worse than that.

"I'm sure having an alleged invasion in the middle of the exhibition did nothing to help."

"No," she said with a laugh. "It was rather poor timing. Look, I'm heading home now but I wanted to come, uh, say hi before I left."

"Thanks. Hi."

"More than that. Sulphur, I heard last night in a tavern about a young woman with short blonde hair from Vinx who did amazing things and become a Mozdol yesterday. That's a big deal. Why didn't you invite your family? I'd have come."

Really? "I *did* invite my family," I said. I suspected I sounded as bitter as I felt, even though I tried not to. "Mom and Dad showed up here in Pilk, but they couldn't find Gypsum, and for reasons I know nothing about, they left with Iolite before my ceremony."

"Oh no. I'm sorry."

"I saw them the night before. They told me they spent half a day looking all over K'ba for you and Celestine so they could bring you with them, but they couldn't find either of you."

"I never told them about this exhibit."

"Why the Heli not?"

"It's … complicated. And I have no idea where Celestine is."

"Mom thinks she's having an affair with some professor at the university. Anyway, Coral and Ryalgar were here in Pilk to meet with Davor and he said he'd invite them too, but it seems he forgot. So, yeah, no family."

"Yet everybody made it to Coral's wedding, didn't they?" she said.

"Yeah. People show up when you do what you're *supposed* to do..."

"... like marry a prince." This sister, one I felt little in common with, finished my sentence for me. "I'm proud of you, Sulphur. Happy for you."

"Are you sure? Dad can hardly look me in the eye now that he knows I killed two men to earn this honor."

Olivine didn't blink. "If you did, I'm sure they needed killing."

"They did. They hurt innocent people, mostly for the fun of it."

"Like I said ..."

I believed her, and it surprised me how even a small showing of support from anyone in my family made a difference. I'm sure I stood taller. I could deal with Issa and her crowd. I could comfort Tamara, manage without Rooslin, and act like royalty because someone in my family was proud of me.

"How's that archery stuff of yours going?" I asked.

"A little like your stuff, but without the accolades. I'm having to examine my own ideas about killing." She didn't offer more explanation except to add, "When a war is coming, it's easier to decide what matters and what doesn't."

It sounded like one of those things the little man with the tinkling wind chimes had said. "You know the best thing about having your house catch on fire?" he'd asked me one morning.

"I can't think of a single good thing," I'd answered.

"There's one. You know at once what is important to you and what is not."

He and Olivine, they had a point.

Tamara walked in not long after Olivine left. She looked smaller, shrunken by the pain of her imprisonment and diminished by her demotion. The long dark-blonde braid that hung almost to the small of her back had come apart in places. She glanced at the beds as if she didn't know which was hers, then she walked over and sat on the edge of mine.

"I guess I'll take this one. It's about to be vacant, isn't it?

I nodded because I couldn't think of the right words to say.

"Did Rooslin tell you his theories about why this all happened to you?" I asked.

"He did. I'm not sure I believe it, but the man does come up with some interesting notions."

"If he's right," I said "I'm not much of a hero, and you're no one who needs forgiveness. We've both been used."

"Yes, but you got used in a far more pleasant way." She said it with a laugh yet I saw the hurt in her eyes.

"Perhaps a bit of ale?" I offered.

She nodded. "Before you get it, tell me. How close did you come to letting me rot in prison while you asked the Svadlu to defend your homeland instead?

"Fairly close." I liked Tamara too well to lie to her. "I like to think I'd give up anyone's life, including my own, to save thousands. But once I understood my gesture for Vinx would do no good, I was glad to ask for your pardon."

She looked at the ceiling and blew out a slow breath. "I'm glad you did."

I expected the kitchen help to argue with me when I asked for a mug of ale in the middle of the day, but the soldier who got it for me only said, "Of course, Mozdol."

Whoa. I'd now be given anything I wanted when I wanted it? Would that change how I saw the world? Of course it would. Fast, if I let it.

Tamara's hands shook as she took the mug from me.

"I owe you my life. Now maybe twice over."

"Please. That's ridiculous."

"No. I need you to know this. No matter what the future holds, no matter what horrible assignment they give me or how closely they watch me, I will help you save your nichna."

"What do you mean?"

"You told me your sister needed Svadlu to take time off and train cow herders and farmers to fight. We'd have to do it in secret, because the Svadlu would never support our involvement in such a thing. As an officer, I didn't think I could risk helping you, but now I can. I'll repay you, Sulphur, I promise. People from Tolo, we're good like that."

81

****

The next day I sought out Davor to find out why my injured friend had been sent on a mission when so many others could have gone instead. Best to have this conversation now as I expected to be put on some sort of detail soon myself.

He wasn't in his office. He wasn't there later in the morning, or in the afternoon. I inquired as to whether he'd been sent out of Pilk or was ill and another Mozdol assured me Davor remained well and in town. Apparently, I could now get information as easily as I could get ale.

When I couldn't find Davor again the next day, I wondered if he hid when he saw me coming. His showing up late and drunk at my Mozdolo with a woman other than my sister, after forgetting or not bothering to invite my sisters, should have embarrassed him. Perhaps it had.

By the third day, I started checking taverns and found him alone in the back corner of one less frequented by the Svadlu. Yes, he was hiding. I got a sheepish and slightly tipsy grin as I walked up to his table.

"I didn't do right by you, Sulphur. I meant to, I did. That varming discussion with your sisters and then the one with all those pus-filled royals and the way it ended, I was so discouraged."

Odd as it was, I understood his frustration. I didn't like the outcome either.

"How could such a bad decision happen?"

He rolled his eyes and blew out a frustrated puff of air.

"We made a lousy deal because no one had a better idea. So, the Svadlu will act like cowards, huddling back behind the wall until the Mongols reach us. The Velka will do whatever they do, and I hope to Heli thousands don't die because of them. The Royals will probably blame everyone else no matter how it turns out. Maybe if we're lucky we'll have a piece of Ilari left to hang onto at the end."

He sounded more discouraged than embarrassed until he added, "Doesn't excuse me acting like a scumphead though."

I recognized it for the apology it was.

"No, it doesn't. I didn't come here because of that, though. I want to know what idiot sent my friend Rooslin, a man with an injured shoulder, off to chase thieves in Faroo."

"Yes. That." He took another long gulp of his ale. "He'll be fine. He's got a few uncomfortable anks ahead of him camping in the worst parts of that damp place, but he *is* with good men who will make sure he doesn't have to fight."

"He better be. Why's he there?"

"The other Mozdols insisted and I couldn't stop them. I did try. Consider it his punishment for being so cynical about our motives in promoting you and in jailing your former commander."

"How would any of them even know about his theories?" I felt my anger towards Davor rising. "Wait. Did you tell them about my suspicions? Why would you do such a thing?"

"I wouldn't, and I didn't. I'm not that stupid. But for once, Rooslin was. He told Tamara his theories in the prison courtyard! Plenty heard him say she and you were both being used by the Mozdols." Davor shook his head. "You don't talk about ideas like that where you can be overheard."

"He must have thought no one was in earshot."

"For a man who's paranoid, he needs to be more suspicious."

"Are his ideas correct?"

"What do you think?" Davor spread his hands apart, palms up, as though waiting for me to produce the right answer.

You don't punish someone for proposing a false theory.

But … a little flash of light went off in my brain, like when fire takes hold of kindling.

"I think he's well-meaning, but his ideas are absurd. The leaders of the Svadlu would never stoop to such a thing. *Never*."

My statement earned me having Davor raise his glass in a toast to me.

"Very good. You *are* smarter than they think. Make sure you clue Rooslin in when he returns."

"I will. So, who does a Mozdol report to? What can I expect to be doing now that the ceremony is over?"

He gestured for me to have a seat. I did.

"Given your lack of experience, you're kind of a probationary Mozdol until you get your feet on the ground. Your fellow Mozdols all agree you need direction and as your sponsor, I'm stuck with the job. So, I'll get you deployed on a few little missions here and there as issues arise. I admit, your reputation for fierceness makes you more useful than most."

"More useful? I don't understand."

He waved to a server and pointed to me, indicating I needed a mug of ale.

"We want people afraid of us so they'll stop their mischief when we get there. It should happen more now that we've got this golden girl who fights like a wildcat. The mere sight of you riding up, flanked of course by plenty of armed men, should prevent bloodshed. It's a worthy calling. Show up and stop trouble."

"Sure. I'll be happy to do it. But what I want to know is how can I help us better prepare for the invasion."

"Oh that." He let out a large and rather rude belch. "Officially? Our stance is we expect the citizens of the eastern nichnas to evacuate when and as ordered. We in no way support the Velka's unauthorized schemes."

"I figured as much."

"Unofficially, your schedule will have an unusual amount of free time. I suggest you use it to impart a modicum of military knowledge to your sisters and those they hope to train. I and the others in command will not question your absences."

"You *want* me to help them?"

"Not particularly, although I do like the idea of fewer lives being lost no matter how. No, I would choose to phrase it more like 'we want to have some idea of what the Heli these old biddies are planning.' Who better to find out for us than our own newest Mozdol, a woman with every reason to help her sisters without them suspecting her?"

I was aghast. "You want me to spy on my sisters for the Svadlu?"

"Spy is such a strong word. Why do you have to take things to extremes? We'd simply like you to keep us informed. Can't you see the advantage of our having an insider who lets us know what's happening? Without that knowledge, we're at a disadvantage once the Mongols come at us. You do want us to be as effective as possible, don't you?"

Okay. He had a point.

I recapped my situation in my head. Giorgi, my ruling prince and new brother, wanted me to act like a good Mozdol by doing whatever the Svadlu asked. He wanted this so I could tell *him* what the Svadlu were doing. He said it was the best way I could help Vinx.

Now, the Svadlu had asked me to act like a good sister by doing whatever the Velka asked. They wanted this so I could keep *them* informed of what the Velka were doing. They said it was the best way I could help Ilari.

Fine. I could keep everyone happy by telling everyone everything. That worked as long as no one insisted I lie to anyone else. Would anyone do that?

I knew what Rooslin would say. My best hope was they wouldn't do it for a while.

~ 13 ~

Unspoken

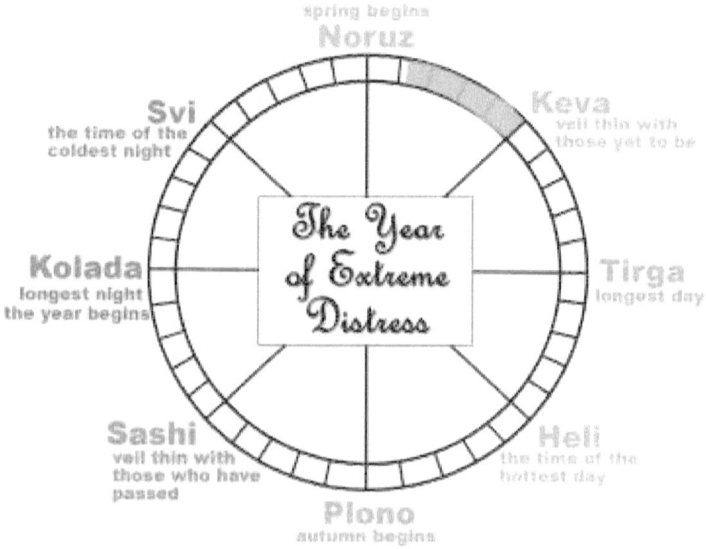

Days later I received a letter from my father. Dad was a thoughtful man, at least if you gave him time to think things through. He apologized for their abrupt departure, explaining how Iolite had the second spell of her life the night before my Mozdolo, and they thought it best to get her far from Pilk Center.

By then, I'd already heard about Iolite's episode from several sources in the Svadlu. Dad confirmed what I'd learned. He and Iolite walked through Pilk Center when the Mongol envoys arrived to deliver their ultimatum, and my sister's episode appeared to have been set off by the presence of the invaders. She connected with them, something frundles occasionally did with strangers, and to the amazement of all she'd served as an interpreter for the interaction. I'd already learned of how much the Svadlu appreciated it.

What I hadn't known, until his letter, was how Iolite's connection to these barbarians frightened Mom and Dad, who then whisked her away in hopes of severing the tie.

Thus, their absence during my big moment.

I suppose their fear-inspired exodus made some sense. Dad apologized for it twice, adding how proud he was of me. Well, at least he knew the right things to say and said them. I tucked the letter away with my personal things.

I now had storage for such keepsakes, with a small chest and an armoire in a little room of my own. I had a wooden chair, too, and a small high window facing the street. It wasn't as nice as the bedroom I'd left behind in Vinx, but it beat the barracks.

There were five of us women in a house built for eight, and we shared a kitchen and dining area staffed by an older housekeeper named Nino. The other four female officers, including the fierce Issa and the woman who'd spoken to me about how relatively undeserving I was, no longer disliked me. My friendship with Tamara, and news of how I'd secured her release, seemed to have bought me some respect.

I appreciated they didn't give me Tamara's old room, but chose to leave it as it was when the guards took her away, so she could come sort through her things in her own time.

"Will you be living here long?" one of the women asked me as we ate the lunch Nino prepared for us. All the women except for Issa ate together; I'd noticed she often missed our meals.

"I think so," I answered her. "I don't need a fancy house of my own and I can't afford such a place anyway. I think it makes sense to stay here at least until the Mongols' ultimatum passes."

The women looked at each other when I mentioned the silent sword at all our throats.

"We want to talk to you about that," another said. "We've heard your sisters persuaded the Royals to let the Svadlu defend only the Western nichnas."

Her tone left me confused as to whether they resented my sisters' efforts or appreciated them.

"The Svadlu know how to keep the people of Ilari safe," the third one said.

"Yeah. The Royals had no business telling us how to run a war to suit their political agendas," another agreed.

Okay, these women liked my sisters' success. Why not find out more?

"Have you heard details of what my sisters are planning?"

They all three shrugged.

"Velka magic."

"Not that we believe in that stuff."

"Yet you gotta give those forest ladies credit for trying."

"I hope they don't all die."

"I hope not either," I said.

The three women exchanged another look.

"We invited Tamara to come have dinner with us tonight."

"We can do that?" I had the impression our table was restricted to officers, but maybe not.

"Who's gonna stop us?" one asked.

"Not me," I said. "She can eat with us every night as far I'm concerned. In fact I wish she would."

"Done," one of the other women said. I'd earned a smile.

"Tonight we thought we'd talk about your sister's ill-advised idea of having farmers and cow herders refuse the Svadlu's order to evacuate."

So maybe this was the problem.

"We think civilians taking up arms is a bad idea."

"But we've been told your sisters won't be dissuaded. They insist they need the help of the locals to carry out their plans."

"Tamara says she's going to help train them. To repay you."

"We want to help Tamara."

"We've more freedom with our time than the enlisted people."

"And more experience teaching people how to fight."

"We don't want Tamara to have to do this alone."

I held up my hands to stop the conversation. "She won't be alone," I said. "I plan to help her."

That earned me smiles from every one of them.

"Then we don't want Tamara and *you* doing this alone."

Shortly after our first meal with Tamara, the higher Mozdols sent me out on the sort of mission Davor described. I led a group over to the border between K'ba and Eds to quell an unneighborly dispute between two angry neighbors. I'd discovered as a teenaged girl that while knowing how to fight is useful, knowing how to prevent a fight is often better.

These particular angry grown men saw the wisdom in calming down once we arrived, and I didn't even need to dismount my horse. If the men sent to ride behind me and look intimidating had any problems doing so while led by a woman, they wisely kept it to themselves.

When I returned to Pilk, Davor supplied me with a schedule. I now had assignments every other ank until Kolada, mostly involving training Svadlu recruits to fight. Then, if not on a peacekeeping assignment, what I did during my anks off was my business.

Well, I certainly had a lot of time to train farmers.

I composed a carefully worded letter to Ryalgar, mentioning how much free time I now had as a Mozdol. I walked over to the nearest market and gave my letter to the Velka. As I handed it over, I understood it committed me to a multilayered and dangerous role. Lives, perhaps a lot of lives, would depend on my ability to figure out what to tell whom.

****

The Svadlu commanders assigned me a small office to conduct my business in during the day. I noted it was less than half the size of Davor's and smaller than all the others, but I figured some sort of seniority system existed. Someday I'd have a larger one.

Besides, it was plenty for my needs. I spent my time in it planning how to teach the recruits, hoping to incorporate some of the odd exercises the man in Vinx had taught me. Funny how I only spent anks training with him and yet thought of his methods often.

A few days before Keva, a messenger came to my door. I hoped he brought a reply from Ryalgar, or maybe word from Rooslin, who'd now been gone longer than planned. But as he stood in front of the small table that served as my desk and began his recitation, I realized it was neither.

"His Royal Highness Giorgi, the ruling prince of Vinx, invites you to join him today for a light lunch and an exceptionally fine pink luncheon wine in the Sparrow Room of the Pilk palace."

Giorgi *had* said he'd see me soon. Looked like it was time to report in. I gathered up my things and began the short walk to the palace.

"With the Mongol envoy and everything happening so fast, I regret I couldn't visit with you after your Mozdolo," he said as he gestured me towards the other chair at a table covered with lavish food. One never eats poorly when they dine with a prince. A waiter filled my goblet as I sat. "And my family sends their regrets that no others could attend. Truly, the timing of that envoy was horrible. Your event should have received more attention."

I raised one eyebrow and took a long swallow of the wine.

"But everyone is delighted with the successful negotiation you conducted in that clash between Eds and K'ba. Oh yes, word spreads quickly. Our new lady Mozdol is a force to be reckoned with."

So now I was the lady Mozdol. Heli, maybe I should have gone with Mozdolrina and been done with it.

"So tell me," he said in what I guessed he considered a conspiratorial whisper. "What's actually happening with the Svadlu." He leaned in towards me as if I'd share the juiciest of gossip.

I knew why my friend Rooslin had been sent off on an uncomfortable mission. I needed to speak as if unseen ears heard everything I said. Yet I needed to satisfy Giorgi by supplying information.

So I told him of my new office, my new housemates, and my new duties training recruits to fight. I left out any mention of Davor, or Rooslin, or anyone's plan to help the Velka.

He listened and nodded. "Sounds like you're fitting in fine."

"I think I am." We smiled at each other.

"So much so that maybe next time we should go for a ride together. Everyone I know from Vinx loves to get out in the open air on a horse."

It was true; most Vinxites did. More to the point, though, there was no easy way to overhear a conversation between two riders. A man who grew up in a palace no doubt understood that advantage.

"Excellent idea. I look forward to it, Your Highness."

"Please, no need for that, you're my relative now. Good luck with training those recruits."

We parted with an unspoken understanding, the best kind under our circumstances.

****

Keva was the most awkward of the holidays for me. The warm spring air and lush greenery often persuaded those disinclined to take part in the year's other sexual celebrations to loosen up and enjoy the pleasures of the day. My approach for years had been to take a journey somewhere alone. I confess, I usually pleasured myself on that day, allowing a release I often abstained from because I thought I fought better when I didn't give in to urges others embraced with alarming frequency.

I'd planned to ride up into the hills of Lev the day before Keva and camp for a night. There was a spot along the Little River, partially forested and not frequented by many, where I thought I could have a solitary picnic and an evening away from prying eyes and unwanted invitations. I'd have my own fun and return when society behaved with more restraint.

I finished gathering my gear as Issa knocked on my door. I confess I worried she sought a partner for the night, but the alarm on her face told me a worse situation beckoned.

"Your friend Rooslin is outside. He wishes to come in."

I'd already learned men could visit us in our rooms if we wished, but no man was allowed without a resident's explicit permission.

"Of course. Is he alright?"

"I'll let you be the judge of it," she said.

I knew as soon as I saw him, he was not. His face had been beaten badly. One eye swelled shut and dried blood caked around his deformed nose. He held his hurt arm like a bird with a broken wing. I suspected his clothes hid many more injuries.

"Prucking bat scump. What happened to you?"

"Please don't say anything to make me laugh."

"Have you seen a doctor?"

"Yes. This morning when I rode in. I've been told there's nothing to be done for me, it will all heal in time. Just bruising."

"That's ridiculous. If the doctors can't help, I know the Velka have poultices to ease your pain and lessen swelling. Let me get over to the market and get you something. It won't take long."

"Not right now. Please, stay with me. Can I sit?"

"Heli yes. Lie down on my bunk."

He did and a shudder of relief ran through his body.

"Did these thieves do this to you?"

"Not directly. My comrades are still chasing them through the muck along the river. They aren't Ilarians but they seem to have an arrangement with some Faroojers, one we suspect is lucrative for all.

"That would complicate the situation."

"It has. We'd have caught these rantillions anks ago if they didn't have help."

As he talked, I placed a pillow under his head and a blanket over his body.

"My shoulder gave me a hard time last night," he said, "so I passed on going out with the others, and got my dinner in the tavern where we stayed. Some of the locals must have been associated with the bunch we chased. They recognized me and picked a fight. I did my best, but it was four on one and I'm only good on one side."

Our housekeeper came to my door.

"Madam? I've put out food for all of you for today and tomorrow. Things that won't spoil. I'll be back the day after Keva."

"Of course. Enjoy your holiday, Nino."

But she wasn't looking at me any longer. Rooslin had her full attention.

"By all incarnations of the Goddess, this man needs medical help. What is he doing here? No offense meant, madam."

"None taken; I agree with you but our doctors already told him to go home and go to bed; he'll heal on his own."

Her hands went to her hips. "Lazy scumpheads. Any other day they'd fall over themselves to help this poor man. I've got supplies here. Will you let me do what I can?"

"Let you? I'd be so grateful."

She hurried off while Rooslin told me of his horrible night nursing his wounds alone at the inn. Apparently the locals feared the men who beat him up; they wouldn't risk helping him or even sending for a doctor after the attack. Rooslin's companions had stayed out late, and when he woke them early in the morning to beg for help they sent him riding back to Pilk for care.

He'd managed the ride, I couldn't imagine how, only to be brushed off here by those anxious to celebrate.

Nino came back with salves and lotions and instructed me on how to apply what where while she did the same. Soon we had Rooslin's shirt removed and his feet bare and much of his body covered in substances meant to ease his pain and help him heal.

When we finished, she gave him something to drink.

"It will make him sleep," she told me. "Sleep is the best thing for him. If he wakes up, give him more. And keep his wounds covered the way I showed you."

I thanked her and sent her on her way. Rooslin already dozed, exhausted from the effort he'd made to get here.

He woke up a few hours later, made his way to the outhouse, then drank a broth Nino had prepared for him before he curled back up on the bed and let me apply all the salves and lotions again. When I finished, I saw him shiver, the way people sometimes do when they're in a lot of pain.

"How can I help you?"

I felt so lost. My powers of fighting would have done him a world of good last night, but now they did nothing at all.

"I can't get warm. I know it's odd, but would you lay next to me and keep me warm?"

"Of course. And I'll get another blanket, too."

The bed wasn't large, but it was wide enough that I managed to lay behind him and wrap my arms around his body. I bent my legs so the front of my thighs were tight against the back of his, while my stomach snuggled against his butt and my chest was tight against his back. That way I gave him the most warm surface I could. I felt his shivering slowly subside as his breathing became slow and regular.

I lay with him through the night, becoming a human blanket, a living heat source who held him like his lover, his mother, his doctor, and his friend. I only moved my arm or leg slightly if it began to cramp. Until dawn came, I willed my strength into his body, soothing him with my touch and with my warm breath on the back of his neck.

~ 14 ~

Safe Ways to Throw Rocks

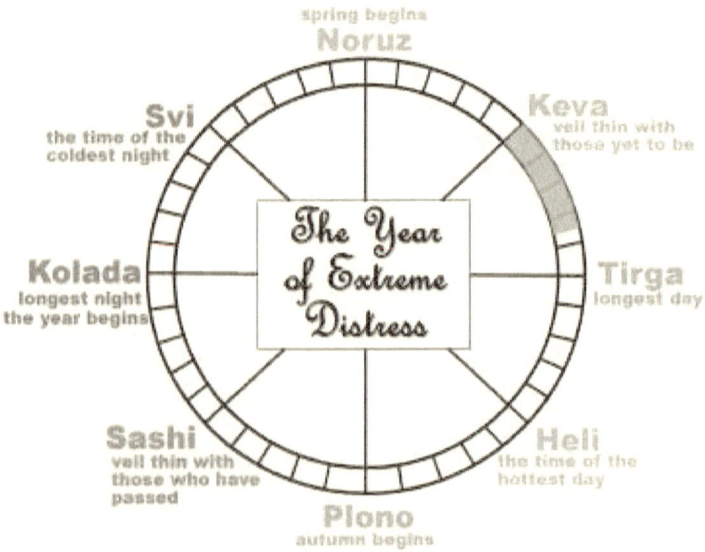

spring begins
Noruz

Svi
the time of the
coldest night

Keva
veil thin with
those yet to be

Kolada
longest night
the year begins

The Year
of Extreme
Distress

Tirga
longest day

Sashi
veil thin with
those who have
passed

Heli
the time of the
hottest day

Plono
autumn begins

All my adult life I'd dreaded Keva, yet I woke that morning feeling comforted and refreshed. I saw Rooslin had rolled over to face me. As my eyes fluttered open he managed a smile with his swollen lips.

"You healed me last night," he said.

I knew I hadn't done that, but between the potions, the sleep, and yes, maybe the comfort I gave, he looked so much better.

I felt self-conscious lying there with him so I sat up and put my feet on the floor.

"Let me tend to my personal needs, then I'll bring us both back some breakfast wine."

I made my way to the outhouse in the back, thinking this particular Keva had brought more intimacy than I'd ever had and with no sex involved. How odd.

Rooslin was fully dressed when I returned, and he took a mug from me and gulped the light fruity beverage most Ilarians drank to begin their day.

"Ahh." His long content breath told me how much he'd improved since yesterday.

I'd also brought some of the cake Nino left for us, and as I nibbled on it, he talked. He had much on his mind, and his conversation kept away the awkwardness trying to creep in.

"The men I traveled with, they couldn't stop talking about the Svadlu's decision to abandon the eastern nichnas when the Mongols return."

"How they'd feel about it?"

"It varied. Two thought it was the best of bad choices, the other two disagreed. They believed we are honor-bound to protect every bit of the realm."

"Let me guess. The unhappy two grew up in nichnas that will be evacuated?"

"Of course. But none of the four liked the idea. And word of the Velka's involvement inspired all kinds of responses."

I could understand why.

"Like what?" I asked as innocently as I could.

"One man said 'good for them' and thought they could make a difference. Even thought we should help them where we could. Another found the idea foolish and hoped they wouldn't all die."

"I see. And the other two?"

"One thought we should forcibly protect them by kidnapping them if we had to, for their safety and ours. The fourth argued they had every right to do as they pleased, but shouldn't ask poor farmers and herders to die with them. He wants the Svadlu to forcibly evacuate all residents, then let the Velka do what they will."

"Quite the variety of ideas. What do you think, Rooslin?"

"I'm from Bisu." He managed a shrug with only one shoulder. "I know my people's land is their life. Asking them to hide while their animals are slaughtered, their fields burned and their homes destroyed? They won't have lives worth going back to. I'll help *anyone* willing to fight for my nichna."

"I hoped you'd feel that way. You remember my sister in the Velka, right?"

"Oh yes. The men guessed she's the one leading this harebrained idea because she met with Davor and Prince Nevik right before the decision was made. One pointed out she went with her sister, your sister, who's supposedly married to Davor but never seen with him. You do have a complicated family, don't you?

I laughed. "You don't know the half of it. But yes, one or more of my sisters is behind this and, because of my loyalty to my family and nichna, I will give my sisters a hand. I think Davor will look the other way, given my circumstances."

"Heli, that's the best news I could have hoped for! Let me work with you. Maybe they'll cut me slack for being your friend."

"Once you've healed."

"No, now. Listen I've been thinking about this. If you had unlimited poorly trained people -- some small, some awkward, some obese, some old – and you wanted to put them into groups and have each bunch subdue one dangerous armed fighter, how would you do it? How many people would you need?

"Some would say no number would be enough."

"But that's ridiculous. Surely a million people could subdue one man, right?"

"Okay. Right. But we don't have a million."

"Could a hundred people subdue one man? If they received instructions about what to do ahead of time?"

"Of course. You'd have casualties though."

"Maybe. How about fifty? With a little practice thrown in?"

"Sure."

"Twenty? With more practice?"

"Okay, I see where you're going with this. What number *do* you have in mind.?"

"I'm starting with ten."

"Ten cow herders? Your warrior is swinging a sword. They can't get close to him."

"That's why people throw rocks at his face, from either side of him. All they need is a good aim. Plenty of fine rock throwers in Bisu, and more in Scrud. Not much else to do there."

"So then our Mongol charges, sword drawn, at one of the people with the rocks."

"Yup. And one throws smaller rocks at his eyes while two new people, small and limber, dive for his legs from behind. We save all the biggest people for grabbing his sword and sitting on him once he falls."

"You thought this up while riding around Faroo trying to catch thieves?"

"Gotta do something while you're on a horse."

Ilari needed Rooslin and his strange mind.

"Okay. You're part of the team secretly helping the Velka. Keep quiet about it though."

"Who else is helping us?"

"So far? Tamara, and the four female officers."

A few days later I got my response from Ryalgar. She chose her words with care, offering respect for the Svadlu's difficult decision and voicing understanding for my conflicting loyalties. She asked if I could spare some of my free time to help her, and if so, would I come into the forest after Tirga to discuss specifics.

I'm sure she knew I'd been offering her my help. Did she know my direct superior gave me the time? Did she worry I'd been asked to spy on her while I did it? Maybe. She was smart.

She also wrote of how someone else in the Velka would handle communications with me. Wise, I thought and I liked her choice.

Joli, Ryalgar's closest friend, had impressed me during my first visit to the forest. She kept her dark brown locks cut above her shoulders and because I'd never met another woman who didn't let her hair grow as long as it could, I felt a kindredness. Plus, she grew up in the cantankerous nichna of Zur, where fighting was considered normal. She'd make a good liaison with the Svadlu.

I crafted an equally polite letter back, telling Ryalgar circumstances left me no choice but to provide her with aid. I'd go into the forest to meet with her and Joli as asked.

I assumed I'd have to keep up the charade of reluctance throughout the meeting. This would be tiresome.

Rooslin asked me to apply the salves to his face. I obliged because I wanted him to heal fast and, to be honest, I wanted to examine his injuries as they healed.

His face inspired me to design something my trainees could wear over *their* faces. This loose-fitting wooden and leather mask with wide slits would be of no use against a sword or knife but it would protect eyes and sensitive parts of the face against accidents while training.

If we used it and padding around the neck and shoulders, we could actually throw rocks at each other. I couldn't wait.

I got Rooslin to start building my face protectors as I continued to think about ways to make the learning go faster. In my mind, being tasked with teaching others to fight was one more way to protect people. Maybe it was the best way to do it.

****

A couple of anks after Keva, I sought out Iolite to make sure she'd had no further episodes, thinking I hadn't been doing a good job of protecting her lately. A bird would have a short journey from Pilk Center over to her school, but because the place was on the other side of a branch of the Little River, a branch with no bridge, it took half a day's journey to get there. No excuse. Farming kept my father busy this time of year and my mother didn't travel alone on horseback. I needed to go.

This exclusive place cost more than most, and I knew my parents had found a way to send Iolite there because of its gentle reputation. Once I finally arrived there, both students and teachers tried to help me but they couldn't.

Iolite had been on track to finish her studies by Tirga, which was typical timing. Then she'd surprised everyone by completing everything early and leaving. She'd said something about meeting her parents in Pilk Center and, given her condition, her friends assumed she'd moved back home. A couple of teachers expressed concern at the abruptness of her departure.

I wished my parents had dropped me a note and let me know about this. You'd think they'd stop in and say hello to me when they were within walking distance of where I lived! Were they that embarrassed by my unique role as the only female Mozdol in the realm? And my father's letter had been so nice.

Their failure to visit me hurt more than I wanted to admit. They'd come halfway across the realm to get my frundle sister and didn't even bother to say hi to me?

It took a day or two before I realized this made no sense. I knew Iolite cared for me as I was, and no honor I received would embarrass her. Why hadn't *she* insisted on visiting me? Perhaps health problems prevented it, and my parents had rushed her home for that reason.

Now I was worried.

I composed a short note to my parents telling them of my trip to the school and inquiring about Iolite's health. Before I could send it off, though, a messenger arrived to summon me to Davor's office. I left the letter on my desk and followed him, not apprehensive but curious.

I noticed the jug on the table and a cup waiting for me. So, this would be a congenial meeting. I sat.

"How's Ilari's finest female Mozdol doing?" he asked, amused at his own cleverness.

"Concerned about one of my sisters, to be honest."

He slapped his knee in delight. "I love how blunt you are. None of this 'fine and how are you, Davor?' bullscump others indulge in."

He'd no doubt already consumed a mug of whatever was in his jug these days.

"So, tell me, which of the fine ladies in your family concerns you on this lovely spring morning?"

"They all do, but I've had some bothersome news about Iolite, the younger one who has health issues."

"The frundle?" he said. It was considered rude to use the word, unless you were a family member. Then I remembered Davor *was* technically a family member. It was easy to forget.

"Yes. She left school early, a few anks ago. She and my parents passed through Pilk Center, and I can't imagine her not saying hello to me."

I got a raised eyebrow and a look of confusion in response. So I charged ahead.

"All I can guess is she must have been so ill they couldn't pause on their journey. I'm sending a letter to my parents now, asking after her health."

"Sulphur." His face became surprisingly serious for a man who'd been drinking hard liquor in the morning. "Don't send the letter. I don't know who gave you this wrong information, but your parents still believe Iolite is in school. We need to keep it that way."

"What?"

"I only learned of this a few days ago. She finished her studies early to join us and supply helpful information about the Mongols. She's fine and working hard on behalf of Ilari. You need to trust her and trust us."

"But my parents …."

"… will never know, I promise. Iolite will return to school soon and write to your parents to come fetch her. It will all be fine. You need to pretend you never learned of this."

"Is that why you summoned me here?"

"Oddly enough, yes. I intended to be less forthcoming, encouraging you to come to me if you discovered any reasons to be concerned about Iolite, but you made that part unnecessary."

"I'd like to speak with her then."

"Not possible. She's not nearby and shouldn't be disturbed until she's done. You can talk to her later."

I didn't like it but what could I do?

"I trust we have your discretion?" he said. He didn't wait for an answer, but raised his mug, finished the contents, and stood. "Excellent. I'll leave you to the rest of your day."

Davor's words bothered me. Before I joined the Svadlu, I'd never needed to worry about my loyalties. Now it seemed every time I turned around someone forced me to decide who I should tell what. As far as the situation with Iolite went, I had no better choice than to give Iolite and the Svadlu my trust. For now. I hoped it wasn't misplaced.

However, I needed a safety net. Someone else in the family had to know the truth, in case something happened to me. I was a soldier. I could die in a skirmish.

Who in my family best kept a secret? Two sisters qualified, but Olivine was hard to find and Coral wasn't.

I waited until I knew Davor would be busy in Pilk and then I rode over to her little cottage in Vinx. I arrived breathless from the ride.

"I need someone I can trust. I must tell you something. Iolite's left school and no one knows it. She's safe somewhere and she shouldn't be disturbed. Especially by mom and dad."

Coral looked bothered so I took a deep breath and started over as I tried to reassure her. She ushered me to a table on her porch and poured us both afternoon wine as she listened.

"She's being incredibly brave, Coral," I said. "And this is her choice."

That seemed to only make Coral *more* worried, so I tried to add some perspective. "Come on. You and everyone else with a part in this inane defense scheme is taking a risk. Why not allow Iolite to help, too?"

She set her goblet down and looked at me. "Do you *know* what part I'm playing?"

Of course I did. My sister Celestine, who told everyone everything, had filled me in on how Coral could do something frightening with her voice, something that allowed her to boss people around with her tone.

"I'm trying to keep this from the people I know," Coral said. "Dad knows but he thinks I should wait to tell Mom. How do think Mom will handle it?"

Not well.

"I'll keep your secret," I said. "You keep mine."

That seemed to work. We raised our goblets to salute our agreement, and for the rest of my visit we spoke of other things.

~ 15 ~

Nobody's Business Where You Sleep

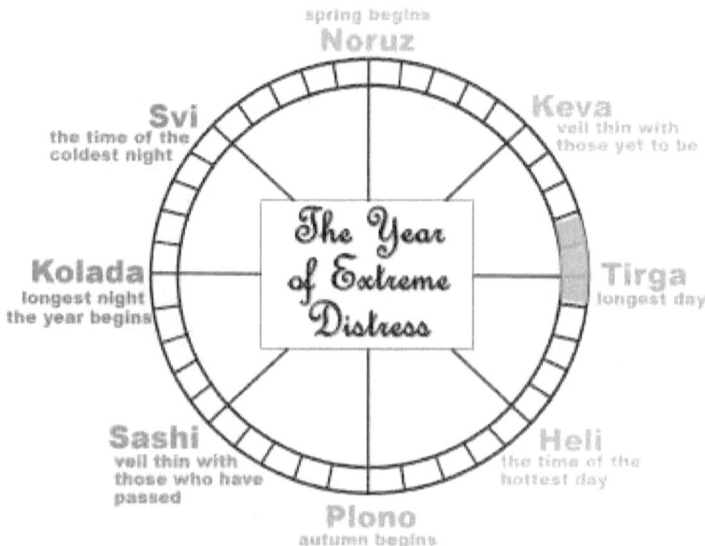

Soon after, Giorgi invited me to join him for a horseback ride, and I knew more intrigue awaited. He lent me as fine a stallion as I'd ever ridden. I stroked the horse's face by way of getting acquainted, and his eyes looked eager for a hard ride.

Giorgi and I made our way to the outer edge of the heavily populated part of Pilk with his ever-present guards close behind. Once we reached an open field, he insisted his guards dismount and have a seat. Then he gave me a signal to follow as he took off across the field at a gallop few horses could match. My mount kept pace with no urging from me. We let the two animals run hard until they tired, then stopped under an apple tree.

I looked behind us to see his guards in the distance mounting their horses in resignation.

"They won't stay back there, even if you asked them to?"

"No. They insist it's for my safety. But these fine horses have bought us a little time."

"Can't you find guards you can trust?"

He laughed. "I've found many. But over time, some get bought, coerced, or threatened. Loyalty is a fleeting commodity; it's a lesson one learns at a young age in a palace."

I thought of my mother's yearning to have each of her daughters marry a prince and wondered if she knew anything about the realities of royal life.

"Who cares so much about what you say and do?"

"Far too many people. My parents, my siblings, my wife. The entire ruling families of the other eleven nichnas. Thieves, traitors, and ne'er-do-wells. The Svadlu and the Velka. Most days I think everyone has an agenda whether they love me or hate me."

This prince has got to meet Rooslin. They'd have a great conversation.

I noticed the two guards had covered about half the ground. We didn't have much more time to talk.

"Who should I be most worried about?" I asked.

"Great question. Listen carefully. Most of the Mozdols mean well even if they're an arrogant bunch. Their worst ideas come from one man who is, unfortunately, their commander. Kazimir is from Kir, and he has wanted to combine, annex, or eliminate the outer nichnas his whole career. He particularly hates Gruen, I've no idea why. The other three commanding Mozdols side with him in most matters and the rest of the Mozdols go along with him when they must. I'd bet my horse he wants your sister's plan to fail, and that he's no fan of yours either."

"Good to know. I'll try to learn more. Anyone else?"

He laughed. "Yeah. My mother. I pissed her off when I stood up to her about you're being a Mozdol. She's turned her anger away from me, her lovable son, to you, a stranger who's easier to hate. You now stand for everything wrong with young women these days. Be careful."

"Great."

"I'm sorry, Sulphur. I probably could have handled your situation better. I'm still learning."

"You're way ahead of me on many things," I said. I wanted to tell this faltering but well-meaning young man something of use, by way of thanking him for what he'd shared and for his trust in me.

"Real quick. Several days ago I found out my sister Iolite ran away from her school to work with the Svadlu. I don't know why or where or on what. My whole family thinks she's still studying and I've been asked to keep my silence. So far I have."

"Good call. And helpful to know."

"Also I'll be going into the forest just after Tirga to plan for training the farmers and cow herders."

"Perfect. Be careful and keep your eyes open."

"The Svadlu have already asked me to do the same thing."

He laughed. "Of course they have."

The two guards pulled up alongside us.

"One last thing," he said to me. "Make sure the other Mozdols are inviting you to *all* of their meetings."

"What? They have meetings?"

He rolled his eyes and nodded as his guards dismounted.

"Please, Your Highness," one said. "Allow us to do our jobs. Your parents would have our heads if anything happened to you, and you know your mother hates it when you ride your steed that fast. One small gopher hole, and you could break your neck."

Prince Giorgi turned to me. "Being the ruling prince of a nichna is *not* all it's cracked up to be."

It was my turn to laugh. "I can see that."

****

I intended to confront Davor about these meetings I'd been excluded from, but when I got back to the officers' quarters, three angry women met me at the door. I didn't see Issa, but the others stood with their arms folded across their chests as they spoke at once.

"We are not going to do it. We're just not."

"Who the Heli do they think they are, getting involved in our house anyway?"

"It's none of their prucking business who sleeps where."

I had no idea what they spoke about, but it didn't sound good.

"Of course it's nobody's business where you sleep," I agreed. "What's going on?"

"Your Mozdol friends are looking out for your newly elevated sensibilities. Can't put a prince, or whatever the Heli you are, in commoner's quarters, right?"

I looked her in the eyes. "They don't want me to live here with you?"

They all answered me.

"Oh no, they'll tolerate that, but only if we 'respect the position' by giving you the best room in the house."

"That's right. They marched in like they owned the place and inspected the rooms!"

"Guess what? Issa has the best and they told her she has to move out today so you can move in tomorrow."

I looked at all three of them. "Do you really think I'd go along with something like that?"

"It doesn't seem your style," one of them agreed.

"Thank you. Issa hasn't started to move her stuff, has she?"

"No, she took off, pissed. Probably wanted to calm down."

Two unrelated pieces of information drifted by each other in my head and connected.

"Where is Issa from?" I asked.

"Gruen. Why?"

"Just, just curious. Don't move anything. I'm going over to my sponsor's office to let him know I won't change rooms. Maybe he can put a stop to this stupidity."

"I can't keep every stupid thing from happening," Davor protested as I walked in.

"This doesn't even make sense," I said. "I like my room. I've never complained. Why would you guys want to piss off all the female officers and make them hate me?"

"That's *not* how the Mozdols see it. Some of us believe we've earned a certain amount of prestige and your being housed in a lesser room than mere officers erodes not only your status, but all of ours as well."

"Sheep scump. You don't believe that, do you?"

"Lady, I can and have slept in a tent, with your sister by the way and that part was great. Didn't diminished my status. Look, I don't care if you sleep in a barn, but those to whom this sort of thing matters won't back down. You risk your position by defying your oath to behave in a manner befitting royalty."

"I swore I'd behave like royalty?"

"You did. At your Mozdolo. I know, I know. No one pays attention to all that scump they make you repeat. But I promise it's in the oath you took."

It probably was, but there was no way in Heli I could kick the beloved Issa out of her room because I was a Mozdol and she was not. I could only think of one solution. I wasn't sure how I'd manage it, but I needed to find a way.

"Could you help me get around this, then?" I asked Davor.

He opened both palms up towards me to say *maybe*.

"My royal arse has decided it is entitled to housing as good as all the other Mozdols. I will be finding and moving into a suitably majestic residence of my own within days. I do not wish to inconvenience my precious regal arse by moving twice, so please tell my fellow Mozdols that I will tolerate my current meager lodging until I can move."

Davor looked at me with genuine appreciation. "Well, I'll be prucked. You're learning sarcasm."

"This place is an effective teacher."

"Uh, if you could use a little short-term loan to make this happen, let me know."

"You bet I could, but why would you help me?"

"Not because I'm a nice guy," he said. "Your creative solution will save me trouble, and it will be entertaining to watch."

He was still grinning at me when I left.

I think the women officers felt sorry for me.

"We didn't mean for you to leave. You're fine here. We just didn't think it was fair to Issa."

"I didn't think it was fair to Issa, either," I said.

"I wish you all would stop worrying about me," Issa yelled from the kitchen. We ignored her.

"This could work out okay," I said. "I'm looking for a roommate now to help with expenses and haven't gotten a chance to talk to Tamara yet, but I was going to ask her if she was interested."

"They're not gonna let some enlisted woman go live with you," Issa yelled again from the other room.

"Really? I know of three other Mozdols who have enlisted women living with them right now and no one's complaining," I said.

"Yeah, but they're, you know ..."

"I know. But so what."

"Wait, are you and Tamara?"

"No, we're not. But what are they going to do? Come make *sure* we're having sex? Insist we do?"

Tamara had much the same reaction.

"Sulphur, I think the world of you, but, well, usually guys are more my thing, and rushing into living together without even ..."

"No, no. I'm not asking you to live with me like that. Just share a place."

"But enlistees don't get to live out of the barracks unless, you know, once in a while ..."

"Yeah, I know. So let people think what they want, and we won't go out of our way to correct them. The other Mozdols can't afford to deny me the same pleasures they take for themselves, not without bringing on problems they don't want. Assumptions about our relationship won't bother me. Will they bother you?"

"Nah. If I want a guy, I can tell him, right. And I can bring him home, can't I?"

"Absolutely. Just pick the kind that knows how to be discrete."

"That's the only kind I like. Okay then, count me in. I've got some savings, thanks to being paid like an officer for years, and it's been hard going back to a tiny bunk and no privacy. Are you sure?"

"We start looking for a place tomorrow."

We did, and it only took a few days to find something that would do and was available soon. After we secured it, I remembered I hadn't yet asked Davor about those meetings I was supposed to have been attending.

Before I had a chance to see him, though, I got a request from Ryalgar and Joli to come to the Velka lodge. They couched it as a social visit, but I understood the meaning. They wished to discuss plans for training our farmers and herders.

Rooslin and Prince Giorgi's counsel gave me pause. How should I approach this? Would watchful eyes and eager ears be straining to learn if the Svadlu and Velka were secretly working together? Would some wonder if I was a spy and could be trusted?

I decided to err on the side of caution. I'd play the role of the angry sister, dismayed at being forced by family obligations to aid a hare-brained scheme I thought had little chance of success. Honestly, that was close enough to the truth.

I knew I was a poor actress but I arrived determined to play my part. I kept my stance defiant and glared as Ryalgar came outside to greet me. Perhaps I overacted a bit.

"It's been too long since we've visited," she said, eyeing my demeanor. "You've had a tough half year?"

Best to stay in character. I rolled my eyes and glared again. In a voice loud enough to be overheard by anyone, I said "Tell me, are you pleased the Svadlu are the cowards you suspected they were?"

"I don't call them cowards," she said in a conciliatory tone. "They have different priorities for defending the realm and the Velka understand. We're trying to work within those realities, to keep everyone safe."

Ryalgar wasn't making this easy. What did she want from me?

I glared harder. "You want my help, don't you? If I don't give it, I betray my own family. If I do, I go against those I've sworn loyalty to." I crossed my arms tight against my chest, doing my best to look like the loyal soldier I was.

"This is never going to work," she said.

Okay, maybe for the benefit of those watching she needed to convince me to help her. I felt like I performed in a play in which my fellow actors had gone off-script. What were my lines now?

"Of course it will work," I said. "I'll help you, and lie to those I fight with about what I do with my free time. I'll do it because your strategies have left me no choice."

Ryalgar looked like she'd made a decision. Her eyes bored into mine.

"Listen. To. Me. The Svadlu already know what we're doing. They're not only okay with it; they've turned our ideas into part of their strategy."

What was she thinking, saying such words aloud? Who knew who listened in?

"Don't add more lies to the mix," I said. "I won't believe them."

"I'm not lying." She simply was *not* going to play this the smart way. Was it possible my intelligent sister didn't know about eavesdroppers and intrigue?

She stepped closer to me and lowered her voice. "We all are working together."

Yeah, but why announce it so everyone could hear? I struggled for a line to clue her in.

"So why haven't you told everybody how the Svadlu and Velka are working together?

"We can't," she said. "Our farmers are taking up arms because they have no choice. Their anger at the army gains us their cooperation. I don't like the deception, either, but it's our best shot at surviving."

I decided to pretend she'd convinced me because I didn't know what else to do. I searched for a believable thing to say.

"Are you scumping me?" I finally said.

"I scump you not. I'd have told you all this sooner, but I know how much you hate lying."

Yeah.

"How much I hate lies," I corrected her.

"Yes. Well, how could we ask you to train people while pretending you didn't know things you did? I wanted to make it easier for you."

"You failed at that."

I wanted to elaborate but Joli came outside to join us. Surely she'd overheard this weird conversation.

"Forget about your well-meaning sister," she said. "I'm the one working with you and we're done lying." Joli turned to Ryalgar. "I'll take over. We'll be fine."

I was so confused I couldn't even look at Ryalgar as she left. After she went inside, Joli started to laugh.

"You were pretending the whole time with her, weren't you?" she whispered.

"Of course," I whispered back. "I thought no one could know that we worked together. I've been learning how there are ears everywhere."

"Well it was quite a performance, but completely unnecessary. We trust each other here in the forest, no one worries about being overheard. Ryalgar didn't understand what you were doing. You two live in different worlds."

I probably still looked confused because she added "We'll straighten this all out later. Right now, we've got a lot to get done."

~ 16 ~

The Wild Animal Within

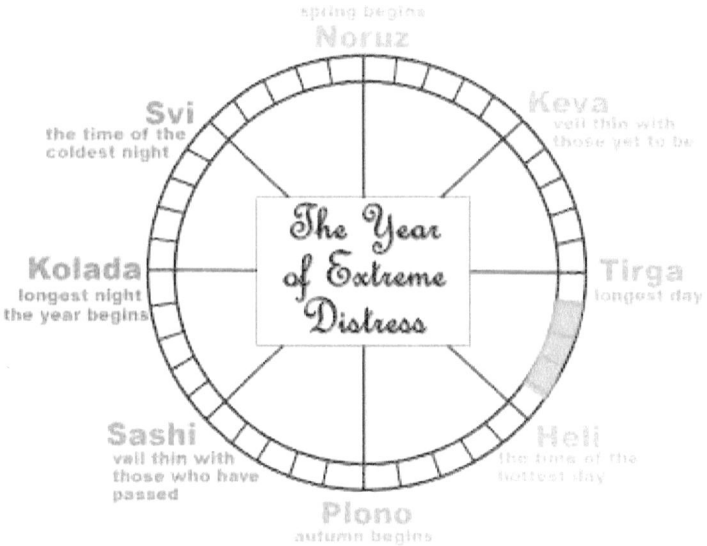

Joli and I understood each other well. She shared my approval of Rooslin's ideas and we made quick plans to begin training the most eager cow herders. In the end, we hoped to roll most able-bodied Eastern Ilarians into our strategy, but we agreed to start small.

Besides her duties coordinating the oomrushers and their efforts to send arrows further, and working with me, Joli also worked with my father and Ryalgar on transforming the landscape of Ilari. I admired a busy woman.

We sat and talked at the market in Vinx in the shade of an old tree, fanning ourselves in the afternoon heat while merchants haggled with customers in the background.

"Here's where we hope to have our first encounter between herders and Mongols," she said, showing me a small hand-drawn copy of Ryalgar's map and pointing to the grasslands of Bisu. "Cow-herders will capture individual invaders after the rest of the horde has moved on, and they'll also secure the horses who survive the poison arrows."

"Rooslin grew up in Bisu," I said. "According to him most Bisuites are uncommonly good on a horse and talented using rope to secure cattle. That should help."

Joli drew a big circle in the middle of Vinx.

"Here is where we stage a second altercation in which the invaders get thrown from their horses, thanks to two of your sisters and people like them. Once done, I'm counting on Vinxites to learn how to capture these men, and I want to add in anyone from Eds willing to help. Do you think Edsers and Vinxites can work together?"

"Sure. Vinxites get along with everyone, and Edsers aren't as bad as you hear."

"I hope you're right. Now," she pointed to the southern edge of the map "the third and final skirmish will be here in Gruen, along the river."

I scooted closer to study her drawing. "How will you get the Mongols there? Ryalgar says they've already scouted the realm. Surely they'll ride from Vinx straight to Pilk."

"That will be what they think they're doing, if our road crews are successful."

"You're going to divert them to the wide river without them knowing it?" This idea impressed me.

"Yup. The road to the river will look uncommonly wide and well-traveled, while the road to Pilk will be a barely visible trail. Once they get to the water's edge and figure out their mistake, we'll have a combination of water-savvy Faroojers, local Gruenites, and K'basta staging all sorts of shenanigans. Well, actually the reczavy will be staging the shenanigans and some of the K'basta will help."

I scooted back so I could look her in the eye.

"Wait – you've got the reczavy involved? Why?"

"Why not? They live here and their lands are being sacrificed, too. Besides, they have tricks up their sleeves we haven't even considered."

"But …." I didn't know where to start. If there was any group in Ilari I had no sympathy for, it was these immature adults who centered their lives around pleasure and play with no thought of their obligations to society.

"Why would Ryalgar stoop to include them? Why would she think she could trust them?"

I could see a light dawning on Joli's face.

"You don't know, do you?"

"Know what?"

"Ryalgar trusts them to deliver because one of your sisters is spearheading the Reczavy's contributions."

"One of my …. oh, Great Goddess." I knew which one it had to be without asking. "That's where Gypsum went? She joined the reczavy? Prucking goat scump. My poor parents must be devastated."

"Ryalgar's says they've handled it as well as could be expected,"

"When?"

"She dropped out of school right before Noruz. Ryalgar's met with her and they came up with this plan." Joli seemed to search for something helpful to say. "It seems to be going well."

At this news, I stood, too distressed to sit. I couldn't imagine ever looking Gypsum in the eye again.

"Give it some time," Joli said. "You'll feel better about it once you get used to the idea."

"No, I won't. Maybe you won't need much help from me for that part of the training."

She had the good sense not to argue.

****

An ank later she, Tamara, Rooslin, and I, along with the three Svadlu officers helping us, met with our first group of trainees. These cow herders from Bisu supplied the coveted beef Ilarians loved, as well as butter and cheese used throughout the realm. They had a certain pride about living at the gateway into Ilari and some had wanted to form a militia to help defend our entrance.

When the Svadlu said no thanks, many felt insulted. Others, like Rooslin, had joined the Svadlu.

We sought out the insulted ones. By this time everyone knew of the Svadlu's plans for Ilari's defense, and had heard at least one variation of what the Velka were doing about it. Opinions varied, but plenty of Bisuites thought doing something was better than doing nothing. We found ten such people.

"Four rock throwers, three tacklers, three to subdue," Rooslin said. "I hope we can go to fewer later, but best for them to start out thinking they can do this."

Joli cast me as the lone invader, outfitted me in the protective gear I'd designed, and gave me a dull wooden sword. Then she and Rooslin convinced the ten unarmed herders they could capture me.

Only they couldn't. I deflected rocks with my arms, then charged at them faster than they could respond. Caught up in the moment, I whacked several of them across the head with my fake weapon.

Joli stopped everything.

"Sulphur. For this *first* training session, could you please act like a slower and less aggressive Mongol?"

"No. I only know one way to fight."

She rolled her eyes.

"Tamara? Do you think you could take a turn at being the invader?"

Tamara nodded and took the gear from me, tucking her long honey-colored braid up into the protective mask as she put it on.

The herders did better. Tamara fought well but she hesitated enough that her opponents finally surrounded and captured her. Joli cheered when they did. In Tamara's defense, it was ten to one and the Bisuites were learning.

One of the other female officers took a turn. Eventually, the Bisuites prevailed again. Then Rooslin became the Mongol. Tall and thin, he had a height advantage and a long arm to go with it. His shoulder had healed, and his better reach forced the herders to struggle. It took longer, but finally, they captured him too.

"Okay, Sulphur. You're up again." Both Rooslin and Joli turned to give the Bisuites more instructions for dealing with me, then Tamara and the officers chimed in with a few more tips. It felt like a sixteen-to-one fight.

I willed my brain into helpfulness, but my body refused to go there. As far as it was concerned, I was surrounded by enemies, without a friend in sight.

The herders came at me, and I have no idea what happened. I went straight at them, hard, with my wooden slick flailing at high speed, wielding it like a scythe. I'm told I gave something of a war-whoop as well. Some of the poor Bisuites ran behind Joli, terrified.

Joli shook her head but she laughed. She turned to the Bisuites in sympathy.

"Heli, I'd run from the likes of that too. Okay, subduing Sulphur will be your final exam, sometime this fall. Today, let's take a little time to go over specific techniques, and then we'll be done. Can you meet here on the second day of every ank for more practice?"

The eight men and two women all nodded.

"Great. Bring any of the like-minded with you and if you've got folks from Scrud working with your herds, they're welcome too."

"How many herders do you think you're going to need for this?" one Bisuite asked.

"Well, if we meet our goal of having two hundred horseless riders, and if we need ten of us for every one of them …."

"Two thousand people," said one of the officers.

"That could be a problem," said one man. "Not sure we've got that many healthy adults in Bisu."

"Then we better figure out how to do this with fewer people. Next ank, we'll try it nine to one."

****

Tamara had dinner with me and the other officers most nights, and on occasion Issa joined us. The other women never mentioned where else Issa ate, and I sensed I shouldn't ask. The night after our first training session in Bisu, she was there.

As we ate, I felt a difference in the way the other officers and Tamara treated me.

"I never saw you attack those two men up in Tolo," Tamara said. By unspoken agreement, we didn't discuss the skirmish that forced her demotion and made me a Mozdol. I wasn't sure how to respond.

"I try not to think about it," I said.

"We understand," another replied. "What we never understood was how you prevailed over both of those men by yourself, and why all the other recruits just stood there and watched you."

"Yeah. But now we get it."

Issa gave me a quizzical look. "You exhibit some sort of fighting magic today?" she asked me.

"I don't think so. Maybe I took things a little too seriously. I've been told I have a problem with that, but I'll try to do better next time."

"You really have no idea how well you fight?" one of the other officers challenged me. Maybe she thought I was being falsely modest.

Tamara jumped in. "I promise you, she doesn't."

I looked at them all in confusion.

"I try to do my best, always. But doesn't everyone?"

"Yes, by and large, but your best is beyond what I've ever seen," one of the women said. "Man, woman, young, old. You don't move like a human when you fight. You move like a wild animal."

Her words made me sad with the memories they brought back. "That's what the boys said when they saw me spar. 'She's no girl. She's an animal. One who gets in fights.' They told me it made me repulsive, and I should learn to control it."

"They were jealous of you," Issa said. "Not all boys are such jerks."

"I know. So why do we pay so much attention to ones who are?" It slipped out of my mouth.

"We've all let that group get under our skin," another officer conceded.

"The wild animal in you is beautiful, I think," Tamara said. I wondered if the other women heard the hint of infatuation in her voice, or whether I'd imagined it.

****

My new house became available the following ank. All the women officers, even Issa, helped Tamara and me move our things. The housekeeper Nino took us aside to share some news. Back pains had made her work more difficult and soon her daughter would take over as housekeeper for the female officers. Nino needed to work less, but she could tend to Tamara and me a few days every ank if we wanted her.

I didn't hesitate. All the men Mozdols had domestic help as far as I knew and while Tamera and I could barely afford our lodging, it would worth it to find a way to have Nino's help once she was available.

"Until then you two will be welcome here for dinners any night," she said.

"We'll probably be here most evenings."

Our new house had three bedrooms, probably intended for a couple, their children, and a live-in servant. Tamara insisted I take the large one, laughing that she didn't want Mozdols inspecting the place and making her change rooms. I intended to pay a larger share of the rent, so I didn't argue.

"And the other bedroom? It's not that bad. We could use it as an office or for guests?" I said.

"You know who'd really appreciate it?"

I knew. Rooslin was having trouble adjusting to life in the barracks. I'd gathered he came from a more well-off family and, like me, had grown up with more personal space than many. He'd never wanted to join the military and I still didn't know why he had, other than his concern about the invasion. I suspected there was more to his story, but neither my questions nor Ilari's best wines had yielded the information. Yet.

He didn't fit in well with the joking and teasing that seemed to rule barracks life for males, and he'd been the brunt of some rather cruel humor when he returned from Faroo beat-up but with no life-threatening injury. He'd weathered it with a certain dry wit, but inside he hurt. I could tell.

"I don't think we can use the usual excuse for including him."

"I don't think we should have to," Tamara answered. "You're a Mozdol. You get to live with who you want, right? If the others complain, they'll bring more problems down on themselves. Think about it. Should those who run the army *really* be sleeping with women under their command? I mean, it seems wrong to me so why would they want to get people thinking too hard about it?"

"Do you think living with two women will make Rooslin's life with the other enlisted men harder?"

"Maybe. But Rooslin might not care."

"Let's ask him."

The invitation made Rooslin as happy as I'd ever seen him.

"Pruck the others. I get a room of my own? In a place with two people I like? How soon can I move in?"

We both shrugged. "Today?"

****

Three days later a messenger summoned me to Davor's office. Good. With all the work involved in moving, I still hadn't asked him about these meetings Giorgi mentioned, and I also wanted to find out when I'd finally get the scarlet cloak I'd been promised. Not that I'd wear it often, but the symbolism of having it, or not having it, mattered.

I hoped he wanted to talk about such things, and not that he'd received word of my unorthodox housing arrangement breaking some other unknown oath.

Instead, he greeted me with "I thought Iolite would be long gone by now. She isn't."

"Can I see her?"

"No, and that's not the problem. The problem is your parents rode all the way over to her school to check on her, and they found out she left long ago. They don't know she's here, and they're worried sick."

"It's not right to do that to them."

"I agree. But now what?"

"Why not have Iolite send them a letter? In her own hand. She can tell them she's with the Svadlu ..."

"No. Absolutely not."

"Okay, then she can just tell them she's safe. Handling important matters. It *is* true. They'll worry but not nearly as much as if they don't even know if she's alive."

"Not a bad idea." Then he added "Sulphur? She doesn't want to see you. It's nothing personal; she's working hard, and says she needs her focus. Okay?"

"You're *sure* she's alright?"

"Yeah." It was the answer I hoped for but a hint of inflection in his voice kept it from carrying the certainty I wanted.

When I stood to go, he said, "You may be asking for trouble with your new roommates."

I sat back down. "Turns out I need help affording my lodging. Did I take an oath to not to share my living space? Or did I promise to only live with people I have sex with, like the other Mozdols?"

He grimaced at the last question. "One could argue having roommates is not behaving like royalty, but then again doing whatever you please is, so I think this one's a toss-up. What you're doing is unorthodox, though, and some people do not like unusual behavior. It makes them nervous."

I thought of Kazimir, our leader who I'd never met, but who everyone described as lacking flexibility. He probably hated my situation. Then there was Prince Giorgi's mother, my new enemy. I thought of the boys who'd taunted me years ago by calling me an animal.

"Yeah. I get a fair amount of that."

"I bet you do. It's strange because you have rather conventional morals. Yet your natural skills put you at odds with people's expectations, even though that's the last place you want to be. It must be tough."

I didn't know what to say as this oft-drunk womanizer tried to see the world through my eyes.

"Heli knows, I've gotten away with far worse than you'll ever try," he said, standing to let me know the conversation was over. "I'll try to have your back on this one." He said that part quietly, and not until I was partway out the door.

Scump, I forgot again. But after the door shut, it didn't seem right to go back in and demand to know why I didn't have a scarlet cloak yet and wasn't being included in meetings.

~ 17 ~

One Heli of a Heli

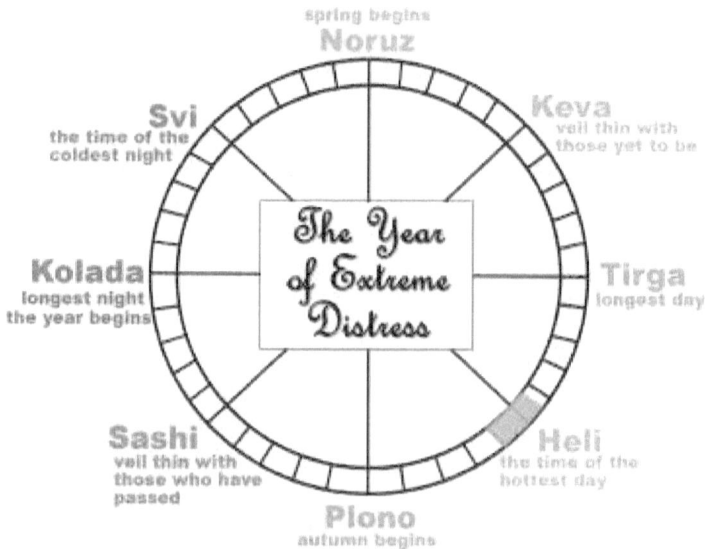

The Year of Extreme Distress

- spring begins — Noruz
- Keva — veil thin with those yet to be
- Svi — the time of the coldest night
- Tirga — longest day
- Kolada — longest night, the year begins
- Heli — the time of the hottest day
- Sashi — veil thin with those who have passed
- Plono — autumn begins

The problem of how cow herders might subdue someone like me intrigued me. I suspected I could have kept fifty of them at a distance through sheer intimidation and felt certain our attackers would have fighters with skills like mine. What does one do to capture a wild animal as fast and fierce as me?

Well, one usually kills it, to be honest, but Ryalgar insisted we could trade live captives for respect and mercy from our would-be conquerors. She hoped not to take a single human life and even planned to use less poison for their horses, believing the safe return of some of their beloved animals would serve the same function.

So, our oomrush-aided archers would put horses to sleep instead of killing them, though some would die because the amount of poison needed to cause death depended on the size, age, and health of the horse. We would err on the heavy side, killing smaller and weaker horses. Could we use a similar strategy to subdue people as well?

I didn't mean all of them, of course. I understood Ryalgar wanted eight hundred of those thousand Mongols to ride on to Vinx to encounter her next trap. But as the cow herders moved in to capture the two hundred or so left behind, why not leave them an archer or two to deal with the most difficult fighters? The people like me.

We could take the opposite approach with the dosage, keeping it light enough to not kill any human, no matter how small or weak, although I doubted the Mongol horde had many small weak people. But even a little poison would slow down the biggest attacker and perhaps reduce our causalities.

A poison arrow would have taken me down. I'd talk to Joli about it the next time I saw her.

****

In Vinx, the heat bounces off the dry earth in the days before Heli and the wind carries it away in the night. In Pilk, however, the heat sinks deep into the stone fences, walls, and streets where the rocks hold it tight. In Pilk, people sweat through the night almost as if it was day, finding no relief before the sun rises and begins the cycle again.

I couldn't wait for Plono.

Most Svadlu didn't work on Heli, and Tamara, Rooslin, and I all were free. Rooslin left the day before, opting to ride to Bisu to spend the day with his family. He hadn't seen them since enlisting and he packed in tense silence before leaving with barely a word.

Tamara suggested she and I celebrate by swimming in the Little River. Throughout the summer, the banks were lined with swimmers, mostly children. Their mothers watched from shore, happy to have a little peace. On Heli, however, entire families and groups of friends would congregate to celebrate, sitting the relative cool of the shade, sharing the lush fruits and vegetables of the season along with plenty of ale and wine.

We got a late start, having made no preparations the day before and having spent a late night celebrating Heli Eve with the women officers in their quarters. Tamara slept unusually late and, by the time she woke, and we found and packed up adequate food, drink, and picnic gear, the heat of the afternoon had passed.

The crowd along the riverbanks began to change not long after we arrived. More couples appeared, walking hand in hand, often wearing less than customary. Parents gathered up their children to leave for home.

Ilarians usually wore special clothes for swimming, particularly if with the other gender. But after the sun of Heli went down, swimming naked in the presence of all would not only be acceptable, it would be encouraged as part of a traditional Heli celebration. I knew this, of course, and hadn't thought much of it. I figured we'd be swimming during the day and home before dark. Now I wondered if Tamara's dawdling had been deliberate.

She drank her wine fast, offering me more every time she poured, and I had a rather good idea of where this was going.

"Want to swim?" She gave me a playful look and pulled her frock up over her head, revealing she wore absolutely nothing under it. Her body was strong and fit, her breasts small and her nipples erect in the cool twilight breeze.

Stop now. Or don't stop at all.

My mind saw the wisdom in stopping, but to my surprise my nether regions had ideas of their own. Tamara was attractive, and what's more, she wanted *me*. Not a boy, not a girl, not some ideal. She might have been the first person in my entire life to specifically desire the body I walked around in. Being wanted turned out to be a powerful aphrodisiac. It rendered me helpless.

I stood up and pulled my shirt over my head.

"Let's go for a swim," I said as I removed the rest of my garments, taking my time so her eyes could linger, too.

After a refreshing and playful dip involving an unusual amount of touch, we dried off together standing on our blanket. Other couples would move on to what came next, counting on the shrubbery and others' preoccupation to provide adequate privacy. But I was mindful that some weren't entirely comfortable with two women together, and my status as a Mozdol required more decorum than was expected of others.

"I think we should go back to our house," I said.

"Oh yes. Definitely." So we did.

I woke up smiling, feeling her head against the soft part of my chest where my underarm met my outer breast. She smelled like the river and wine and all the good memories of the day before. That's when I heard footsteps in the house. Was Rooslin back already? He'd planned to stay in Bisu for two days, but perhaps he'd cut his visit short.

I tried to squirm out from under Tamara without waking her when Rooslin pulled back the thick tapestry covering my door.

"There you are," he said, his eyes glad to see me until they wandered from my face to the face right below.

"Oh my. I'm so sorry." He pulled the drape closed with embarrassment and something else. Anger? Was he mad at finding Tamara and me in bed together after a holiday? Why? What could be more natural?

This sort of drama was what had prompted my mind to suggest I stop this before it started. Now, it was too late. I sighed and closed my eyes again. I'd have a long talk with Rooslin later and try to discover what the real problem was. For the moment, I only wanted to close my eyes and spend a few more minutes savoring the warm happy feeling inside me.

Rooslin disappeared by the time I got up, and we didn't see him for the rest of the day. Tamara was friendly but not affectionate, letting me know she considered our closeness to have been a celebration of the day, nothing more. I agreed that approach was for the best and felt glad she could keep a clear head on her shoulders. I liked her the better for it.

I'd alerted her to Rooslin's ill-timed entrance and a possible need to ease his embarrassment, but by bedtime, he hadn't come home. She and I each retired to our rooms, both a little worried.

Early the next morning a messenger summoned me to Davor's office. I followed him without delay. I needed to have a serious conversation with Davor, too. As I entered his office, though, he greeted me with, "You're welcome."

"For?"

"For giving you another easy chance to show off and to polish your legend. I've been told there's a minor altercation going on along the border between Pilk and Faroo, down along the Wide

River. It started during yesterday's celebration and still hasn't been resolved. We need you to hurry over there and make it go away."

"Aren't you going to send soldiers with me?"

"We don't have time to assemble a group. Come on, it's less than an hour's ride. You can go find out what the problem is, then come back and get help if you need it."

His words made perfect sense when he said them. Only later would the instructions seem odd.

The stable boy saddled my horse as I gathered a knife, my sword, and a jug of water for the ride. The morning air had a hint of coolness, making my stallion friskier than he'd been since the heat descended over an eighth ago. I rode to the spot Davor described, but I saw no problems anywhere along the Wide River's banks. Here the wall separating Faroo from Pilk was short, no higher than my waist. My mount jumped it with ease. I looked around but could see nothing amiss on the Faroo side either.

I was about to return to Pilk and report that the problem had solved itself when a young boy standing behind me under a grove of trees called out. He had the reddish skin tones and shiny black hair of many Faroojers. As I got closer I saw the metallic iron eyes as well.

"Please, sir. Can you get my cat out of the tree? She's scared, and she won't come down."

My hair confused a lot of children; I didn't bother to correct him about my gender. Instead, I rode over to see how high the problem pet had managed to climb. I couldn't see a cat up there anywhere.

"You can't see her from there; you have to stand here under this low branch. Let me hold your horse. Please. She's not very high up."

I should have known better. If Rooslin had been with me, he'd never have fallen for it. But I was in good mood, confident and at peace with the world. So I gave the kid my reins and walked to the spot he showed me, intending to do a good deed before I returned home.

When it fell on top of me, I didn't know what it was. Not at first, at least, only that it was heavy, made from rope, and was being pulled tight around my legs, holding me bound so I couldn't fight. This wouldn't have been a problem except that a dozen or so young men surrounded me, yelling taunts and holding buckets of what looked like fish guts. Some of them had heavy Faroojer accents and I couldn't make out their exact words, but the gist of it had to do with me showing them how tough I was now.

Flaming scump, this reminded me entirely too much of my youth.

My sword was useless in my current bound state, so I pulled out my knife and started slashing through the heavy rope around me. A fishing net? I'd never seen one but given I was in Faroo it made sense. Turned out every tiny square was meticulously knotted together, meaning I'd have to cut through tens of them before I'd free myself. I looked up. I'd be soaked in fish guts long before that.

Then, as the slimy, bloody mess in each bucket flew towards me, I realized something.

"You guys are brilliant!" I shouted. "This is terrific."

Splat. I couldn't even look at what covered me, it was so disgusting, but I didn't care.

"Do you have any idea how useful this is?"

The dozen or so youths looked at each other confused. I supposed they expected me to be futilely fighting, or maybe cursing or crying. I'm not sure which of the three would have brought them the most pleasure but I didn't care.

"Get me out of here, or I'll get myself out eventually. Either way, I've *got* to talk to you. You young men have a key role to play in saving the realm."

A couple of them came forward, and one was nice enough to brush some of the worst of it off me. They undid the noose around my ankles and helped me out.

"Are you crazy, lady? Everyone knows Faroojers aren't good for anything."

"Four of you and one of these here nets could bring down the toughest fighters in the world. Do you know what a difference you could make?"

"You're part of that scheme to save the Eastern half of Ilari, aren't you?"

"Yup. Do you really want to be stuck in a realm with nothing but people from Pilk, Kir, Lev, and Tolo?" I asked.

"If you put it that way ...." one of them laughed.

"You and your nets have no idea how important you are. Thank you for showing me what you can do." I flipped something disgusting off my shoulder. "Despite this scump."

As I looked up, I saw a scarlet-caped older man in an ornate uniform watching us from a short distance. He had to be Svadlu, and important Svadlu at that. Why hadn't he come to help me?

"Who's that?"

"Him? He's the guy who put us up to this. Paid each of us some pretty coins."

"He may want some of them back," another said. "We didn't finish the job."

"You were supposed to do more?"

"Yeah, he wanted us to get you down and kick you in the face a few times. He said not to hurt you bad, just make sure everyone who looked at you knew you'd lost a fight."

"I see. Did he say who he was?"

"He didn't have to. *You* don't know him?"

All the young men looked at me like they didn't believe me.

"That's Kazimir, the head of the Svadlu." one said. "Where have you been hiding?"

"Yeah," another added. "He said this was an important training thing and it happened all the time and not to worry. They really train Mozdols this way?"

"No. They don't. But thanks for telling me. You keep your coins and I'll make it right with him."

I looked behind me. The little boy was nowhere to be seen but my faithful horse happily munched grass and waited for me. I intended to ride over and confront Kazimir, who'd not only had failed to conduct my Mozdolo as was the custom, but who'd also not bothered to introduce himself or welcome me in any way in the three eights since then. Enough was enough.

But when I turned back around, the man was gone. I rode back to Pilk to talk to Davor instead.

~ 18 ~

Hard to Hate

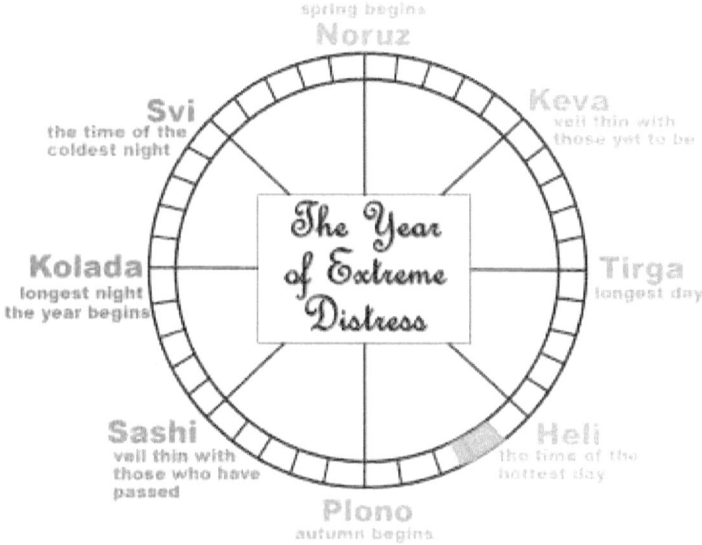

spring begins
Noruz

Keva
veil thin with
those yet to be

Svi
the time of the
coldest night

The Year
of Extreme
Distress

Kolada
longest night
the year begins

Tirga
longest day

Sashi
veil thin with
those who have
passed

Heli
the time of the
hottest day

Plono
autumn begins

"Did you think it was funny?"

I blew into Davor's office like a sudden storm, a fury out of nowhere.

"Think *what* was funny? And wash yourself in my basin, please. Sacred scump, you smell of fish. What happened to you?

"A dozen young Faroojer delinquents happened. Ones paid to capture me in a net and throw fish parts at me. What I want to know is, were you part of it? Is this some sort of hazing ritual? Because if it isn't I'm going to go beat the living crap out of someone. So please answer carefully."

"You do still report to me, soldier."

127

"That's Mozdol, not soldier, and at the moment I don't give a rats arse who I report to."

He sighed, long and slow.

"We do not haze Mozdols. That would be beneath their royal dignity."

"So I thought. Who told you to send me on this errand?"

Davor didn't answer.

"Who?"

"The one Svadlu you'd best not vent your wrath on. Listen, Sulphur. Kazimir asked me to send you. Told me it ought to be easy for you to handle a few boisterous Faroojers; said he'd ride over and watch you to see why everyone made such a fuss about your fighting. He wanted to introduce himself afterward, long overdue in my opinion, and buy you an ale and fill you in about your new position." Davor gave a what-could-I-do shrug. "It seemed reasonable enough."

"He had something else in mind. He paid these guys to kick me in the face, so the whole world would know I'd been bested."

Davor squinted at me. "Doesn't look like they did a very good job of it."

"They didn't. The good news is those fishing nets will hold any fighter, no matter how capable, plenty long enough to be restrained. I got the Faroojers talking about how they could help Ilari win, and they got so excited they didn't bother kicking me."

Davor rubbed both of his temples with his knuckles.

"We need to worry about why Kazimir did this," he said.

"Oh, believe me, I'm worried. I'm also tired of being treated like I'm half a Mozdol. I've heard you all have meetings, and no one bothers to invite me. Either I belong or I don't. If I don't, Vinx needs to be made aware that they are without representation."

"For once, you and I are in complete agreement. You know who needs to fix this?"

"You," I said.

"No, not me. I'll just get us both in trouble. This is the sort of problem that takes finesse, a quality I've heard I lack and so do you. You need to go around the problem, not at it."

"I don't know how to do that."

He laughed. "You need to complain loudly to Prince Giorgi and his entire family. Tell them exactly what you told me.

Emphasize the lack of respect being shown to Vinx via your treatment."

"But his mother hates me."

"Oh come on. You're hard to hate, Sulphur. Take it from a man who's really tried. Go meet mama, let the whole family know how much you love your nichna, and beg for their help on behalf of everyone."

He was right, but I didn't like it.

Rooslin was home when I got there. He gave me a casual hello from across the room without meeting my eye. I suppose if my day had gone differently I might have shown some of the finesse Davor thought I lacked. But it hadn't. I still stunk of fish, and I'd just agreed to go make nice with an important woman who disliked me. I wanted to kick something. Hard.

"Did you have a good visit with your parents?" I managed.

"It was okay." He busied himself with something and said no more.

"What the pruck is your problem?!" Yes, I yelled it at him and he probably didn't deserve that, but....

"What the pruck is yours?" He whispered it back, but his tone had far more venom.

"Are you pissed at me because I finally did what nearly every other adult around here does on every prucking holiday?"

"No. I'm flustered because you did it with Tamara. I thought we had a nice arrangement here. No complications, just three friends looking out for each other. Simple and unemotional and refreshing. But no, of course not. People aren't made that way. My fault for wanting something more."

"What more did you want?"

"Family. I wanted a varming family, Sulphur, and family members don't pruck each other."

"You've got a family, in Bisu."

"Not anymore. I won't be going back. Ever."

I didn't know what to say. Finally I asked, "What's your family got against you? Or you against them?"

"Not every family is as open-minded as yours. Perhaps you guessed I prefer guys. I joined the Svadlu after two of my brothers found me in the barn with ...." He trailed off but he didn't have to finish. I got the picture.

It surprised me. Most Ilarians tolerated others for what they were. Most wasn't all, though.

"I'm sorry to hear it."

"It's alright." His shrug said it didn't matter but his voice said otherwise. "I used this visit to say goodbye to the young man I've cared about for years." He held up his hand to stop any well-meant expression of sympathy from me. "It's okay, we've grown apart anyway. He won't leave Bisu, and I know we can't be together there, even discreetly, even once in a while. Not with my three brothers on the warpath about it. They proved that."

"I'm so …"

He cut me off. "It just is, okay? I don't need your sympathy. I don't need your anything."

"Me and Tamara didn't help?"

"I suppose not. Shouldn't hold bad timing against you."

"I think it was a one-time thing, you know. If it matters."

"Do what you want, Sulphur. The least I can do is show you the tolerance my own kin won't show me. Give me few days. Okay?"

"Take all the time you want."

I could have been wrong, but I think we both felt better after the conversation.

****

The next day I sent a letter to my ruling sovereign, Prince Giorgi, asking for the courtesy of an audience at his palace to discuss issues of importance. I suspected he'd be baffled, but would agree. I didn't expect he'd send my sister Celestine to talk to me about it.

Celestine always shows up when you don't expect her. She's a musician and performs with a popular trio in the classier places out in K'ba and all over Pilk. She writes her own songs, which I do respect, and she wears the most beautiful clothes in the realm, which I think is waste of time and money.

She claims looking good makes her more popular and being well-liked is essential to her success as a musician. She doesn't seem to realize she could wear potato sacks and achieve the same results, for she was blessed, or cursed, with a degree of classic beauty well beyond any of the rest of us. Her features are delicate and her thick, wavy black hair contrasts with large bright blue eyes. I've seen every male in sight stop and stare at her.

Prince Giorgi's mother was among her many fans. Of course. Gorgeous Celestine embodied everything wonderful about womanhood.

To Giorgi's credit, he'd tried to make my visit easier by inviting Celestine and me at the same time. She could perform a special song for his mother, one commissioned by the prince as a birthday gift for his mom. If that didn't put her in a good mood, nothing would.

I could give Giorgi my report, and attempt to let the old dragon know I was as sweet and harmless as my sister, just a little different. It was a reasonable hope.

Celestine and I shared afternoon wine, both expressing our regrets for not seeing more of each other during all the time we both spent in Pilk. In truth, we both knew we had little in common, so all the regretting was sort of an act. It was a way of saying we cared for each other, even if we didn't particularly want to spend time together.

I was surprised to learn how involved she was with the second diversion of the Mongols. Celestine had traveled around the realm, enlisting other singers to help with their convoluted scheme to get the Mongols' horses to throw their riders. I doubted any number of singers could force these expert riders off their mounts, but I kept my doubts to myself.

We made plans to travel to Vinx together in a few days.

****

I'd missed the previous practice session with Joli and the herders, and I wanted to see how the group had advanced. I noticed they'd reduced their ratio to eight to one, now using three rock throwers, two tacklers, and three to subdue. Better. The herders showed more confidence, too, and we now trained thirty-two herders instead of ten.

As the four groups of eight practiced, Joli took me aside.

"This is getting more complicated," she warned me. "We're now training cow herders on the second day of the ank and we've started training farmers in Vinx on the fourth. Soon we'll be working with the K'basta and Faroojers in Gruen. I'm going to assign you and Issa to this group because Rooslin sent word he doesn't want to work in Bisu. I'll put him and the Scrudite officer in Vinx and put Tamara and the remaining officer in Gruen if that's okay with you."

"Wherever you need us."

"So this first piece here is being called 'The Snake'."

"Odd name."

"Your sister's choice. She'd decided to call the whole plan a Chimera. It's a mythical animal made up of three parts…"

"I know what a Chimera is." I'd gone to school. Why did people assume soldiers were ignorant? "Which part is Vinx?"

"The lion."

"That's nice." I was glad Vinx wasn't the goat.

"Gruen is the goat. We'll need to train some Gruenites, but not as many because a lot of the captures are going to take place in the river. The Reczavy are working with the fisherfolk of Faroo on that. Some young Faroojers got the idea that their nets would work well for taking prisoners and I think they're right. It's a brilliant idea."

I might have had something to do with that.

Because one of my proposals was already being used, I told her of my other suggestion.

"Why don't we look into using barely poisoned arrows to shoot difficult to capture fighters? You know, people like me. If I was throwing up, I couldn't fight as hard."

"I like it. I'll move that idea along. You know, we could put back-up squads in all three places, people with extra tools and weapons, maybe even a mace or two, and train them to step in when complications occur. Because problems will happen."

"Then we better put healers in both locations, for our folks and theirs."

"Absolutely. Maybe even antidotes to the poisons if there are any. I'll find out."

I promised Joli I'd be at least every other practice and I asked her to let me know of any other ways I could help.

"Our biggest problem right now is getting more people to come train. Four groups subdue four Mongols. What am I supposed to do about the remaining one hundred and ninety-six of them?"

****

On the day of our audience with the Vinx Royals, Celestine and I rode together to their castle. Although Vinxites called the home of Giorgi's family a palace, it was a country manor with a lovely stone tower on one side for effect. I'd been told the tower held a nice library.

The large stone lodge sat on beautifully maintained grounds, and an entourage of servants rode out to take our horses and escort us inside. There, the royal family greeted us with royal politeness but enough warmth to acknowledge my semi-royal status.

Lady Patela, Giorgi's mom, knew how to put on a good face. She'd been doing it for most of her adult life. If Giorgi hadn't warned me, I'd have assumed she liked me fine.

Giorgi had younger twin sisters, still girls though they neared adulthood, and a shy brother of nine or ten. The young boy disappeared after greeting us, but the twin girls latched onto me as I entered and they stuck to my side.

"A lady Mozdol!" They jumped up and down with the sort of happiness reserved for children. I hoped their enthusiasm wouldn't annoy their mother and make her hate me more, but I needn't have worried. Celestine knew how to charm people. She charmed her audiences and her fans, and as our visit began she charmed Lady Patela. I saw my sister's subtle but effective actions as she listened to the woman and complimented her and made her feel important without ever looking as if she tried.

Giorgi's wife and his father were warier, but as the evening wore on and the wine flowed, the overall ambiance grew warmer. The specially commissioned song was a bit over-emotional for my tastes, but its intended audience of one listened to it with happy tears and asked Celestine to sing it again.

I'd been asked to wait until after the maid served dessert wine before bringing up my issues. Given the quality of the roast mutton and many fresh vegetables, I'd complied without complaint. When Giorgi's young wife expressed fatigue and a need to check on her child, I understood her exit meant my turn had come.

I shared my issues openly with Prince Giorgi and his parents, telling them of how I wasn't included in these Mozdol meetings Giorgi mentioned, and how Kazimir pretended I didn't exist. I didn't even have my scarlet cape yet. My sponsor from Lev was frustrated but powerless to help.

"That man only cares about Kir," Prince Giorgi's father said in disgust. "And Pilk and Lev probably, but no place else. We opposed Kazimir's appointment back when, but others were so glad to finally see a commander from somewhere other than Pilk that they voted him in anyway."

"He's always been a bad choice," Lady Patela agreed. "Yet given Kazimir's position, we need to make him less of an enemy, not more of one."

"Then this seems an appropriate issue for the royals from Kir," the dad said. "He's their man after all. They need to know his biases are threatening the delicate alliance they have with the outer nichnas. If Vinx is treated poorly, so poorly that their own Mozdol is ignored, who knows how this whole structure might dissolve, and at the worst of times."

"I'm friends with the ruling Prince of Kir," Giorgi said. "He's older than I, but we studied together and he's new to his throne, too. I'll talk to him."

Mom and Dad both looked at their son with surprise and a touch of pride.

I slept poorly as the former ruler of Vinx's words circled in my head. *Who knows how this whole structure might dissolve, and at the worst of times?* He had a point. My sister, no, all of Ilari, put their faith in a complicated scheme.

"You look worried," Celestine said as we rode away from the castle. "Everything okay?"

"It's better than it was yesterday. Thanks for easing things with Giorgi's mother."

"No problem. She confided to me this morning that now that she's met you, she understands why you didn't want to be an honorary princess. It's about you and the kind of person you are, she said, and not about how you think she or other women should behave."

"She's right." I had to smile. "You have a nice way with people."

"So what's on your mind this morning?"

"Bisu has thirty-two volunteers we're training. We need a thousand, maybe more. I can't even imagine how we get enough people in time. The truth is sheer numbers matter here, and we don't have them."

"Why didn't you mention this sooner?"

"To you? Why would I?"

She laughed. "Sulphur, I have a following. A big one. If I want to get word out about something, I can do it."

"You can?" This was a side of my sister I didn't know.

"Give me more specifics. How many people, what kind of people, and where do you need them. I'll write a song for it."

"You'll do what?" I could have sworn I heard her say she'd write a song.

"Nothing moves people like music. Something short. A jingle, with the meeting time and place and maybe a little punch to make people want to go."

"Sure. I mean it sounds silly, but if you think it can help, do it. I'll send a message to Joli, and she'll get you specifics."

"I promise you. Once my songs start to circulate, you'll have more people than you need."

I didn't believe her, of course, but what did I know about music?

~ 19 ~

The Power of a Song

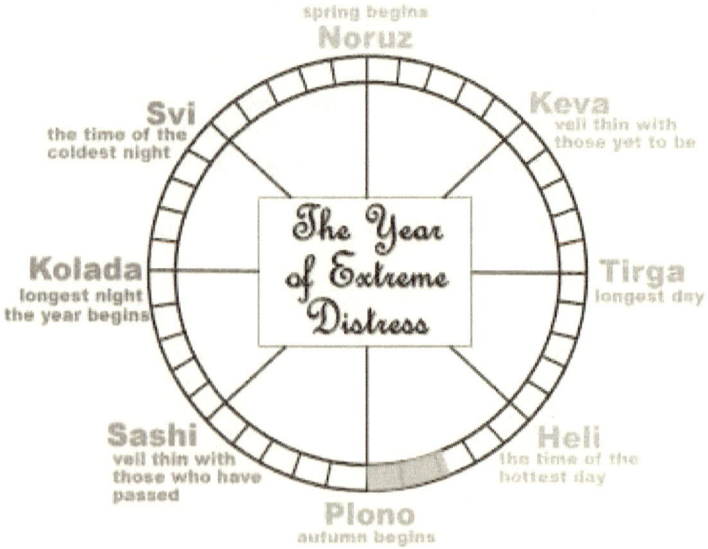

spring begins
Noruz

Svi
the time of the
coldest night

Keva
veil thin with
those yet to be

*The Year
of Extreme
Distress*

Kolada
longest night
the year begins

Tirga
longest day

Sashi
veil thin with
those who have
passed

Heli
the time of the
hottest day

Plono
autumn begins

I'd seen the new ruling prince of Kir from a distance but had never met him. Because he was new to his role, I expected him to be as cautious as Giorgi, but he wasn't.

Three days after I complained to the Royals of Vinx, Kazimir summoned me to his office, gestured me into a chair, and wasted no time making his point.

"I've been informed that I have inadvertently mistreated you, madam. I apologize."

I stared at him. He was an older man, with uncommonly short grey hair, but he remained well-muscled and he held himself as though he ran the world. In a way, I guess he did.

I wanted to say to him "Why in Heli would you pay people to beat me up? How about apologizing for that." Or better yet "What do you mean 'you've been informed?' You didn't notice you haven't spoken once to your new Mozdol? There only are nineteen of us. Are you too stupid to count that high?"

I said neither.

He waited. I *was* expected to say something. What?

"Thank you, sir. I understand you've been busy lately."

He beamed, delighted.

"Quite busy. Serious matters we have to tend to these days, right?"

"Right." I wanted to punch him in the face but I clenched my fists instead.

"You've become a Mozdol at a highly opportune time for Vinx. I want to make sure you're given every chance to represent your nichna, as well as to serve the entire realm. You understand that is my hope, right?"

"Of course it is, sir."

That remark earned me a raised eyebrow. Perhaps I *had* let a dribble of sarcasm into my voice. He chose to ignore it.

"Excellent. To that end, I'm going to overrule your sponsor. It is my prerogative, you know. I'm going to take you off Davor's assignment of training recruits and, with perhaps the rare exception, assign you full-time to providing support to whatever it is the Velka and common folk think they're doing. We'd as soon not see too many of them die, right? So. You go do everything you can to provide them expertise."

"Yes, sir. One problem, sir. Most people are unaware the Svadlu support this effort. Up to now, I've told people I'm using my time off and helping out because of respect for my family. How do I explain my full-time availability?"

"Well, go ahead and tell them what I told you. We're aware of what's happening and unable to stop it, so we've okayed your assistance. I think we're far enough into this that they'll accept that."

"Yes, sir. I'm sure my sisters will appreciate more of my time."

"I hope they do. One more thing, Sulphur. I've been understandably reticent to include you in Svadlu business up till now. It wasn't personal. You're so young, and you were barely a

Svadlu at your Mozdolo, much less an officer, as new Mozdols almost always are. Yet, these are extreme times. I would never, never want Vinx to think I left you out deliberately. So from now on, I will expect you at every gathering we have. At each one, we will expect a complete report from you on everything the Velka are doing. You understand?"

I did now.

After my Mozdolo, Davor had asked me to keep an eye on the Velka's plans and report back to him. His request made me uncomfortable, but so far I'd managed to pass along whatever seemed helpful to the Svadlu and harmless for the Velka. Most information fell into that category, so my role as informant hadn't caused any problems. Yet.

But now, I'd be grilled by all eighteen Mozdols every time we met. My role as an informant could get considerably less comfortable. I needed Rooslin's guidance before I did something stupid without realizing it.

****

I wanted to arrive early at the next practice session in Bisu, so I could tell Joli about my full-time availability. We'd become friends, so I also wanted her counsel on my function as the Svadlu's official observer. At the least, I needed to make sure she knew about it.

The day before, I rode to my parents' farm to make the travel easier. They were surprised but happy to see me, and I sat on the porch with the two of them, enjoying a breeze and an afternoon wine. It was hard to believe we hadn't spoken since Noruz, when they disappeared before my Mozdolo. We barely spoke of that day, but opted for the easier conversation of reminiscing about times long passed.

As we ate, we exchanged family news. Iolite had finally told them she worked for the Svadlu. Did I know what she did? No, I knew no more about it than they did. I'd been told to stay out of it. Yes, I'd visited Coral back in Keva, as business took me close to her house. No, I hadn't seen Ryalgar in a long while.

Dad told me of his involvement with a group he called "the road crew" and of his unprecedented trip to visit the Velka during Tirga. He made me proud, the way he'd chosen to take an active part in saving his realm. Mom had less to say, and I noticed how the worry lines on her face had grown.

A night sleeping in my old room reminded me of how only a year ago I'd been desperate to join the Svadlu, practicing my skills nearly every day in hopes I'd get my chance. My eagerness seemed naïve to the person I'd become. I wished I could go back and whisper in the ear of young Sulphur, "Really, it's not all you expect it to be," but she probably wouldn't believe me.

The next morning, at the first sign of light, I rode towards the large barn in Bisu that served as the training center for the cow herders. As I made it to the top of the last rolling hill before the barn, I stopped.

A few hundred men and women stood around talking and laughing. A few hundred! Honestly, there can't have been that many Bisuites back home in their beds.

I looked closer and saw a quarter of the group wore the distinctive rag-based clothes of Scrudites. For once they intermingled with the Bisuites, a common goal soothing the unspoken class distinction that normally kept them apart.

How in the world had Joli managed to gather nearly ten times the number of people in two anks?

Then I remembered. She hadn't. This crowd had to be the result of Celestine's efforts. What had she called her song? A jingle. Could a jingle make hundreds of people show up somewhere?

As I rode closer I heard people singing. More joined in. Before I'd gotten to the barn, half the crowd hummed, whistled, or sang.

> By the big brown barn in Bisu
> On the ank's second day
> Come stand up for your nichna
> Make the Mongols go away.
>
> Bisuites and Scrudites
> Come do what must be done
> Arrive at dawn, learn to fight
> Winning will be fun.

They got tired of it after about eight more times, but no one there was going to forget when and where to practice, or how important it was. And once I'd heard it, I couldn't keep the melody from repeating itself in my head.

I think I'd seriously underestimated Celestine.

I stayed at my parents' farm for two more nights so I could check out at the practice in Vinx on the fourth day of the ank as well. Joli had been delighted to learn of my new assignment, particularly now that we had so many people to train. She had also brushed aside my worries about the Svadlu, confident we could supply plenty of information to them without causing problems. I didn't share her optimistic assessment, but I hoped she was right. I still planned to consult Rooslin.

On the fourth day I expected a lot of people again, but we had nearly twice as many as last time. Vinx had a bigger population, though, and Celestine had had a couple more days to spread the message. Then as I got closer to the center of the crowd, I saw the real draw. Celestine sat on a makeshift stage with other musicians, playing their instruments and singing.

For all I was grateful to her, we couldn't work with a group this big. We needed to divide up the people and break the training into smaller pieces.

"Sulphur! Help!" Joli called out from behind the stage.

"Yeah. I have an idea. Tamara, go through the crowd and pick out fifty or so likely rock throwers and take them off to one side." I turned to the Scrudite Svadlu officer. "You've got tacklers. Young and limber. Go claim fifty of 'em. I'll take all the big people as subduers."

Rooslin rode up as I spoke.

"Heli, I am glad to see you."

"Rode out here to see what size crowd your sister would draw. All anyone in Pilk talked about last night was this thing and how she'd be performing at it."

"Can you help us?"

"Of course."

"Great. Find yourself fifty horse chasers. Good riders with strong mounts. Get them away from his group and come up with ideas."

I turned to Joli. "That ought to cut the crowd size down. Once we've pulled all of ours out, let the rest pick which group they want to join, or give them the option of working with you on building a force to handle special problems. We'll move people around later as we need to."

By the time the chaos got sorted, somewhat, and I found myself with eighty-three burly people, I was exhausted. I wondered if Celestine could write us a "we need you but don't come for a couple more anks" song.

I knew that on the sixth day of the ank Gruenites and Faroojers met along the wide river to train for the third diversion being designed by the reczavy. I didn't want to go. I didn't want to meet real live reczavy in the flesh, and I didn't want to have to speak with Gypsum. But this was now my job.

I arrived late and kept my distance, observing a dozen or so men and women in clothing that was skimpier than anything I'd wear but did cover the essentials and was probably cool and comfortable on this hot summer day. They worked at the river's edge, yelling to several dozen Faroojers out on rafts. The discussion appeared to center around using the same fishing nets that had recently caused me such trouble. Curiosity pulled me closer.

I didn't see Gypsum among them, but a young man who seemed to be in charge turned to me. "You Sulphur?"

"I am. Is Gypsum here?"

"Not today. Back at camp, scheming new schemes. You here to help?"

"If you need me. If not, I'm here to tell you I *will* help whenever you do."

That earned me a grin.

"We do water first, while it's hot. Land stuff after Plono."

There was a certain logic to his reasoning.

"I can help with land stuff. Tell Gypsum to contact me when it's time. I'll come. I'll help."

"Bye, sister."

He turned back to his problems and I left. I didn't know the first thing about fishing nets other than that they were varmin strong and the more of them we could use against the invaders, the better.

The following ank when I arrived at the barn in Bisu, just as many people came but this time they at least knew their roles. We tried going down to groups of six and although the smaller number left the participants more intimidated, I hoped in the end we could use this ratio of six to one.

As I walked through, making sure each group had the right components, I sought out Joli with my eyes and got a surprise. Off in the distance, she rode her horse next to someone who had to be Ryalgar. So, the Velka mastermind had come down from her cloud to see what us little people were doing? It was about time.

We started the exercise as Ryalgar came towards me. The six nearest to me played their parts well. As she rode up, my rock throwers and tacklers tied my pretend attacker's hands while my subduers hogtied his feet.

I searched for a way to include Ryalgar in the scenario and remembered Joli had said she was working with a man who spoke some Mongolian.

"This is where you come in," I said to Ryalgar. "These people will need words like 'surrender and we won't hurt you.' Maybe even 'you'll be returned to your Khan so don't be stupid.' Whatever you can manage to teach them. When are these words coming?"

She told me of her complications in the matter but how we'd all be taught Mongolian phrases soon. I tried to say something nice, something to bridge the gulf formed by the many awkward parts of our situation.

"Good. Thanks for handling your part."

She pointed at the many teams talking and practicing among themselves.

"Looks like you've got a solid plan. Thanks for handling yours."

We said no more, but at least we acknowledged our mutual respect.

****

I came home the day before Plono, dusty and dirty. The holiday fell alongside an ank break, so I'd have four glorious days off the road. Our house boasted a nice washtub and, despite the heat, I started a fire to warm enough water for a pleasant bath.

No one else was home. Rooslin had been developing a social circle in Pilk, mostly of men who weren't Svadlu. His mood improved as his number of buddies grew, and he likely celebrated Plono Eve with his new friends.

Tamara had said something about going up to Tolo to celebrate with her family. I suspected she also wanted to circumvent the awkward question of whether she and I had a date together every holiday. I didn't like expectations and it looked like she didn't either. Maybe someday, down the road, a repeat of our intimacy would appeal to us both. Maybe not. I hoped we could navigate those waters with friendship and kindness, however it worked out.

I'd settled into the bath in the middle of the kitchen when I heard the door open. Scump. Who was it?

Rooslin walked into the kitchen looking and smelling like he'd started his party early in the day.

"Oops. Sulphur. I'm so sorry. I came home to lie down for a while. May go out again later." He turned about-face and headed out of the kitchen, then turned around again.

"Wait. It's Plono's Eve. And there you are, without a glass of wine." He walked into the pantry. "Hmmm. Is it still correct to serve an afternoon green fizzy? No … I think it's time for a dinner red." He turned to me with a grin. "You can't bathe on a holiday without wine. I've heard it's a law."

"You're drunk, Rooslin."

"No. I'm having fun, Sulphur. Red or green. Pick one or I'll mix them and pour them both down your throat." He laughed, clearly having no intention of doing any such thing.

"I'd like to see you try. However, a little red wine would be good."

"Your wish is my command." He presented me with a full goblet, then stopped to look at my body in the tub.

"So that's what you look like naked."

"Do you mind not staring?"

"Hey. I was curious. No big deal."

"Go lay down, Rooslin."

"Yes, madam."

I drank the wine in a few gulps, my thirst getting the better of me. I wanted more, so I stepped out of my bath, dried off, and poured another goblet full.

It went down almost as fast.

As I walked by Rooslin's door, I heard him snoring and smiled. His being happy made me happy too. I saw he hadn't bothered to pull his tapestry closed so I reached to do it for him but paused.

I don't know why I did what I did next. Maybe the memory of the night we lay together at Keva overtook me and I wanted to feel that warmth and connection again. Maybe two glasses of wine on an empty stomach addled my judgment. Maybe having him look at me naked awakened something inside.

Whatever the reason, I lay down next to him on his bed, without clothes, and wrapped my body around him and held him the way I had that night at Keva when he'd come home so injured and so discouraged.

I fell asleep.

We both woke up much later. I'm not sure who began. It didn't matter. My hands were on him and his on me and in the dark, we found ways to pleasure each other that may not have been typical for a man and a woman but worked for the two of us. We managed it all without saying a word.

Only when we were done and lying next to each other, with a bit of dawn showing in the sky, did I ask, "Do you want me to go back to my own bed?"

"Not really. Lay with me the way we did at Keva."

So, that night had mattered to him too.

"Sulphur? This isn't usually what I'm into."

"I know. Me neither. Let's call this a one-time thing."

"I like that."

"Me, too."

~ 20 ~

What Kind of Man?

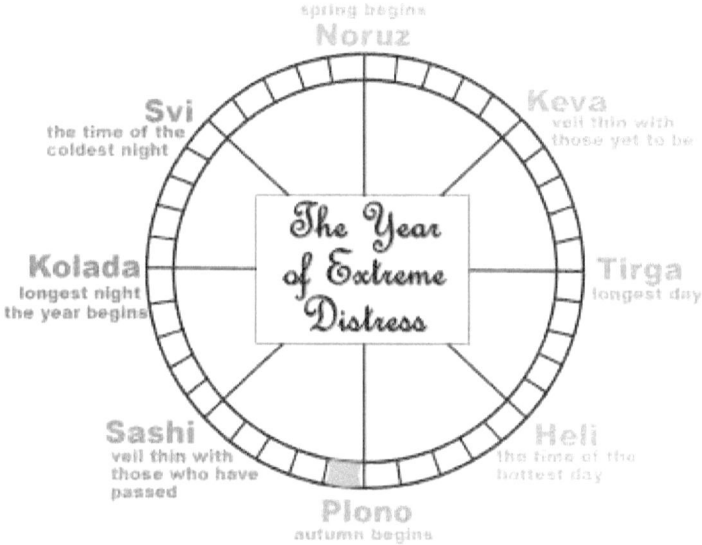

I woke up the morning of Plono to two realizations.

One, I was lying alone in Rooslin's bed because I'd now engaged in sex with both of my roommates. This might not have been a problem for someone else, but it was for me. I didn't behave this way.

Two, today was Plono. In exactly two eighths, ninety short days, a lot of armed people would arrive on horseback expecting tribute from my people. They'd get none, and they'd be pissed. We all knew what they did when they were angry.

On that day, everyone I cared for would have to fight for their own life, one way or another. Our collective success, in part, would depend on how well I managed to teach basic brawling skills to a whole lot of people who lacked the knowledge, practice, or inclination to fight well.

And I was laying around in bed worried about my sex life.

I needed to get up.

****

The next day, with the holiday behind us, I sought out Celestine in the part of Pilk where musicians performed. She was about to go on stage when I walked in. Surprise flashed across her face.

"I didn't think you came to this part of town," she said, adding a laugh to soften it. "I've never taken you for a fan of the troubadour scene."

"I guess I'm not. I didn't come to watch you."

"Oh." Disappointment tried to hide in her lowered eyes.

"I came to thank you. The turn-out you produced for us was amazing. I can't imagine any other way we'd have gotten so many people."

"You seemed rather flustered by the large numbers. I couldn't tell if you were happy about it or not."

"We weren't prepared for it. But don't worry, we will find ways to use every person you brought us. You did fantastic, Celestine. Thanks."

She looked proud, and she should have.

"I've been thinking. Perhaps Ryalgar has more things you could help her with," I said. "Things I don't even know about. Why not check in with her and see? I'm fairly sure she has no idea what you can do, either."

Celestine shook her head. "Her highness the boss is too busy for me. If I do run into her, she criticizes my shoes. I don't need that."

"Forget shoes. This is important." My revelation from yesterday still haunted me. "If we pruck this up, we're dead. Everyone we love is dead. Our world is gone. We've got to get past our petty differences and start doing everything we can. Now, while we have the time."

She pulled her head back in surprise. "Well, aren't you cheery this evening?"

"Celestine, I'm serious. If every one of us does we all we can, it still might not be enough. Do you understand?"

She answered, softer now. "Yes. Yes, I do. I know people who …. I may understand better than you do."

"You'll think about seeing if Ryalgar could use your help?"

"I'll talk to her soon, I promise."

****

Kazimir kept his word in one regard at least. A sealed formal letter sat on my desk the next morning, inviting me to the royal palace in Pilk in three days for a gathering of Mozdols. It said we would hear Prince Nevik of Pilk review plans for our defense from the point of view of the Royals. The letter went on to claim, in quite ornate handwriting, that I would also present a thorough review of what the Velka were up to.

Well, I guess I would.

I found one of the messengers kept in Pilk by Vinx's royal family. I'd been encouraged to use them because the Royals assumed their loyalty to Vinx remained above reproach.

"Read this and memorize it," I insisted, showing her the letter from Kazimir. "I need you to repeat it back to Prince Giorgi word for word. Then tell him I said three things. One. Thanks for getting me invited to this. Two. Any advice? And, three, I'll let you know how it goes."

She repeated my three things back to me, and then repeated the contents of my letter. I wished I had a mind half as good as these messengers did.

"Hurry. I'll make myself easy to find the next few days in case he has an answer."

Then I went looking for Rooslin.

Rooslin and I had worked our way through those few awkward days after Plono, then fallen back into the patterns of our old friendship. I suspected he had a lover, maybe two, among the men he hung out with. I suspected Tamara wanted a full-time lover even less than I did, and I understood Tamara's lover would be a he if she found him. Tamara had no wish for the life of an outlier.

Our three-way understanding would baffle some, but as the welcome cool breezes of autumn blew through our little home, we moved forward appreciating the household we had. For whatever any outsider might say about us, our home was filled with love.

Rooslin now knew of my run-ins with Kazimir. He believed the fishnet incident was nothing more than a powerful old man looking to discredit a talented young upstart.

"Think about it. The first thing he wanted to do was make it clear to all you're not the fighter they think you are," he told me. "He doesn't hate you, Sulphur, not in the classic sense, anyway. He fears you."

"That's ridiculous," I replied. But later, as I thought of how my uncanny abilities in battle might appear to a waning warrior trying to hold onto power, I understood what Rooslin meant. I represented the future, a future in which Kazimir was no longer in charge. Heli, I'd probably fear me too.

Rooslin surprised me by sharing Joli's upbeat assessment of my orders to spy on the Velka.

"It scares me a little that you're starting to see devious intent where even I see none," he said, "but honestly I don't think this can be called spying. You're communicating, Sulphur. Letting one group know what the other is doing. Communication is a good thing. Why do you have such a bad feeling about it?"

It was a fair question. No one but me had used the word spying.

"I know why." Suddenly I understood. "Because I hold loyalty to all three parties. Vinx. My sisters. The Svadlu. I don't lie to people I'm loyal to and I'm afraid someone somewhere is going to do something that they will beg or order me not to reveal. I won't know what to do."

He nodded. "It's not an unreasonable fear. But it hasn't happened yet, has it?"

"So?"

"So go to your meeting and tell Kazimir and the others what you know. Assure them the Velka are doing better than hoped and could even be of some help in slowing the Mongols down. At worst their efforts will cause casualties, but the Svadlu already know some of the Easterners will die. Then tell Giorgi everything the Svadlu say. No one has secrets."

"And what do I do when someone does?"

He smiled, the same soft sad smile he had back when we rode together to move rocks to build the wall between Gruen and Pilk.

"Come tell me. I'll help you navigate this. I promise. Until then, you're *not* a spy."

I repeated it. "I'm not a spy."

It went okay. Prince Nevik wasn't as full of himself as so many Royals; I could understand what Ryalgar once saw in him. Kazimir was noticeably dismissive of me when I spoke, but his three underlings were less so.

I recognized two of them. Irakli, the quiet man who was the highest ranked after Kazimir, had presided over my Mozdolo. He greeted me with some warmth, maybe because he felt responsible for my career moving forward. And the other, less senior commander from Pilk, had spoken to me at the Svadlu's information booth long ago. I could tell he didn't remember me at all.

I understood that these men's egos precluded them from acknowledging the Velka could be any help. As far as they were concerned, the Velka's sole use had been to persuade the Royals to back off the plan to defend the outer nichnas. Yet I tried, gently, to let them know that some value could come of these magic-infused diversions. The other Mozdols let me know, less gently, that I was being unrealistically generous. I didn't argue with them.

Davor hadn't been listed on the formal agenda in my letter because he always updated the group on the Svadlu's training progress. He made something of a show of sitting next to me and welcoming me. Perhaps he liked sticking it to Kazimir a little, or maybe he saw my achievements as adding to his glory. Either way, I appreciated any support I could get.

I was happy when the meeting ended with no real problems. I sent one dispatch to Prince Giorgi, who hadn't responded to my first letter, and another to Ryalgar. Both messages summarized the information without giving my opinions on anything. I'd at least figured out that opinions were best delivered in person and in private.

Two days later Kazimir assigned me to handle a small brawl in a pub just inside Kir, less than an hour's ride away. The messenger he sent told me a group of Levish had taken over the place and threatened to burn it down because of some grievance about payment for wine.

Once again, no soldiers were sent with me. Given my last assignment, I was nervous but I arrived to find what the messenger claimed. Three large Levish men stood inside the entrance. One explained that they'd been sent to get payment and if they didn't have the coins in their hands by nightfall they'd been told to torch the place.

I walked past them to the proprietor, a small man who kept wringing out a wet cloth and wiping the counter. He insisted he'd arranged with the vineyard to pay for half the wine at Tirga, which he had done, and the rest at Kolada, which he would do. He didn't owe any money now.

I turned back to the Levish.

"This doesn't involve you," one of them said.

"Yeah. We don't want to hurt a lady. Leave now and we'll reason with this man."

I guess they hadn't heard about me.

"Is what the proprietor says true?" I asked.

"Yes," one of them admitted, "but the way our boss sees it, owing money at Kolada is like owing money at never. I mean, who's going to pay debts on that day?"

He had a point. "Probably no one. Your boss may have to wait until things settle down before he gets his coins."

"Yeah, and what if things don't settle down? Our boss would like to have his money now, just in case, you know?"

I understood. "But that's not the agreement. This man doesn't have to pay you now."

"Well, we say he does, and if he knows what good for him, he'll do it."

I crossed my arms over my chest and gave the three my sternest look. "Go tell your boss the Svadlu say you've no right to hurt this place, and we'll post a guard outside of it until Kolada if necessary."

"The Svadlu, huh? You speak for them? A girl soldier? Here all alone?"

They were starting to piss me off. "I do."

Unfortunately, they stood between me and the door and I wanted to take this fight outside so I didn't damage this poor man's pub. I could have drawn my sword, but the odds of bloodshed went way up once metal got involved. I needed one of those less direct approaches.

"You're right," I said. "Me against three men is ridiculous. How about I fight one of you. Outside. No sword, no knives. If I lose, I'll *help* you make the proprietor pay. If I win, you go home."

They laughed. "Sure, why not. Any one of us will be happy to get you on the ground yelling for mercy. You'll give us the Svadlu's backing once we do?"

I smiled. "You have my word."

It took me less time to get the first man on the ground with his arm bent up high behind him than it takes me to gulp a mug of water. I gave him a hard kick in the nuts as I released him. I'd normally never do that, but I wanted him out of commission when the other two came at me.

I hadn't thought for a minute that they'd keep their end of the bargain, and I was right. Two on one was harder, but it was better than three, and I'd grabbed a broom as I followed them outside. One whack across the head turned it into a one-on-one fight. I'd said no metal, I hadn't said anything about brooms.

By the time the third man went down, a friend of the proprietor had helped secure the first two. A few Svadlu rode up, a bit conveniently, to escort them away. Had they been nearby the whole time? I bet they had. Well, at least they promised me they'd keep watch over the bar for the rest of the night.

As I rode back to Pilk, my suspicions ran high. Ten or more soldiers should have been sent to dispel this problem without bloodshed. Why send only me, a Mozdol with other duties? I'd have to see if Rooslin could imagine what Kazimir hoped to gain.

Of course Rooslin had an answer.

"Last time, he set you up to fail. An obvious choice, but it went poorly, even though you did get caught in the net."

"True, so why not do it again? He knows I can be defeated. He just needs meaner people doing it."

"Maybe enough others heard about it and now he can't risk purposefully harming one of his own. So this time, he set you up to succeed. I mean, there were only three of them and they weren't trained fighters He knew you could best them."

"That's stupid. Why would a man who fears me want me to win a fight in front of other people?"

"Ah, now that's the question."

"Do you have an answer?"

"My theory is that Kazimir has some way of spinning this to make you look bad. We won't find out what unless Ilari emerges victorious, and he needs to make *sure* you don't come out of this as a beloved hero."

"What kind of man plans and plots in advance like that?"

Rooslin laughed.

"The kind who ends up running the Svadlu."

~ 21 ~

Three Meetings
and a Lot of Commotion

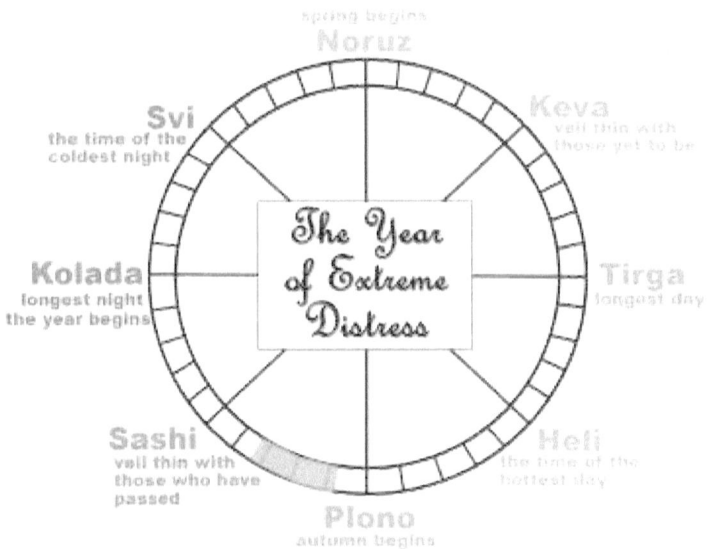

Within a day I learned these strategy sessions occurred every ank, but the last one had been unusual because of Prince Nevik's presence. Normally, Kazimir made Irakli run the meeting so he could observe and ask questions. Furthermore, they'd all been on good behavior in front of the prince, keeping their reports free of specifics to prevent discussion in front of a Royal.

The second meeting was just us Mozdols, and I felt the increase in tension. This was where men argued about how to save lives.

Everyone in the room could count. There had been ten anks until Kolada at the last meeting and now there were nine. We debated when to evacuate the eastern nichnas and how to keep the refugees safe in the forest of Zur and the mountains of Tolo.

"Pilk, Kir, and Lev ought to take their share, too!" a Mozdol from Tolo insisted. "What? You think you all are too good to have refugees to care for when this is over and the outer nichnas have been torched?"

"Let's not assume anything will be burned."

"Better plan for it," the man insisted.

"We need a better estimate on numbers! Exactly how many people from each nichna are we talking about? We can't plan anything until we know that," said Kazimir's fellow Mozdol from Kir.

"Sulphur!" Irakli turned to me. "Get the Velka to give us estimates of how many are staying behind in each nichna by the next meeting."

"Yes sir. But I can give them to you now if you want."

"You can?"

"Bisu. About twelve hundred are being trained to capture the estimated two hundred Mongols without horses. Another hundred will stay behind to tend to the horses who wake up, and two hundred will aid in moving the subdued Mongols to their individual homes. Another hundred have agreed to stay to handle communication, help healers, and carry out other emergency functions. It's all voluntary. That leaves just under half of Bisu evacuating, including all the small children, the very old, the sick, the injured, the pregnant, and a hundred or so of the more able-bodied who will assist them. My sisters are sending people door to door to make rosters and ensure everyone knows their role."

"I see. Hmm. It sounds like this is well in hand."

"I think so, Sir. Now in Scrud, about two hundred are …"

"Sulphur. If you have that level of detail, you and I can go over the numbers after the meeting."

"No. Wait." Kazimir interrupted. "Are you saying over half of Bisu has volunteered to stay behind? That's absurd!"

"I agree," another leader chimed in. "When we approved this Velka nonsense, we got the impression a few hundred people would remain to help the Velka with their crazy notions. I'm not comfortable sacrificing these sorts of numbers."

"But they all *want* to stay and fight, sir," I said. I knew Ryalgar hadn't considered that she might recruit too many farm folk for the Svadlu to accept.

"Well, we could make them evacuate, for their own good," a younger Mozdol from Pilk suggested. "You know, there are plenty who think we should force every resident of the outer nichnas, and all the Velka, to go to safety. It's one thing to let them come up with schemes to keep themselves busy, it's quite another to let them all die doing it!"

"True words!" another said.

"Pruck your sanctimonious scump!" the lone Mozdol from Eds shouted at him. "If my Edsers want to stay and fight, they *will* stay and fight. You lost the right to tell them what to do when you decided to forfeit their lands. We in Eds will consider any attempt to interfere in our plans to be an act of aggression upon our sovereignty."

He looked at me. "Right, Sulphur?"

Goat scump. Davor was watching me with an amused expression on his face.

Don't go straight at the problem. For once, come at it another way.

I swallowed and cleared my throat. I wanted my voice to be strong, and I needed the extra bit of time to form my words.

"The Svadlu have a proud and respected history of protecting the citizens of our realm."

Everyone in the room sat up a little straighter and looked at me as though they expected my next sentence to reaffirm their own opinion. Half would be disappointed.

"We would stain that reputation, no we would damage it forever, if we forced citizens to choose safety over a chance to defend their homes. That is not our role. We *offer* protection. We don't coerce behavior that good men and women consider cowardly in their own hearts."

I turned to Kazimir and looked him in the eye, "We have the reputation of the Svadlu to consider."

He arched his eyebrow.

"You continue to surprise me, Sulphur. How wise of one so young to recognize the value of a good reputation." He smiled at the other men. "Our youngest and most female member," he chuckled at his own wittiness "rightly sees the damage such a policy would do to us. Not to mention the extreme drain on resources at a crucial time, when our soldiers need to be preparing for the battle of their lives."

He turned to Irakli and spoke as if I wasn't there. "Meet with Sulphur and confirm her numbers. Verify that the evacuation plan is progressing well under its current auspices. If it is, I see no need for the Svadlu to interfere. We have better things to do, and those who survive will thank us mightily for carrying day when all is done."

"See you next ank, gentlemen." He got up to leave. The meeting was over.

Rooslin literally jumped up and down with excitement when I gave him a word-by-word account of my big moment.

"You are my star pupil," he said.

"I'm your only pupil."

"It doesn't matter. You handled that perfectly. See? Kazimir doesn't care whether people live or die. I mean, he'd as soon they live, but what he really cares about is how the Svadlu come out of this. You spoke to his biggest concern in a way he couldn't easily refute. And, believe me when I tell you everybody liked your answer, except for those idealistic young Mozdols making a misguided attempt to save lives, of course."

"Do you think they're right? Should we be evacuating everyone?"

"Of course not. The Svadlu's fears are based on their egocentric assumption that the Velka will fail. You and I, we're doing our best to see that won't happen. Thanks to your cleverness, the Mozdols can go back to preparing to win the final battle. You pushed them into the most advantageous of all decisions." He gave me a friendly punch on the arm. "I'm so proud."

Then, as if he remembered something.

"Oh, you know that comment Kazimir made about you recognizing the value of a good reputation? I know what he was talking about...."

"Huh?"

"He's trying to destroy yours."

"That's horrible. What do you mean?"

"Oh, don't worry, he's not doing a particularly good job of it. But a couple of my buddies heard of your adventures in Kir a few days ago, only with an interesting twist. There's a handful claiming your uncanny fighting abilities resulted from some nasty spell the Velka performed on you. Do people really believe in such things? Silly question. Of course they do. Anyway, Kazimir couldn't use your losing against you, so he tried to use your winning."

"Should I worry?"

"Nah. If he'd had more confidence in you and put you up against nine big men and you won, which you could have, then this rumor might get some traction. But Kazimir was too cautious. Worst you did was beat up on one big thug at a time, and any woman who gets into the Svadlu ought to be able to do that much."

He took me by both shoulders.

"Sulphur, It's okay. You're. Doing. Great."

"Thanks."

No matter how well one does, sometimes they need a friend to tell them that.

****

An ank later the nights had grown cool and the leaves held glints of yellow. Our meeting began with a spirited discussion of whether we should hurl burning oil off the wall between Pilk and Gruen. We argued about the specific fighting techniques to be used and how many soldiers to have trained for each. Archers sat at the top of our list, of course, because we now had a thick tall wall to place them upon. Some worried about relying on archers too much because we'd been told the Mongols wore hard-to-pierce leather clothing. Thus the hot oil option.

"Is it true your Velka are making poison arrows? Could we get some of those?" Irakli asked me. I'd realized by now that he wasn't trying to put me on the spot with his questions. His demands for information came from the courtesy of inclusion.

"Historically the Velka have refused to give poisons to anyone else."

"But surely under the circumstances ...," the lone Mozdol from Faroo said, his arms out wide with his palms pointed to the sky in frustration.

"I know. Don't forget, the Velka hope we Svadlu don't have to fight at all. Their plan is for us to appear so formidable, and for the Mongols to be so spooked, that we negotiate without firing an arrow. But I understand no one here would dream of relying on that outcome. So, I'll ask them if they'd be flexible with the poison arrows, given the danger."

The conversation moved on to what the Svadlu considered the inevitable hand-to-hand combat. Should we train more knife fighters or more swordsmen? Tolovians prided themselves on their knife-fighting abilities. Thus, the two Mozdols from Tolo lobbied for knives having a greater prominence in the battle.

I wondered how many strategic decisions we made to appease the vanity of those involved. I could ask Rooslin, but I thought I knew what his answer would be.

****

By the following ank mornings held on to the coolness of the previous night, and most leaves had turned gold and few a shimmered with hints of orange. We focused on the start of the battle. For us.

"Sulphur, tell us more about the third and last diversion. Our information on it is sketchy at best."

"As is mine, sir."

"What's the problem? Are the Velka holding out on you about this one? Hiding something?" Kazimir asked.

"That is totally unacceptable!" yelled one of the Mozdols from Pilk. "Our agreement included them keeping us fully informed of their plans."

"No one is hiding anything." I sighed. I should have been better prepared for this question. "The Velka have handed the third diversion over to another group, so they don't know much about what is being planned either. This other group is rather secretive."

"Another group? What sort of nonsense is this? How many groups do we have in our realm?" Irakli asked.

"We didn't okay the participation of anyone else. Why would they do such a thing?" Kazimir was visibly annoyed at not having been consulted.

"I don't think they planned to do this, sir, but as things progressed …."

"Sulphur. Why don't you tell them who the group is?" Davor said. I knew he knew. I wondered if he was trying to embarrass me, or simply curious how I would handle it. It was hard to tell with him.

"It's the reczavy," I said as plainly as I could and without lowering my gaze in embarrassment. The room erupted with a combination of obscene remarks and angry disbelief.

"Why has this not come to our attention?" Irakli wanted to know.

"It's never come up, sir. The… the reczavy volunteered for this, they told the Velka they valued their freedom as much as anyone."

I ignored several guffaws and rude comments about what they did with that freedom.

"They told us they could stage a confrontation that would shock and disorient the remainder of the horde," I said. "With any luck, they'll leave the Mongols too spooked to fight, prompting the possible surrender and negotiations the Velka hope for. Given the alternatives, the Velka agreed to let the reczavy design their most outrageous diversion."

Conversations erupted again but Davor cut through them all. "I knew about it," he said. Much of the group turned to stare at him, but I noticed a few continued to watch me. "I knew most of you wouldn't like it when you found out, but if you gave it some thought you'd realize it makes sense. These people, and they are people, they are willing to lay down their lives to send confused, maybe even panicked, enemies on to you. It's something they can do. Why not take the gift?"

"We'd heard of this, too," one of the two Mozdols from K'ba confirmed. "The reczavy live on the fringes of our nichna, but we support and commend them for this effort."

"Only a fool would turn down help in such desperate times," added the Mozdol from Bisu.

Kazimir shrugged. "Does what they're planning involve naked women? That would be a nice change. It's probably just naked men, though, isn't it?"

"All I know is they plan to drive many of the Mongols into the river, and work with Faroojers on rafts to capture them."

"Is this true?" Irakli asked the lone Mozdol from Faroo.

"I heard that some of my people have bravely offered their skills in the water. I wasn't aware of these details, however."

"What makes you think we can trust this group of delinquents?" the other Mozdol commander from Pilk asked me. "Are they responsible enough to show up? Who's in charge of them? What makes you think you can rely on him?"

That did it. I'd had enough.

"I know I can rely on *him* because she's my sister."

For the length of a cock's crow, the room went absolutely silent. Finally one of the Mozdols from K'ba asked me in a pleasant voice, "You have a sister in the reczavy?"

"Yes, I do. She's putting this third diversion together."

"Do *you* trust her?"

I thought. To say she and I had never been close would be an understatement. Yet, I'd watched her grow and seen her struggles in our family. I'd noticed her strength and courage amidst her rebellion.

"With my life," I said.

"Anyone a Mozdol would trust with his life is worthy of our trust," the Zurian Mozdol replied. I didn't think I'd ever heard him speak before.

"Of course," Kazimir said. He waited, as if he expected someone else to pick up the problem from there.

After a heartbeat, Irakli did.

"Make haste to see your sister and get all the details you can before our next meeting. We need to know what we're going to find on our doorstep when this happens."

My body went numb as I nodded my assent. Now I had no choice but to do something I couldn't imagine doing. I had to go visit the reczavy.

~ 22 ~

Finding a Spot

Yes, I threw things at the wall in my room. I'm not proud of it, but I didn't know what to do with the anger boiling over inside.

I fumed at Gypsum for joining the reczavy and putting me in this embarrassing situation. Wasn't it hard enough being a female in the Svadlu? Didn't I have enough obstacles to face as the only woman Mozdol? Why did she have to bring endless crude jokes into my life on top of everything else?

Of course, if she'd just quietly joined up and kept a low profile, her choices wouldn't have affected my life much. But no. The women in my family appeared to be exceedingly bad at keeping a low profile.

I thought of the drunk man on a holiday long past who'd ruined our family outing by calling us pruskas. Even now, I wasn't sure exactly what a pruska was, though I'd once beaten a boy's face bloody for calling me one.

Could the drunk man have been some sort of traveling wizard? Had he cursed all seven of us with his mumbled insult? What a horrible thought. Maybe we'd be nice normal women today if my mother had never stepped into his path.

I stopped my tantrum and stared at the mess I'd made in my room. A soft knock on my door proceeded two voices.

"Sulphur?" Rooslin said.

"Are you okay?" Tamara added.

They walked in uninvited.

Rooslin looked around and laughed.

"What the pruck?" Tamara asked me as she surveyed the debris strewn everywhere.

So, what could I do? Out came the details of the most recent Mozdol meeting and my frustrations with my sister. No, with all my sisters. I even told them of the stupid family incident years ago and my irrational fears we'd been cursed to grow into troublemakers.

"If that's the case, this wizard must have sobered up and tried to atone for his actions," Rooslin said.

"What do you mean?"

"Well, it seems to me as if each of you girls received a gift, too. Several really, and all different. That's exactly what I'd do if I was a guilty wizard."

"What are you talking about? I mean, sure, Ryalgar can do that oomrush thing but I don't see how it's ever helped her."

"Ryalgar is uncommonly smart," Tamara said. "And doesn't your sister Coral have some talent being used?"

"Yeah. She and Celestine can make animals do things. I don't understand it, but it doesn't seem all that useful either."

"Coral seems uncommonly empathetic. Celestine is charismatic. I don't know the others well enough to comment but …"

"Okay, okay, so maybe everyone but me got something out of this varmin curse. Fine. It's a great theory."

They both looked at me like I was stupid. I'm *not* stupid and I don't like being looked at that way.

"What?" I said.

Rooslin turned to Tamara. "Being able to move like the wind and fight like a tigress isn't much of a gift, I guess."

"Not a useful one at least," she agreed.

"Stop it. Yes, I know I can do things but it's not because of any varmin wizard. I worked prucking hard at it." When they just stood there and didn't leave, I added. "I've got to pick this place up and get packed."

"Where are you going?"

"Oh. I didn't finish my story. I've been *ordered* to go to the reczavy to talk to my sister."

They were both quiet.

"That does explain your outburst," Tamara said as she turned to leave.

"Hope it goes better than you expect," Rooslin added as he pulled the door closed behind him.

****

"Sister's here!" I heard a male voice yell out as my horse neared the large colorful tents that housed the reczavy.

"Which one?" Gypsum's voice responded.

"The other tall blonde," a female answered.

"Are you *sure*?"

I smelled smoke as I entered the clearing. It was midday and a completely naked man and woman both stared up at me on my horse. They were washing dishes in a cauldron hung over a small fire. Looked like he was scrubbing and she was drying. A tall pile of clean pots and pans was stacked beside her.

"Positive," they yelled back together.

"Send her in."

After turning my horse over to the helpful woman, I pulled back the flap of the tent, not sure what I would see. Gypsum wore a long robe and sat on a pile of soft blankets, sewing small items together. She smiled up at me.

"You are the last visitor I expected. I mean, after Mom but she doesn't count because she never goes anywhere."

I looked around. "Where are the others?

"Out. Have a seat." She made one more stitch, tied a knot in the thread, and laid her sewing down. "What brings you to the doorstep of those you once described to me as, I think I quote correctly, 'perpetual children with no sense of responsibility or obligation to their fellow humans?'"

"I've been ordered to get more information about what you're planning. The Svadlu are concerned about the handoff of the battle."

She laughed, and I realized how seldom I'd heard this sister laugh as a child.

"There will be no hand-off. It's simple, really. Dad and his crew are making the road down to the Wide River look like the road going to Pilk. Those plant women with the Velka are helping. Once the Mongols see the river ahead of them, they'll know they've been tricked and they're not where they want to be. At that point, we pull out all stops to drive as many of them into the water as we can, and as many of their horses too."

"I saw a practice with the Faroojers."

"I heard."

"Looks like they'll be pretty effective at forcing fighters and horses to the other side. Is there any plan past that?"

"Why would there be? Mongols aren't swimmers, and they don't cross big rivers on horseback. Few will try to come back. At that spot, the other side is nothing but marsh in either direction. Where they go and what they do once they get through that muck is their problem. Ryalgar told us to make a lot of them gone. A lot of them will be."

"I see. And those who don't go? What's to keep them from killing you?"

"We'll be hard to find because Gruenites dug tunnels for us. We've got exploding powder we'll use to push the rest on to Pilk, too. I guess that's your handoff."

"So I tell the Svadlu to expect somewhere between one and a thousand Mongols to ride up to the wall and demand tribute? And at that point, it's the Svadlu's show?"

"Pretty much."

"Gypsum, I need more details."

She looked frustrated. "I don't have more. That's not how we work."

"Okay. What does 'pull out all stops' mean?"

"We're not sure yet. A lot of illusions and weirdness. It's a free-form performance, not the sort of thing you choreograph ahead of time. I know it will work, Sulphur, but you have to trust us."

Something in me snapped at being asked to trust the reczavy. I did trust Gypsum, but her new friends didn't inspire the same confidence. They washed dishes in the nude!

She wanted me to trust people who'd sleep with anyone. In any combination? If you couldn't count on them to behave themselves sexually, how could you possibly trust them in other areas?

I started to say so when I thought of my night with Tamara. And my night with Rooslin. Great Goddess, someone could make the same claim about me but I wasn't like that. My word was worth gold.

So instead I said "You know they call you all the goat? The goat part of the Chimera, that is?"

She laughed again. "Yes, I heard. I'm sure it's a reference to the sex stuff. Funny how we do so much more, yet the whole realm seems obsessed with that one aspect of us."

At a loss for a response, I borrowed one from Rooslin.

"That's people for you."

Then I realized how Gypsum *could* help me.

"Look, just give me a few phrases about the kind of stuff you'll do, enough so I can get the other Mozdols off my back."

"Oh, I've got lots of notes about the things we're considering. You want that?"

"Let me take a look." I sat down next to my sister and we worked together. Gypsum was well organized and she gave me answers that would suffice. As she did, she gave me something else, perhaps something I needed more. She gave me a new perspective about where my loyalties lay.

It wasn't with my kin, the Renata Glonti family, as I'd once thought. It wasn't with Ilari, exactly, or with the Svadlu, or Vinx, or the Royals, or the Velka. They all were important pieces to consider, but the Chimera itself had taken over as my top priority.

I loved the way the name sounded. "Kuh. Mare. Uh." I loved what it stood for -- a dazzling idea to protect the innocent. I'd always been all about protecting the innocent.

So as Gypsum and I schemed to construct a plan the Svadlu would believe, I no longer felt torn. Despite my respect for my many allegiances, at this moment in time, one responsibility outshone the others.

I would protect the Chimera above all, so it could protect us.

****

I spoke at the next Mozdol meeting. The men squirmed in their seats, a little too eager to hear of my trip, but I ignored the leers that crept onto many of their faces as I talked. I would stick to the relevant facts.

"My sister has done an admirable job. She's choosing from several planned diversions involving noise, fire, smoke, live snakes, and costumed creatures, among other ideas."

"What sorts of *other* ideas?" Several muttered the question with unwarranted eagerness.

"Well, maybe eggs filled with itching powder. It's still being tested but Gypsum says it holds a lot of promise."

"Isn't, uh, nakedness involved somehow?" The young Mozdol from Pilk went ahead and asked the question that seemed to be on everyone's minds.

"No. Not unless the Mongols chose to disrobe because of the itching powder." Most of the men looked disappointed. I kept myself from laughing.

I did explain how weather and time of day would factor into the ultimate plan as would the number of riders remaining. The reczavy prepared to deal with up to a thousand attackers and as few as a hundred dispirited or angry foes. They'd drive as many into the river as possible.

"And those they don't drive into the water? I think the remaining Mongols will slaughter the reczavy," a Mozdol from Lev declared.

"That's what I thought, too. It may surprise you to learn the reczavy are willing to make that sacrifice, for the sake of Ilari."

This caused several looks of discomfort as the thought of such a noble sacrifice collided with a lifetime of contempt in the Mozdols' minds.

"But it probably won't happen. The Gruenites dug them small tunnels to hide in, with multiple entrances and, at worst, not enough width for a horse or the use of a sword. It will even out the fight if there must be one.

"We hope when the attackers don't see foes to go after, and that fancy Chinese powder starts exploding, the remaining invaders will ride on to Pilk to demand what they came for."

"Good report," Kazimir said. "Whatever remains and comes to us will be slaughtered and this will be the end of it."

I looked at him like we spoke two different languages. "What about the agreed-upon attempt to secure surrender and negotiations? We'll have prisoners to return. Possibly horses, too."

"Right. Look, if the infamous Mongol horde rides up and says 'hey nice people, we'd like to surrender to you,' we'll be happy to have that conversation." This came from the other Mozdol from Kir, Kazimir's comrade. Kazimir slapped his knee in mirth and approval.

"Exactly," he said. "Let me be clear, Sulphur. The Velka, and a lot of Ilarians, want to believe we can negotiate with these barbarians. We don't believe it for a minute. We don't even believe we are going to *have* a significant number of prisoners to offer them. It's a harmless fantasy, but those of us in this room, we're preparing for reality. You're one of us now, by your own choice. Keep these conversations to yourself, and let others think what they want. Do you understand me?"

"Absolutely, sir."

"Do you have any problem with what I'm saying?"

"Of course not. The ultimate survival of Ilari is my number one concern. Sir." I looked him straight in the eye as if I meant every word I'd just said. Anything to keep the Chimera alive.

****

As Sashi, approached, Rooslin told us he planned to spend it with his new friends and one of them could end up in our home the next morning.

"No problem, right?"

No, none. Tamara and I both encouraged him to have a wonderful celebration and bring home any man he liked.

Tamara later confided to me she was seeing someone. No, not a soldier, but a widower and history teacher. He had his own home; she could be gone for a night, perhaps two. I shouldn't worry.

"I'm happy for you," I said. And I was. She wanted such a relationship.

But it did leave the awkward yet familiar problem of what to do with Sulphur. As a Mozdol, I could hardly go party with the enlisted soldiers. I'd dampen their celebrations by being there. I didn't want to do that.

The other Mozdols were mostly married. I assumed they'd spend the holiday evening with their wives, though perhaps the night before they'd go out together and have a little fun as a group. I wouldn't be invited because I'd put a damper on their celebrations, too.

Once again, there wasn't a spot for me anywhere.

I spent Sashi eve at home, trying to pretend it was just another night, but on the day itself, I needed to get out of the house. I wandered around Pilk center until the sunlight grew dusky.

Although we honor the dead on Sashi, we also feel a smug joy for not being one of the deceased. Sashi is the day on which Ilarians are most prone to drunk and dangerous behavior simply to prove they are alive. And every celebrator knew Sashi was only five short anks before Kolada.

I kept walking, listening to the noise of the crowds and noticing the growing rowdiness. I needed to get off the street. I'd wandered into the part of town featuring live entertainment. What had Celestine called it? The troubadour scene. Music drifted out of various doors. I'd never been a fan, but tonight the sounds soothed something that ached inside me.

I heard a familiar voice. Did Celestine perform here? I pushed my way through a crowded doorway and saw my sister on stage with her other musicians. She drew a big crowd. People filled every seat and left no room to stand. No place for me here. Either.

I sighed and turned to go when I heard my name.

"Sulphur! Over here. Join us," Issa yelled to me. She and the other three women officers had a table in the back, and one of them pointed to a small unoccupied stool. I pushed my way over to them, happy to be greeted with their hugs.

One grabbed a waiter by the arm, demanding an ale for me. I settled onto my stool, enjoying the music, the warmth, and yes, the sense of having a spot where I belonged, at least for the evening.

~ 23 ~

A Clear Purpose

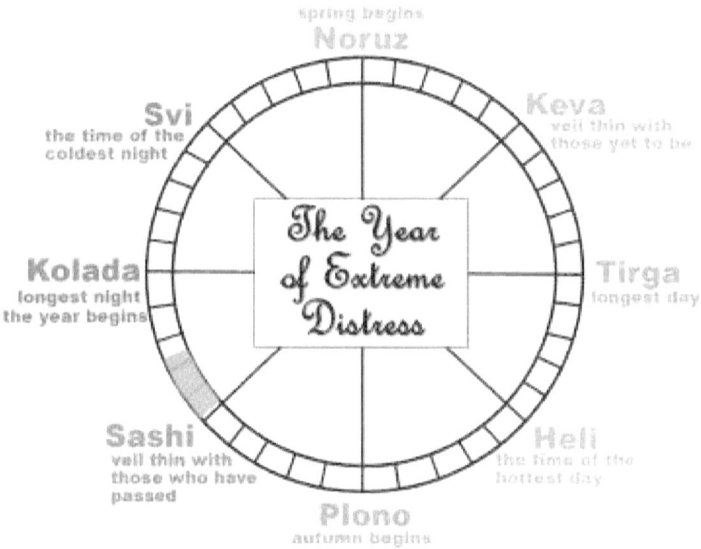

After Sashi my life had a clear purpose as I dedicated my efforts to protecting the Chimera. The outright scorn of the Svadlu for negotiating with the Mongols concerned me most. Someone needed to be alerted, but who? I turned to an expert.

"My instincts are to tell Ryalgar," I told Rooslin.

"No! Don't you dare tell anyone in the Velka," he answered.

"Why not?"

"They're working their arses off to accomplish something incredible. Your news could derail everything. No, you need to …"

"Let me guess. Come at the problem from another direction?"

He chuckled. "You're learning. Tell me, what do you think of living in a realm ruled by royalty?"

"Who else would rule it?" I asked.

"I don't know. Have you considered other options?"

"Honestly, no. Our system is complicated, and skewed towards men, but most of our rulers are decent and power is divided so no one can do too much damage."

"Exactly. Kingdoms, places where one man called a king rules everything, are full of problems. You must have studied them in school. Here, power is shared amongst the twelve principalities, even if Pilk has more sway. Within a royal family, it's often shared between the ruling prince and his father, the former ruler, and sometimes even the grandfather. Wives, mothers, and sisters have influence, too, though I agree they ought to have as much outright control as the men."

"That's not going to change any time soon," I said.

"Probably not. But power is shared elsewhere, too. Ilarians pride themselves on their education, giving teachers some clout. Your sister Celestine has shown the power of fame. But who are the other two big power holders in Ilari?"

Did he want me to guess? "It would have to be the Svadlu and the Velka," I said.

"Another point for my star pupil. In truth, we split power three ways: among the Royals, who are the most obvious holders, the Svadlu, who are the next most obvious because they walk around with weapons, and the Velka. Now, if one of these three groups is planning to do something bad to another, and you want to prevent it, who do you tell?"

I got it.

"You go to the group that's *not* involved and try to get them on your side. It's so simple when you say it that way."

"Isn't it though? It's like military strategy."

"So, Giorgi would be best, wouldn't he?"

"He is your Royal."

"But what can he do?"

"I've no idea, but he may know. Do you have an excuse to go to Vinx for a few days?"

"Lots of them. Now that I attend these Mozdol meetings every ank, I've neglected the training. It's time I checked in. Then there's my family, who I've barely seen."

Rooslin smiled. "It sounds like a lovely trip.

****

Giorgi sent a letter back insisting I stay at the palace in Vinx and informing me his mother would host a dinner party for me during my stay and invite my family.

"She says your achievement should have received more attention, even more so because you now spend your time as a Mozdol helping ordinary people learn to defend themselves. She thinks that sort of altruism would only come from a woman Mozdol." Giorgi had gone so far as to draw a winking eye in his letter after that last remark.

Ah well. At least I could now count Giorgi's mother among my allies and hope the honor of a dinner at the palace would bring my own mother some joy. I saddled up my horse at dawn and left.

The morning sun shone in a cloudless, intense blue sky as I rode and the air sparkled with that dryness that affirms fall's presence. The remaining leaves had all turned one shade of orange or another, while those that had fallen crunched under my horse's feet.

The most sumptuous guest room awaited me, along with the constant company of the twelve-year-old twins who'd stuck by my side the last time I visited. When they begged me, I let them hold my sword and knives but kept close watch while they did.

Then I cleaned up and put on my best frock. It wasn't much, but it identified me as female as I joined Giorgi's mother, his wife, and his grown sister for ladies' afternoon wine. A year ago I'd have politely declined, hoping to rest up after my ride and guessing the conversation would be boring. Thanks to Rooslin's coaching, however, I understood that my inclusion mattered. My participation told the other women I considered them worth my time and such a message made me their champion, not their enemy. I didn't need extra enemies.

It went reasonably well, and after a short break, we freshened up for dinner. I didn't know what other women did to "freshen" but I stretched out on my bed and took a nap.

As soon as I arrived in the great room for dinner, Lady Patela placed me in a receiving line. I looked. The line wound out the door and down the hill. Goat scump, they'd invited half the nichna. I guess such things were possible when you had a royal staff to scurry around and cook a feast.

But all the handshaking and commenting wasn't as boring as I expected. Many of the men and women I'd helped train passed through the greeting line, telling me of how they'd improved with practice.

"You should see this woman throw rocks now!" one man said proudly, putting his arm around his wife. I tried to praise them all, and offer encouragement.

Finally, my parents, Coral, Olivine, and Celestine arrived together, looking a bit harried

"Whew! We made it," Mom greeted me in the line. "Not a lot of time to get ready."

"I'm glad you came."

She looked around at the large hall, packed with people.

"Of course we came. This is to honor you, our daughter. Look. Look at what you've accomplished."

My father clasped my hands and his eyes sparkled. "Don't listen to her. Your mother had the time of her life getting ready for this."

Coral followed, holding a baby that looked more like Davor than ever. The child cooed at everyone, responding to any attention with baby giggles that made all the adults melt.

Olivine took my hand as her fierce green eyes met mine. "A well-deserved reward for excelling in the life *you* chose," she said.

"Thank you. I hope you'll get the same." We understood each other.

Celestine brought up the rear. "I just want to warn you, I wrote a song for the evening and the lavish praise in it *could* embarrass you."

I thanked her. What else could I do?

Before the dinner began, Lady Patela stood to speak.

"I have something long overdue to present, something made by two of Sulphur's sisters, on behalf of her family."

I noticed Coral beamed with pride as Lady Patela brought forward a cape made from thick linen and died the brightest scarlet red. As she held it out I saw a hint of softness in its style, but otherwise it spoke of strength. It was perfect for me, and more beautiful than any garment I'd ever worn.

"In days gone by, these capes were often made for a Mozdol by his own family. I'm happy to revive this fine tradition."

She gestured for me to come forward, and I tried not to feel self-conscious as she placed the exquisite cloak over my shoulders. It fit perfectly. Of course it did.

A praise-filled proclamation from Giorgi's father followed, then Celestine sang her embarrassingly sentimental song and I was finally allowed to sit. After I calmed down, I enjoyed more exceptional food and wine than I'd had in a long time.

I knew tonight had been my real Mozdolo.

The next morning Giorgi met me with two goblets of breakfast wine and suggested we walk through the gardens. If he felt safe talking there, then I did too, so I told him of the Mozdol meetings, giving details I'd considered wise to leave out of my letters.

"We have a major disconnect in how the Svadlu and the Velka see this attack ending," I concluded.

"Which approach works best?"

"I don't know. If the Velka's part goes as horrible as the Svadlu expect, Kazimir is right. There's no negotiating. We better be prepared to fight. But he needs to consider that the Velka could have enough of an effect to matter."

"Which is the better outcome? Svadlu victory or Velka negotiations? I tend to favor victory."

"You'd think, but not for a tiny nation. We'll never have more than a thousand Svadlu. Yet if we win, next winter another thousand will attack us. And the winter after, a thousand more. If we hold them off and they get annoyed, they send ten thousand to put a stop to the nonsense."

"I see. The Svadlu think if we win once, the Mongols won't return. But given their size and resources, there's no reason to think that, is there? But then, why would they negotiate with us either?"

"Two reasons," I said. "Ryalgar hopes our magic and illusions will spook them, convince them we can always cause more trouble than we're worth. And, her research tells her they have a code of honor. Not like ours, of course. We'd hardly invade other realms and burn them to the ground. But she believes if we establish we have honor, too, by returning their men and horses to them, they'll consider a truce with us."

"And why should we trust a truce with them?"

I answered him with a truth I'd yet to say aloud. But it needed to be said.

"If we can't trust them? Then we are, and always have been, completely prucked. If we can't trust them, we will eventually be their slaves or be dead, no matter how hard we fight or what we do."

He looked at me. I looked at him.

"Our only chance for prolonged survival never lay with the Svadlu?" he said.

"I used to think it did, but the more I've learned, the more I realize it doesn't."

"So the Svadlu's real role in this?"

"Is to look intimidating, and be the last straw that coaxes them into a negotiation."

"Obviously, that's not a role they embrace," he said.

"But they have to. What do we do?"

"Well, we definitely don't tell the Svadlu what you've told me. You go be a good Mozdol and act like you believe the Svadlu will save the realm."

"That's what I've done so far."

He tapped a knuckle against his lips, as if the motion would help him think.

"Wait. This might help. Tell the other Mozdols that they have to meet with the Velka for appearance's sake."

"I can do that, but what good will a meeting do?"

"Advise them that this is an official meeting to discuss the battle hand-off and possible negotiations. Who would handle them and how. Tell them the Velka need to hear a plan, or they'll start to raise a ruckus and with Kolada only four anks away, any ruckus would be stupid. So convince them this harmless event placates women doing a fine job of keeping the countryside calm. Calm is good. Right?"

"Yes," I said. "Calm is good. I can convince them we need a meeting. Getting them to plan, or even pretend to plan, for negotiations will be harder. Maybe you could get other Royals to lean on their Mozdols about how important it is to keep people from panicking over the next few anks."

"I can do that. Easy."

"Good. In places like Bisu and Gruen, where people like the Velka's plans, you could maybe get your fellow Royals to push their Mozdols for an actual negotiation option in the Svadlu's thinking."

"I'll see what I can do," Giorgi said.

"As will I. Perhaps the act of planning will open up the possibility."

"Sulphur? Do you honestly think we are, and always have been, completely prucked by this?"

I gave him the most honest answer I could.

"I have no idea."

After a few days at the palace, I made an appearance at practice sessions in Bisu and in Vinx. They now happened every other day, often run by the participants. Afternoons grew colder now, and only dark red leaves remained on the trees. As practices ended, groups huddled around fires to discuss what to do if this happened, or how to react if that happened, the same way the officers and Mozdols talked through military strategy.

These untrained volunteers had become far more than inept foot soldiers. In over half a year, they'd turned themselves into their own kind of military force, one in which determined civilians used unconventional tactics to challenge a much larger and better-equipped army. I thought the idea had merit for warfare in general.

I stopped in to visit Mom and Dad and went over to Coral's cottage to play with my nephew and see how things went for her. Despite my worries, it comforted me to spend time with my kin. As I rode back to Pilk, with my belly full and my heart happy, I kept thinking ... *this ... this is what we are fighting for.*

****

Rooslin loved the meeting Giorgi and I concocted and he coached me as I wrote Ryalgar about it and as I lobbied my fellow Mozdols to set it up. We scheduled it for two and a half anks before Kolada.

I met resistance when I tried to coax Kazimir into putting negotiation discussions on the agenda. His refusal to do such a simple thing baffled me. His stubbornness only brought conflict into the realm at a delicate time. Surely he could see that.

I finally decided that he could, but this was one of those acts that defied common sense. He would not admit, to me at least, that my sister could possibly succeed. The more I pushed, the less likely he was to cooperate.

So I said no more. Davor dropped by my little office late in the day.

"If you're going to be a real Mozdol, you need to keep some hooch hidden around here. At least enough to offer someone a drink right before the ank break."

"I'll make a note to get some."

"Look, I know what you're trying to do with Kazimir and why, but he's a stubborn old coot who doesn't like women telling him what to do. You and your sister in combo really make his hackles rise."

"I've backed off," I said.

"Good. I'm going to have a few words with him. It shouldn't have to work that way, but sometimes ..."

"I know."

After he left, I sat wishing I did have something strong to drink. Before I had time to go look for some, Davor came back.

"Never got to talk to Kazimir," he said. "Turns out three other Mozdols beat me to it. Three. All of them got urgent letters from their ruling princes insisting peace had to be kept with the Velka at all costs, even if it meant discussing negotiations."

"They did? That's great."

"Don't you think it's odd three ruling princes would write pretty much the same varmin letter?"

"A little."

"I notice you spent some time in Vinx last ank. Did you and Giorgi talk?"

"We always talk."

He laughed. "Well played. And here I thought you needed my help. You just might get the hang of this Mozdol thing yet."

The nice thing was that Davor seemed fine with it if I did.

~ 24 ~

Pointing Out the Obvious

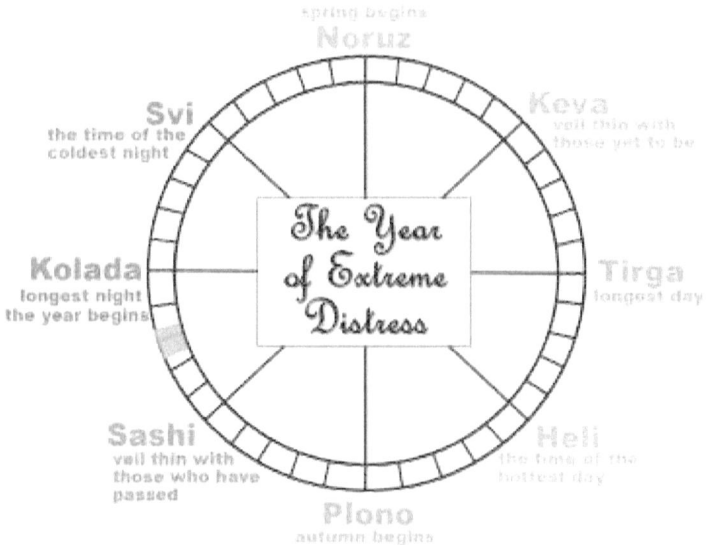

The day of the big meeting came.

As Ryalgar walked in, I realized I'd never told her I'd become a Mozdol. I assumed my family had, but her surprised look when she saw me seated with the others, wearing my red cape, said otherwise.

"I've risen through the ranks," I said. She blinked in surprise but said nothing. I guessed she couldn't afford to appear anything but informed in front of this crowd.

Before others could redirect the discussion, I began with what I always did; I gave an overview of the training in the outer nichnas.

"Are they ready for what they need to do?" Ryalgar asked.

"As ready as they can be, under the circumstances."

Her smile was genuine. "You've done an amazing job."

Several men squirmed at her comment. Nobody gave compliments in these meetings. Pruck 'em. I considered all my big sister had done in the past year.

"You've done an amazing job, too." I grinned inside when they all squirmed a little more.

When Irakli took over the meeting he changed the topic to the flow of the battle. He emphasized how all the Chimera would need to back off once the attackers moved away from the river's edge and headed towards Pilk. After that, the army would handle everything, irrespective of the circumstances.

"Kazimir, our chief commander," he pointed to Kazimir as he spoke, "will be prepared to negotiate as per your instructions *if* the circumstances warrant it. In such a case, he will read the letter you drafted, outlining terms and the process for our return of their prisoners. We plan to use the translator you found, as well as your sister Iolite."

"Oh there's no need for Iolite to be involved." Ryalgar and I said in unison. Irakli pursed his lips and smiled slightly.

"We'll have her on standby, and will only involve her if necessary.

Ryalgar turned to Kazimir. Her words surprised me.

"You really *will* do this negotiation, won't you?" she asked.

No one ever questioned Kazimir like this. I expected him to be offended, but he wasn't.

"Such a highly irregular operation is so unprecedented, the Svadlu have no way of predicting what manner of foe we will face after you get done with them," he answered. "But yes, I agree to try to secure the terms you want *if* it seems warranted. However, the uncertainty of your success makes it equally important that you promise me all civilians will get out of the way and let us do our jobs."

"They will. You have my word."

"We accept your word," Davor said as he stood up and took over the meeting as if it was completely natural that he do so. "And we give you ours. I'll do my best to get those under my command to behave as we've agreed." He looked around at all of us. "Now, is there anyone in this room who thinks we will have complete control over anything once this invasion starts?"

I held my tongue and so did everyone else.

"Good. At least we have a bunch of realists here. This is going to be chaos from beginning to end. Let's all hope when the confusion settles, we still have Ilari."

He reached across the table and offered Ryalgar his hand.

"Madam, I wish you every success," he said.

"I wish you the same," she answered.

It was as much agreement as I could have hoped for.

****

For the next several days I felt unusually optimistic. Ryalgar and Davor had shaken hands. Kazimir had agreed to work with the Velka. Despite Davor's proclamation that the attack would be filled with unpredictable chaos, I found it believable that Ilari could emerge safe and whole. Just the possibility we might prevail was enough.

Rooslin noticed the improvement in my outlook, and eight days before Kolada he commented on it.

"All those fears you had about spying on people and being forced to lie. I'm guessing things turned out better than expected, huh?"

"It seems so. The commanders couldn't have been more reasonable concerning the Velka."

Rooslin sat in our small eating area, sipping breakfast wine and sprinkling dried fruits on the porridge Nino prepared for us. Winter food. He didn't say anything.

"Am I missing something?"

His face told me he considered my question.

Nino, who seldom spoke, gestured to me to sit and have some breakfast. She now tended to us four mornings each ank, and came over three evenings to prepare dinner. I don't know what we'd have done without her.

Today I would have passed on breakfast but her adamant gestures encouraged me to sit.

Rooslin answered me. "I'd say 'no' but the 'couldn't have been more reasonable' part bothers me. I'd feel better if they'd been more pissy. You know?"

"Well, they were a little. I mean they kept telling Ryalgar how unpredictable the day would be so they couldn't guarantee anything. It's true, though, so how can one object to Kazimir pointing out the obvious? Even if he did it a few times."

Tamara came in and joined us. Nino poured her wine and placed eating utensils in front of her, too. Nino's unusual attentiveness bothered me; she seldom waited on us like this.

"Is something on your mind, Nino?" Rooslin asked.

"Umm... Well... I suppose ... Tamara's friend Issa came to visit her yesterday."

"She did? I haven't seen her in so long. Why didn't you tell me?" Tamara said.

"Because she asked me not to, madam. When you weren't here, she said 'I don't know what I was thinking and made me promise not to tell you she'd come by."

"And yet ...." Rooslin smiled. Nino gave him a barely veiled glare.

"Well, she can't expect me to lie out loud to you, now, can she? I mean, you did ask me what was on my mind."

"We did do that." Rooslin seemed amused.

"I'll go find her this evening," Tamara said. "I wonder what she wanted to talk about."

"Don't go tonight," Nino replied. "I mean, she mentioned she's not staying at her house tonight. Your old house. She's, she's at the other place she goes."

I had the feeling this conversation made more sense to Nino and Tamara than it did to me.

"Where *is* the other place Issa goes?" I'd wondered about that since I'd lived in my previous house, and I couldn't think of a reason not to ask about it now.

Rooslin gave me a disappointed look. "I thought I raised you better," he whispered.

"She has a relationship she prefers to keep private," Tamara answered. "Those of us who care for her respect that wish."

"How about those of us who think the timing of her visit yesterday along with her change of heart makes it sound suspiciously like she has vital information she's considering sharing?" I asked.

Rooslin shook his head but he started to smile. "She has a point," he told Tamara. "Who exactly is the fierce Issa cuddling with? An enlisted man? A kitchen maid? A messenger from another realm?"

Tamara rolled her eyes. "One of the four commanding Mozdols."

"What? And those rantillions won't make her a Mozdol too?" This news made me pissed on Issa's behalf.

"That's part of the problem. Issa and he have been together for years, and everyone thinks promoting his sweetheart to Mozdol wouldn't look good."

"Batscump. She's a fighter not a sweetheart, and they'd promote him in a heartbeat if *she* was a Mozdol."

"It's more complicated," Tamara said, making every effort to soothe me with her voice. "He's the commander from Tolo and he's often out of step with the other three so he can't push things. Besides, Kazimir doesn't like her because ... well ... I shouldn't bring this up ..."

My mind started playing scenarios of what awful thing Issa could have done in battle or while training others.

"Kazimir fell in love with Issa's sister years ago, but the sister didn't fall in love with him."

"What? Are you prucking me? He hates Issa enough to deny her a well-earned position because of what her *sister* did?"

My blood froze. With six of them out there, this could so easily have happened to me. How unfair.

"Issa's accepted it, and her lover has too. I think they'd have married by now but Kazimir's also put pressure on the man to never marry Issa. Denying him the full measure of what he can't have for himself, I guess. Anyway, Issa is sensitive about the whole mess. We never discussed it at the house."

"Of course she's sensitive about it," I said. "It's her life."

Then the larger picture began to make sense.

"Wait. She's living part-time with one of the four commanders of the Svadlu, *and* she has something she thought the better of telling you? Don't you think it could be important?"

Nino coughed loudly.

"What is it, Nino?" Rooslin asked.

"Nothing. I didn't say a word." Nina began to scrub the table with vigor.

"We're still eating," Rooslin pointed out.

"Oh, I'm sorry. I thought you were leaving to go find Issa over at Svadlu headquarters while she was at work. Maybe invite her back here for lunch. I could have a nice one ready."

Nino had made her point. We all got up to go.

Tamara wanted to approach Issa alone, so I went to my small office to work. I now had sketches of the locations of underground tunnels and trenches the herders had dug in Bisu and of the shrubbery-hidden hide-outs they'd worked with the Velka to devise.

Joli tasked me with designing a plan for how many groups of six should be hidden where. We had two hundred such groups. It was a tough question given we didn't know exactly where our enemy would stop for the night, or how those left behind would spend their time the next morning.

Whatever they did, our herders would have to come out of hiding before too long and approach before their targets banded together or, worse yet, began to shoot arrows that made our rock throwers useless.

We'd decided the first rock thrower of each group would choose her group's target with her first throw. The rest of her team would follow her lead. Or his lead, but honestly most of our first throwers were women and we'd trained them specifically on how to pick their group's target.

Then we'd practiced scenarios wherein two made the same choice simultaneously and one had to pick again. We'd devised protocols for who did choose. The taller women picked a new target. Same height? The woman with darker hair. Same hair? The younger of the two. And so on. It wasn't perfect, but we hoped it could prevent some of the chaos, because there just would not be time to talk.

The groups needed to emerge at good locations but I had no idea how to guess where a nomadic fighter from the mountains of Asia would choose to be.

Wait.

Of course I did.

He'd pretty much be where I would, sitting anywhere nature provided a seat. On a stump. Or a large rock. Or a big old dead tree stretched out along the grass.

I couldn't go placing too many of these things in the middle of a prairie, of course, lest the whole place start to look like a picnic area. But even if one man sat on a rock, others tended to join him. Why not put the most subtle of invitations where I wanted them, then assume an average of six men would congregate there? Seemed like a good number. So I'd hide six teams nearby.

This was hardly foolproof, but it seemed a big improvement over having no plan at all. Did we have time to get this done? We expected the attack in less than an ank now, but a few days ought to be plenty for the sort of remodeling I had in mind.

I started to diagram where I wanted my seating areas, but Tamara interrupted me.

"Issa wants to talk now, but she doesn't want to be seen with either of us. We need to get back to the house. She'll meet us there."

Nino had left for the day, but a pleasant-looking cold lunch lay on the table. Rooslin had taken his portion; I figured he ate in his room, the one behind the curtain just off the kitchen, intended for a servant. No doubt he listened in.

"This gets me kicked out of the Svadlu and probably ends my relationship with the man I love," Issa began. "The only reason I changed my mind and came here to talk is I figure those things don't matter if I'm dead."

Tamara didn't respond. She knew Issa better so I followed her lead but Issa outwaited both of us as she chewed loudly on some rather tough roasted duck and washed it down with a gulp of pink lunch wine.

As Issa picked up a drumstick, preparing to repeat the performance, Tamara lost patience and asked "What makes you think you're going to die?"

"I pay attention," Issa said, gesturing with the drumstick in her hand. She jabbed the fat end of it towards Tamara. "Too much attention. Enough to know *some* people would rather be dead, rather have us all dead, than to let the Svadlu fail to be the ones who save us. Pride can do that, you know."

"I don't think anyone has a say in the matter of who saves us," I said.

She laughed. "You're so naïve. There is no way, at all, that any of your sisters are going to be allowed to carry out their crazy ideas. You thought they would?"

Yes. I'd been told so many times.

"Well, they won't. Their likely failure will be given as the reason, but the real one is that they might succeed."

Tamara looked as shocked as I felt.

"Who's going to stop them?" she asked. "This plan is too far along for Kazimir to end it, and the people wouldn't stand for it if he tried."

"You don't comprehend the power he has, do you? Some in the Svadlu would hesitate to carry out his orders, especially under the circumstances, but plenty of others will obey blindly, as they've sworn to do."

I stopped eating and my stomach felt as if it wanted to return what food I'd already given it. So all I had accomplished with my meeting was to get the Royals to force Kazimir to publicly lie to Ryalgar? Kazimir's word meant nothing? It had all been a show?

Why hadn't I been more suspicious when they'd been so agreeable? Heli, Rooslin should have been more suspicious, too.

"As to the civilians?" Issa went on. "When the head of the Svadlu claims he knows things they do not, and is acting in everyone's best interest, who's going to prove him wrong? Who's even going to try?"

"Do you know how, or when, he plans to do this?" I asked. "What will he tell the people? The Velka? The Svadlu?"

"I'm not even sure he knows yet. But he's counting on his two commander friends to back him up and has let my man know he best get on board with the other commanders or stay out of the way. 'Those crazy women will not be involved in our defense.' He's promised them this."

"And what about the Royals?" Tamara asked. "Many of them seem to have some faith in the Velka."

She nodded. "They do. And many will be frustrated and suspicious when Kazimir claims he must act on his insider knowledge for the sake of us all. It won't matter though. He's going to do exactly what he wants."

I'd gone from nauseous to numb. "But, Issa. We all understand the Svadlu can't beat these invaders. Even Kazimir has to have figured that much out by now."

"He has. I mean, he hopes the Svadlu will surprise everyone, including him, by prevailing, but he knows the size of the odds against us. He thinks it's better to die in glorious battle than participate in some ignoble circus that will make the Mongols laugh at us before they kill us."

I took a swallow of my wine and then another. "And you?"

"I'm here, aren't I? A brave person dies for honor. I'd have done that ten times over by now if I had to. A foolish one dies for pride, and I like to think I'm no fool."

Issa had always had my respect. She still did.

"And we both think there is a difference between the two," I added.

"Well said. Today, I can do no more. If I learn something that matters, you both will know it too."

At her friend's words, Tamara stood to walk Issa out the door, in part, I thought, to get her away from me before this entire disaster sunk in, and I began to ask more questions.

I had one, though, I couldn't hold back.

"Davor? Can I trust him or is he Kazimir's man?"

"He's never been that," she said. "Davor thinks for himself but he likes to be on the winning side. You can't necessarily trust him but you can't predict him either."

That fit what I'd seen.

With that Tamara put her arm around her friend and ushered her out. I sank into one of the chairs, wondering what I could possibly do to avert the catastrophe barreling down upon my beloved Ilari in eight days.

~ 25 ~

Expectations and Desires

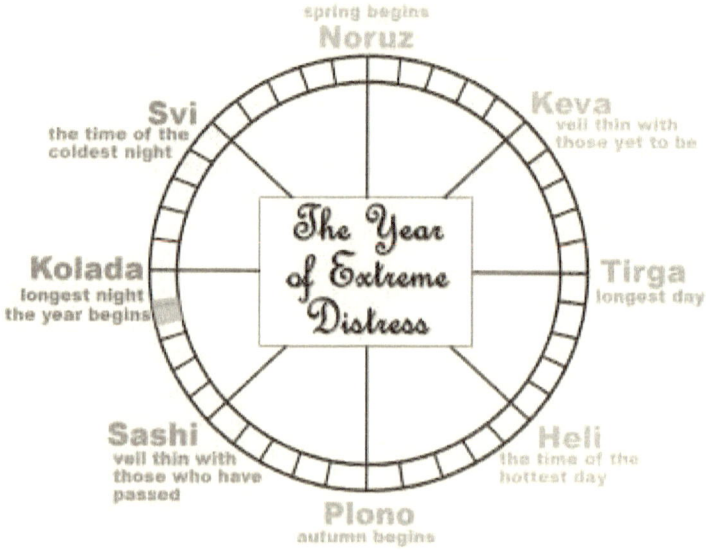

I knew it didn't make sense but I was angry at Rooslin. When he entered the eating area after Tamara left with Issa, I met him with my fists in tight balls and my eyes on fire.

"Why didn't you see this coming?"

He took a step back and looked at me.

"Whoa. I did. I told you I didn't like how agreeable Kazimir had been."

"No. I mean earlier. You promised to alert me to things. I never imagined the Svadlu would let Ryalgar get this far and *then* sabotage her at the very end."

"I didn't either."

"You're not making sense. Did you or did you not you see this coming?"

He put one of his hands on each of my shoulders, and looked me in the eye.

"Sulphur. Listen."

I glared back but I stopped talking.

"Everybody with half a brain worried the Svadlu would put a stop to Ryalgar's plans. They may have wanted to, but her Chimera kept people busy and placated the Royals. At no time would the Svadlu have been better off if they stopped the Velka. So they didn't."

"I agree."

"Okay then. That hasn't kept me from worrying they would, but my concerns were hardly news."

My fury dropped a notch.

"At this point," he said, "I didn't expect Kazimir to squash Ryalgar's plans because it's so much easier for him to let this whole Chimera thing happen. Better for him, too, as it gives him greater odds of living. I assume people act in their own best interest. Sometimes that fuels despicable behavior, and I recognize that. Where I fail, Sulphur, is during those rare times when people choose to shoot an arrow into their own foot for reasons I don't understand."

I took Rooslin's hands off my shoulders and stepped back. I understood what he meant.

"You mean you don't know why Kazimir would rather die than be embarrassed in front of the Mongols?"

"Exactly. Perhaps he admires their fighting prowess. Who doesn't? Maybe the idea of staging pranks when they attack mortifies him? I don't know."

"Do you think Issa is right? Does he does have enough power to stop Ryalgar?"

"Of course he does," Tamara said as she came back into the house.

"You should leave, Tamara." Rooslin held out an arm to block her from coming in further. "Go somewhere else. The things Sulphur and I are about to discuss … it's better off if you're not part of them. For your sake."

I saw the anger in her eyes.

"Not a chance. We three, we're partners of a type few ever are. I won't abandon you two now. Talk in front of me or try to remove me." Her stance moved to that of a fighter. "Go ahead."

Rooslin's sigh was long and deep. "For Heli's sake. You and I are not going to fight. I'm trying to protect you, Tamara."

"I don't want your protection. I intend to help."

He shook his head. "Your choice, but I'm telling you it's a bad one. Here's the deal."

Rooslin sat as he explained the analysis he'd made while listening to Issa from his room.

"Someone like Kazimir can compel others with his rank, his bullying, and his threats. But the question we must answer is does anyone really agree with him? Would others prefer a near-certain death, too? Or will they simply do what he commands out of fear or obligation?"

I understood. "You're asking if the other commanders would carry out his wishes without him."

"Exactly. If we remove Kazimir, do we remove the problem?"

"Because if another would carry on," Tamara added, "we have to remove him too."

"Wait. What are you planning to do to Kazimir?" I asked.

Rooslin gestured to me to join him in taking a seat. When he spoke next, he said each word clearly, as if he talked to a child who might have trouble understanding his concept.

"If Kazimir is the only one who'd rather die than let Ryalgar save the realm, then the most effective solution for everyone is to kill Kazimir."

"Kill him? Why get that drastic? Why can't we tie him up and put him in someone's barn until this is over?"

"Because that's not foolproof, and we can't leave room for failure."

"But you're talking about murder!"

"I'm talking about saving the realm," he responded. "Kazimir *could* change his mind and chicken out, but I'm not willing to bet my whole world on that happening. It's more likely he'll find a way to do as Issa said, and a good chance he'll be successful. If we knew his exact plan, we could counter it. But if we start to make moves now, he'll alter his approach. In his position, he has so many things he can claim are true, so many options for how to go about this. We can't stop them all. We can only stop him."

"So what if one or two of the other commanders feels as strongly?" Tamara asked. "How far will we take this?" Unlike me, she'd already accepted Rooslin's plan.

"If it's one or two, we take them out too. If he's got half the Mozdols ready to die, then the problem is far bigger than us. We'll have to involve the Royals and maybe the Velka too."

"Okay, look." I had to talk my friends out of this murdering spree, no matter what the stakes. "Let's involve the Royals and Velka now. Get their help. We can stop Kazimir without killing anyone."

"No." Rooslin didn't hesitate. "Every person we talk to compromises us and endangers them. Every person we involve makes it more likely Kazimir will find ways to outmaneuver us, and maybe remove us from the playing field. He would have any or all of us killed without hesitation."

The two of them looked at me. They both believed it.

"Nothing will happen for at least a few days," Rooslin said in a more conciliatory tone. "Kazimir knows he'll be most effective if it's close to Kolada when he makes his move. As the invasion nears, there will be more confusion, more fear, less time for others to verify things, and more inclination to panic. That gives us a little time. For now, say nothing. Please, Sulphur. Because we can't unsay it."

"We'll learn more," Tamara chimed in. "I'll ask Issa to see if her man knows how the other two commanders would handle this in Kazimir's absence. The second in command, Irakli, would likely take over and he seems to be less about pride and more about preserving lives."

Rooslin nodded. "Once we know the scope of our problem, we'll talk options."

I held the highest military rank of the three of us, but at that moment I understood this wasn't a military operation. The other had two outvoted me. I could go along with them, or I could set off on my own.

On my own, I'd probably go to Giorgi and Ryalgar and tell all. Would that save the day? Or would it only put an assassin on my heels and on theirs?

I decided I could at least sleep on it and decide in the morning.

****

Sitting in my office the next day, I tried to find safe places my thoughts could go. Places other than fixating on the possibility of murdering the commander of the Svadlu.

I forced my mind back to designing what I called my "seating areas" for the horseless fighters about to be captured. The Mongols were certainly smart enough to recognize what I was doing, if they had the inclination to look for it. But they wouldn't. Nothing in my schooling or my military training suggested any nation had met an invasion with our approach.

They would expect to be in the middle of a meadow, so a meadow is what they would see. I felt certain humans all shared this trait.

If I didn't overdo it.

And as long as my hidden civilians understood their lives depended on their silence. Distance and the wind had to be great enough to cover the inevitable muffled cough. And if it didn't? We'd rehearsed scenarios where our attackers discovered one group of herders. If it happened, the others knew to attack at once. There would be more casualties then, of course, but hesitation only worsened it. We needed as much surprise as possible.

What was I thinking? There would be casualties no matter what happened. On our side. On theirs. More than Ryalgar expected or wanted. I knew it.

So. Why all the concern about Kazimir? What was one more death when added to all the others?

Why was I not only allowed to command mothers and fathers, daughters and sons to train for an operation that would certainly leave some of them dead, but even get praised for doing it? Why was I celebrated for training one set of humans on how to kill another? Plenty would commend me for every Mongol who died. Weren't every one of these invaders someone's relative too?

But let me kill one mean unhappy old man who had the power to bring death down on us all, and that made me a murderer. I'd hang for it, if we still had hangings in Ilari. Heli, they might bring hangings back just for me.

Does a good soldier murder a man to save her country?
I wished I knew.

****

That evening Nino was off and we made our own meal.

"How much do you think Nino knows?" Rooslin asked Tamara while we cleaned up in the kitchen.

It hadn't occurred to me Nino knew anything, but given her odd behavior yesterday morning …. maybe.

"She and Issa were always close," Tamara said. "I think Issa confided in Nino. She may know a lot."

This bothered Rooslin. "Will she be a liability if we have to … have to do something unsavory?"

"Oh Heli no. Nino thinks Kazimir is the height of cruelness for the way he's treated Issa, and others too. Not that she'd condone anything really … unsavory. But she'd never get in our way."

Rooslin nodded. Neither said more.

We finished the dishes in silence.

"Talk to me," I said to both as we left the kitchen. "I won't be shut out of this just because I'm trying to figure out what's right."

"We've been thinking," Tamara said. "Maybe it's better if you're not involved." She looked at Rooslin and he nodded. "First woman Mozdol in two hundred years. You carry responsibility. You shouldn't throw your career away. Rooslin and I have less riding on our shoulders."

"And if we're going to go that way," Rooslin added, "we gain nothing by making you an accessory. What I'm saying is that when I tried to keep Tamara out of this, I worried about the wrong person. It's you I should have kept out of it."

What? I now had people trying to protect me because I was a Mozdol? No, that was all wrong. I protected people, not the other way around.

"You talked about going to Vinx five days before Kolada, so you could focus on placing those you trained," Tamara said. Her voice had turned soothing, "Why not go a day early? You could leave tomorrow and Rooslin and I will handle this. We'll join you three days before Kolada, as planned."

Yes, I'd hoped to be in Vinx the day after tomorrow, but I couldn't possibly leave the problem of Kazimir in the hands of others. Especially not others I cared about.

Then I realized that if I went to Vinx, I didn't have to stay at my parents' house. The outer nichnas had already evacuated the sick, the young, and the old. I'd heard that my mother left with my sister's baby, to keep him safe in the forest. I assumed my father, Coral, Celestine, and Olivine all stayed at the farm, though I wasn't sure who was there now. I *was* sure I couldn't possibly bear all their questions and scrutiny at a time like this.

But I was technically a member of the Vinx royal family, too. I could go "home" to Giorgi's castle. His family would probably be heading to safety, but I didn't need them or their servants, just four walls and a roof while I put the finishing touches on my part of the plan.

Giorgi's castle had two other fine qualities. One, it had Giorgi. And his parents. No matter what Rooslin said, they were good, smart people and as much as anyone they wanted Ryalgar to take her shot at saving us. Perhaps they'd have a better idea for thwarting Kazimir. I could ask them.

Two, the castle sat at the edge of the forest, quite near the Vinx market. Though I doubted much happened in the market as the deadline for the tribute approached, there was no easier place for getting word to the Velka. I hadn't spoken to Joli in far too long, and Ryalgar in even longer. Getting them some hint about the dangers brewing could only result in good.

Yes. I'm going to ignore Rooslin's advice for once and go with my instincts.

"You may be right," I agreed.

"Huh?" Tamara and Rooslin both said it.

"I mean, I hate the idea of putting this on your shoulders. You knew I would. But if we're willing to do anything to allow the Chimera to happen, then I need to do everything I can to ensure my civilians do their job."

Varmin, I was a bad liar, and I didn't expect either to believe a word I said. Yet, if the Mongols wouldn't notice pre-arranged seating areas where they didn't expect to find them, then Rooslin and Tamara wouldn't hear a lie where they didn't expect to hear one. They wanted me to go. Amazing how expectations and desires overruled good judgment.

I started to say, "I'll send a fast messenger to Giorgi in the morning telling him to expect me by tomorrow night." But I caught myself. Telling them I'd be with the Royals might raise suspicions.

So instead I said, "It will be nice to have a few days at home before this all happens."

"Good choice, Sulphur."

"We'll handle everything."

Not if I can help it.

I fully intended to solve the Kazimir problem before either of my two best friends had to kill anyone.

~ 26 ~

Never Stoop to Such a Thing

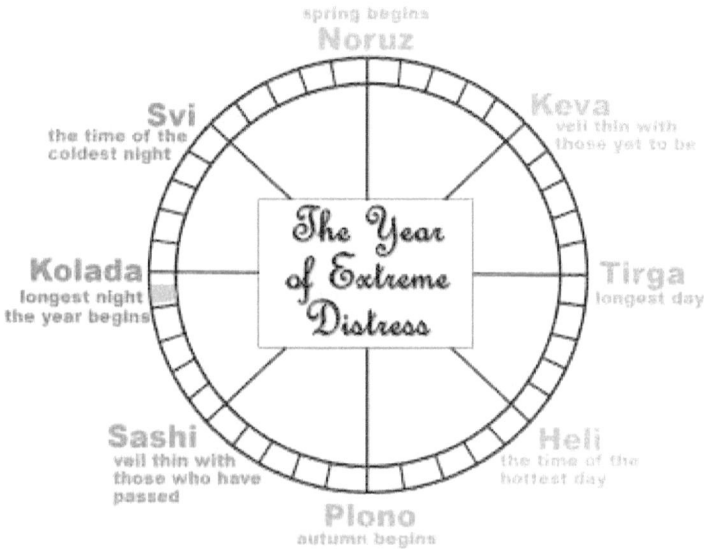

I sent my message to the Vinx castle early the next morning then sought out Davor before I left Pilk. He'd already given me leave to be with my civilian trainees whenever I chose, so this wasn't about permission. It was about saying goodbye.

As the man in charge of training our forces, Davor would serve as the field commander for our troops, with several other Mozdols as his seconds and with our four *real* commanders "leading" from the safety of a command post. In other words, Davor would potentially be the first Svadlu killed by the invaders.

His sobriety surprised me. He seemed lost in thought as he studied pages of diagrams strewn across his desk. He looked up as if he expected someone else in his doorway.

"You? Thought you'd be long gone by now."

"I'm heading to Vinx today. I just stopped by to say …" *What did I want to say? Good luck seemed too tame.*

"Yeah." His half smile told me he understood. "Same to you."

He looked back down at his work, certain our conversation had ended, but I didn't move. I couldn't get my legs to go.

"Something else, Sulphur?"

Yeah. There was. Rooslin wasn't going to like this, but at least I'd make him proud with my indirect approach.

"Kazimir seems to be a man steeped in military tradition," I said.

Davor laid down the papers he held, a small recognition that this would be a longer conversation than he'd hoped. "So?"

"I wondered… Do you think he might try to stop Ryalgar and all the plans she's put in motion?"

Davor looked surprised. "I think even Kazimir understands how much she improves our odds, so why would he?"

"Because …" I shrugged and searched for words.

"No, I get what you're saying," he said. "You know, I thought he might, but I expected it much sooner. Everything's gone too far now for him to stop it."

"Has it? Or could Kazimir better manage such a drastic step with the increased fear and confusion as Kolada arrives? I mean, if a squadron of the Svadlu showed up in Bisu four days before Kolada, with Kazimir in the lead, and he declared he had new information that required all the herders to go hide the forest, do you think anyone would argue with him?"

Davor raised an eyebrow. "You continue to surprise me, Sulphur."

"Once he got rid of the locals, then he could demand the Velka go back to the forest. He could have any who defy him arrested."

"I hope you're wrong." He picked up his papers again and I figured the conversation was over, but then he added, almost under his breath, "And I hope you live through this. You could do

Ilari a scumpload of good if you took charge of the Svadlu someday."

"What? Me?" The idea of a woman as chief commander was more than I could fathom. "They'd never …"

"Probably not, but there's a lot you'd make right if given the chance. And with any luck I'd be retired by then, which is good because I don't think I could handle reporting to a woman." He grinned at me to let me know he joked, at least somewhat.

"As to Kazimir …" I returned to our immediate problem.

"Yeah, yeah. Something like what you describe could be possible. I'm sort of busy here but I'll look into things. I doubt he's up to anything, but if I did need to get word to you, you'd be at your parents' farm, right?"

"No. Too many sisters there already. I'll be at Giorgi's castle instead."

"Interesting choice. Listen. If I were you, I'd make sure I kept this theory of mine …"

"Worry. It's a worry of mine …"

"Okay, I'd make sure I kept this worry to myself. Don't need the Royals involved, right?"

"Right," I said, but only because I knew it was the answer he wanted to hear.

Yes, I now behaved like a spy and no one had forced me to do so. Whom did I work for? For the Chimera. When I walked into Davor's office, I'd assigned myself to the Chimera's espionage corps, a department of one.

****

I stopped at the Vinx market on the way to the castle. A few merchants remained, mostly selling smoked meats and cheeses. One sold pastries and fruit preserves. Well, people had to eat, even in the days before an invasion.

Most merchants, though, had shuttered their stalls. The many vendors who sold wares out of carts and wagons had taken those home. A cold wind blew debris through the open areas they'd left behind.

The Velka had a large permanent stall, usually with an adjacent tent, but today I saw no sign of them and their tent was gone. I'd always communicated with the Velka through their merchants and I had no idea how else to find them. I doubted I could even get into the forest on my own, much less find their lodge.

So much for seeking out Joli and Ryalgar, which had been my next plan. Perhaps Giorgi would know how to reach them.

Part of me desperately wanted to stop at my parents' farm. I knew my mother left days ago, but I wanted to hug my father and whatever sisters stayed with him. Say goodbye, maybe. Just sleep one night in my room and feel like the person I'd been two years ago, back when being a Svadlu meant protecting people. Not killing them. Not dying.

And that was the problem. I knew I couldn't afford to feel like the me of two years ago, lest it cloud my judgment and keep me from doing what I must.

With sadness, I turned my horse towards the Vinx castle, remembering the dinner Lady Patela hosted for me. I'd decided to consider that evening my real Mozdolo. I hadn't known it, but it had been my goodbye to my family as well.

The sun neared the horizon by the time a servant met me at the gate to the castle.

"We've been expecting you since mid-afternoon," he said. I felt sure I didn't imagine his peeved expression as he showed me inside. Rather unseemly given my status.

"Is all well?"

"No, it certainly is not. Giorgi and his Royal father await you in the main room. Please go quickly."

As I entered the room, I saw Giorgi had one arm wrapped around his father's shoulders as the older man wept.

"What's wrong? How can I help?" These people were now my family and I'd help them as readily as the one I grew up with.

"You can get your sister to call off this entire nonsense, forcing our people to risk their lives throwing rocks and tackling killers," the older man rasped. "What were we thinking going along with such rubbish?"

My first thought was that Kazimir had somehow gotten to Giorgi's family. Had he threatened them? Was he holding some of them captive? No wonder the man was distraught.

"Where is everybody? Who's safe?" We'd start there.

197

"My wife, Giorgi's wife, her baby, and our youngest son, all left days ago with our older servants. They were part of the group sent deep into Zur."

"They're fine?"

"I've no reason to think not. Have you heard otherwise?"

"No, of course not. The others?" I looked around. Then I listened. The massive stone lodge was quiet.

"I sent the other servants off yesterday, so they could tend to their families' needs. Karl stayed here, I thought he could get the twins into the forest with the Velka this morning and then care for me and Giorgi. The woman in the market promised us she'd take the twins with her when she left."

"Why didn't they go with their mother?" I knew some their age had signed up to fight, but not all. They were barely old enough and were Royals as well. Everyone would have expected them to evacuate with the rest of the family.

"They begged me to stay a few more days. They've been helping the farmers practice since last summer, and they were so happy to play a part. One threw rocks. The other dove for men's knees. Bizarre behavior for young girls … uh." He seemed to suddenly realize to whom he was speaking. "Most young girls, anyway. Me, I thought being outside doing something physical would help them cope. I encouraged it, as long as they were only part of the practices."

"I think you were wise." The look he gave me indicated he didn't much care what I thought.

"Their mother wanted them with her, but, but I convinced her they'd be fine with me. She …" the sobs started again "she believed me."

"And this morning?"

"This morning I find a note in their bed-chamber saying they haven't been helping with practice, they've been learning these skills so they, *they* can be part of our army of farmers. My girls! They left before dawn to join the others, leaving me a note begging me not to waste the resources to find them. Saying their role was with our people, fighting beside them."

Honestly, these girls impressed me, but I had the sense not to say so.

"I don't know where to begin to look!" their father said. "Then when I got your message saying you rode to see us, I thought the Goddess herself had sent you."

Oh no. I saw where this was headed.

"You've got two choices, Sulphur, and I care not which you choose. Either contact your sister and make her stop this entire nonsense, or find my two daughters and get them to safety."

I don't know why I asked my next question. Instinct, I suppose.

"What about Giorgi? Will he fight alongside his people?"

"Absolutely not. We must preserve the royal line. All the crown princes who are near to ascending the throne, or the recently crowned ones like Giorgi, are all being sent to a hidden cabin in Zur, to remain until we are positive Ilari is safe. That way each lineage of the twelve royal families will continue. That's essential."

To his credit, Giorgi's expression showed me his displeasure at being sidelined. He was no fighter, but he understood how the people he ruled needed him.

"And you?" I asked the father, my voice turning gentle because I thought I knew his answer.

"I will stay in my castle. If my people prevail, I will ride out to greet them, to cheer them, after the horde moves on. They need support, and I'm the one to give it. Or to die in my castle if I must."

Was he also the one to give up the lives of his daughters? Plenty others would lose children loved no less, and I felt certain the presence of these two young Royals would bring courage to all who saw them fight. Yet, I had no children and was hardly in a position to counsel another about making such a sacrifice.

"I've no way to contact Ryalgar," I told him. At least this part of my answer was easy. And true. "I arrived here later than I hoped because I stopped at the market, only to find the last of the Velka already retreated into the forest. I have no way to stop what they've set in motion."

Now for the hard part. Was I going to tell my royal family how another person wished to stop the Chimera, too? That he hoped to affect the same outcome of bringing Ryalgar's plans to a halt, but for less noble reasons?

No, I wasn't.

Ilari needed the Chimera to have any chance of surviving, and I had no intention of uniting people who wanted to squelch it, no matter what their motives. Of course, that meant I couldn't ask Giorgi or his father to aid me in stopping Kazimir, either. I was on my own with this rather major problem, and I didn't have time to waste looking for two twelve-year-olds trying to do something courageous.

I stopped and counted on my fingers.

"Kolada will be here five days from tomorrow. The cow herders who will capture the first group are my primary responsibility. I leave for Bisu in the morning to tend to matters of their placement. Three days before Kolada, others will come from Pilk to help me. Two of them work specifically with your farmers in Vinx."

He started to object but I interrupted.

"Your daughters are in no danger for the next two days. Why not allow them to practice and, more importantly, to continue to inspire your people? Once I have officers in Vinx, I'll task them with finding your twins and urging them to take refuge in the castle with you on the day of the attack."

"The castle may not be safe. I'd rather they get into the forest."

"True but no one can take them inside and hiding along the edge may be more dangerous. If you prefer, I can ask my officer to keep your daughters at the periphery of the action. That may be their safest option."

The look of pain on his face told me he didn't like any of his choices.

"I give you my word we will do our best for them. I can't promise ..."

Giorgi interrupted. "No one can. Father understands that. If you have officers there you trust, we will rely on them to do all they can for my sisters' safety. Right, Dad?"

His dad nodded.

I retired to my room shortly after, and spent a restless night worrying about what I'd become.

Within the last day, I'd talked to Davor about Kazimir, though obliquely, and I'd tried to involve both the Velka and the Royals as well, despite a promise to Rooslin and Tamara to do nothing of the kind. It was hardly to my credit that I'd failed at the latter two.

Then I'd withheld information from my rulers, information they certainly would have wanted to know. And tomorrow, I had every intention of circling back to Pilk and murdering the commander of the Svadlu before either of my friends had a chance to do it. I might not even tell them after I finished, just to keep them safe.

My concern about what other people would force me to stoop to shouldn't have caused me so much worry. I'd managed to come up with all this bad behavior entirely on my own.

~ 27 ~

Three Candles

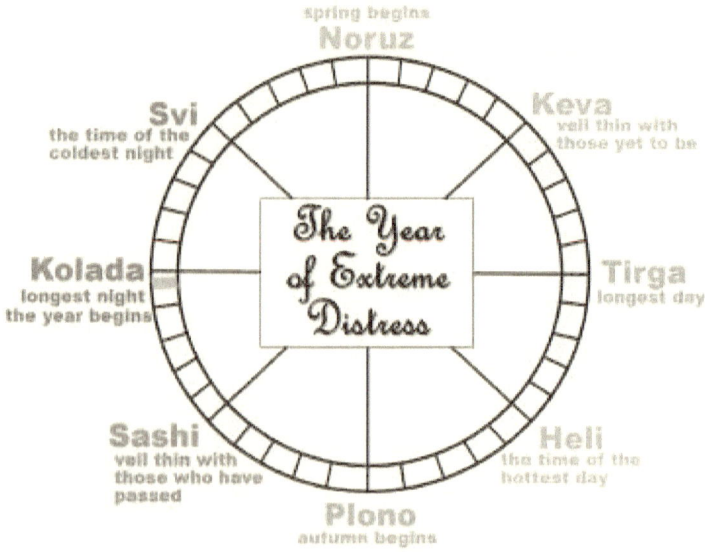

I left before the sun rose. The frost on the ground crackled with my footsteps and my horse whinnied with delight when he saw me. I hushed him and looked over my shoulder. If any of the three men still at the castle of Vinx heard me leave, none wanted an explanation enough to come out into the cold and ask.

I hadn't slept much. For all the moral and mental gymnastics I'd done most of the night, the fact remained. I mounted my horse to go confront a man I believed threatened the existence of all I held dear. I might have to kill this man, and I didn't know if I could do it.

Did I believe Kazimir capable of doing what I feared he'd do? Yes. I found Issa trustworthy and her accusations fit with all I'd seen and heard from Kazimir. Besides, the whole concept had a certain odd logic. As an older warrior, he feared losing his position and his respect. If he stopped Ryalgar and by some miracle the Svadlu prevailed, he'd be a hero for the rest of his life. And if we all died instead, who would complain?

I wished I had another option. I thought the idea of locking Kazimir in a barn somewhere held merit and if my two closest friends felt less cynical about how well that would work, I'd have done it. But hiding Kazimir wouldn't satisfy them so they'd find him and kill him to save Ilari.

Which brought me to the crux of the problem and the reason I now pushed my horse into a slow gallop I hoped he could maintain. Tamara and Rooslin were trying to protect me, and I couldn't let them. Some people let others dirty their hands for them, some perhaps rightfully. I tried not to judge; we all had different roles to play. But me? I didn't need protection. I took care of what had to be done. So I rode on.

At Svadlu headquarters, I tethered my horse and made my way towards the commanders' offices. It neared midday. I felt certain Tamara and Rooslin wouldn't choose to act until tomorrow, as they'd promised to find out more about the other commanders' leanings. Yet, things could change quickly. I needed to find Kazimir before they did, and before I lost my nerve.

His office was empty. Irakli saw me outside the door.

"Thought you left yesterday," he said as he approached. He didn't look particularly happy to see me.

"I did. I came back. Something I need to handle here."

He looked at me. I looked at him.

"Kazimir hasn't been in all morning," he said. "A lot going on right now, as I'm sure you understand."

"Of course. But I do need to speak to him."

"Answer a question for me. I need your best guess about the effectiveness of your sister's efforts. A military opinion, not a relative's assessment."

There wasn't a question in the world I wanted to answer more.

"I'm glad you asked. I doubt she'll be as effective as she hopes. Her ideas have never been tested in real life. They're all theoretical."

"I see. So you think agreeing to her involvement was a mistake?"

"Not at all. Even if she does half as well as she hopes, and I think she'll do better than that, she'll manage to turn an almost certain defeat into a possible victory. Her plans give us chance. Without them we have none."

"That is your assessment as a soldier?" he clarified.

"Yes, sir. As her sister, I'm scared for her."

He managed a small smile. "I'm sure you are. As a father, a brother, and a husband, I'm scared for all of us." It was the first human-sounding thing I'd heard the man say. "Thank you for your analysis."

I turned to leave, but he stopped me.

"Would you do anything to stay alive, soldier?"

Anything? I had enough imagination to come up with atrocities I'd rather die than commit. "I hope not."

Again the small smile.

"Would you do anything to save the lives of those you love?"

"I hope so."

"I'm coming to appreciate your honesty, Sulphur. Kazimir told me yesterday he planned to work from his home this morning. It's a large estate, north of here along the river, not far. If you go now, I'm sure you'll find him there."

"Thank you." I meant it, though after his strange questions, I wasn't entirely sure what I thanked him for.

I'd heard enough about Kazimir's estate to know I'd arrived at the right place. The large stone house sounded empty. No servants, no animals. Odd. While the eastern nichnas had already evacuated those who would leave, almost no one in Pilk or anywhere west planned to abandon their homes. Possibly Kazimir had chosen to send his kin into hiding anyway?

I listened. There was a good bit of noise coming from the barn. Not conversation, but not animal noises either. Grunts, groans, even, if I listened closely, the sound of metal clanking. I moved towards the nearest of the barn windows and crouched down, hoping to see in without being seen.

*Please don't let Rooslin be in there fighting Kazimir. Or
Tamara.*

I eased my head up above the sill as my right hand went to
the handle of my sword by instinct.

Kazimir stood at the far end of the barn, in a fighting stance
with his sword drawn. He concentrated too hard on his opponent
to notice me. I froze anyway.

His opponent faced away from me, as he and Kazimir
prepared to resume a fight which, judging from their torn clothing
and the small cuts on both, appeared to have gone on for some
time.

It wasn't Tamara, her long braid and female build would
have been unmistakable. It wasn't Rooslin. I'd have recognized
his tall lanky body as easily as Tamara's.

This man was shorter, stocky, and well-muscled. He moved
like he'd fought all his life, and his thick coal-black hair
confirmed his identity. I blinked, and Davor and Kazimir lunged
towards each other, each emitting a growl that left no doubt about
the intended outcome of this fight.

Kazimir swung his sword first, Davor stopped the blow with
the flat of his blade and each took a step back. They began
circling. Then their blades clanged together again in moves too
fast for me to follow, but somehow at the end of the maneuver
Kazimir's sword ran through Davor's armpit and shoulder. I saw
the surprise on Davor's face as he crumpled and fell to the ground.

I sprung up and threw my body through the open window to
land at Davor's side. He lay in the dirt, barely conscious. He bled,
but not as heavily as if he'd been hit elsewhere. If he got medical
care soon, he might live. I started to tie a cloth around his injury,
to slow down his blood loss.

I looked up to see Kazimir moving towards us, his sword
pointed at Davor's heart, moving in finish the job.

"Stop!" I stood and drew my sword, ready to back up my
demand with my arm if necessary.

Kazimir did the worst thing he could have. He stopped, he
looked at me, and he laughed.

"Get out of my way. I don't get bewitched at the sight of a
girl fighting the way some men do. No female has ever been a
match for me, and I'd rather not hurt you."

"Then why are you trying to kill one of your best men?" I countered. Once I got his answer, I'd let my sword respond to his insults.

"Davor has challenged my orders, challenged my rights as commander. He must die."

"And I say he must live."

I looked closer. Despite his bravado, Kazimir breathed heavily and sweat ran down his face. His grueling fight with Davor had exhausted him. Given his condition, I could best him with ease. The fight wouldn't even be fair.

"Back down now," I said. "Let me finish binding his wound and put him on my horse, get him help. I'll say nothing of how he was injured. Ilari needs every soldier it has, and we hardly need to lose the man trained to lead our troops in a few days."

"Another can be found. One who knows the meaning of loyalty." Kazimir's voice had almost dropped back into the growl I'd heard earlier.

"Stand down while I tend to his needs."

"Step aside while I run my sword through his cowardly heart."

"You'll do no such thing." My stance changed, weight slightly forward, evenly distributed between both feet. Balance made all the difference in a fight.

Kazimir's stance matched mine as he placed his sword over his shoulder to rest his arm and moved in a little closer. I began circling, keeping my distance from him. Then he lunged suddenly, and I met his steel with a parry.

"So. You have reflexes. I'd expect no less from one we've trained."

He could say whatever he wished. I'd stopped talking.

We continued to circle, each cautious for our own reasons. He barely feinted. I responded with the slightest of moves. I feinted. He acted in kind. We both knew *I* was trying to learn his style of fighting. We both understood *he* was trying to regain his strength.

Under other circumstances, we'd have kept this up for a while but our slow pace posed a major problem. A man, a good soldier, slowly bled to death only a few paces away. I not only needed to kill Kazimir, but I had to do it now.

I lunged at him as if the life of someone I cared about depended on it. My sword darted past his blade as he sought to parry, and without another thought I thrust it hard into his left chest above his ribcage, where I'd been told his heart resided. Kazimir gasped and fell to his knees.

"You're no woman," he said. "You're an animal, a ..." He weakened as he spoke, so I never heard the last word.

I left him where he fell, wasting no time getting back to Davor. He still breathed. Good. I finished my makeshift bandage, ready to face the problem of getting him onto my horse and into town.

"Who's hurt?"

The voice calling out to me sounded familiar, but in my dazed state I couldn't place it. It came from atop a horse trotting up the long entrance to the home and as the horse got closer I recognized Irakli.

"I couldn't sit by and let you handle this. It's just not right."

"What are you doing here?" Although I asked, it didn't matter, really. Just so he was quick about helping me get Davor on a horse.

"I knew what Kazimir intended to do and I knew Davor somehow found out this morning. When I told Davor where he could find Kazimir, I worried the two of them would come to blows."

I'd removed a small jug of water from my horse and I poured the liquid into Davor's mouth as I listened. The man kept talking.

"I thought when you showed up, sending you out here was brilliant. Your arrival would stop the fighting and maybe you and Davor together could talk some sense into Kazimir. But I should never have sent you out here alone. By yourself."

"Tell me later."

Then he looked around. His eyes took in the bleeding and barely conscious Davor. He stared hard at Kazimir's body, lying in a pool of blood too large for life to be a possibility.

"I see." He swallowed hard, gathering his composure. "I followed you after we spoke, but I stopped to bring a doctor along in case someone needed medical attention. I didn't, I didn't expect this." He pointed to Kazimir's body. "I'm sorry I sent you into this mess."

"Don't be." I meant it. "Given all the other ways this could have ended, I'm glad you sent me."

Behind him I saw the doctor riding up the entryway, his saddlebags thick with supplies. That's when I sat on the ground and shook with relief.

As the spasms passed, I looked for my sword, knowing I had to hurry to make it back to Vinx before dark.

No. Wait. I have important business here to finish first.

And I did. Someone had to ensure Davor got the care he needed. I had to tell Tamara and Rooslin the full story. I didn't think our new chief commander had any plans to follow in his former boss's footsteps, but my friends would need to make sure he didn't. Also, it wouldn't hurt to spend the night in Pilk recovering from the day.

****

Tamara and Rooslin met me and my narrative with all the emotions I expected: surprise, disgust, amazement, and relief. And one that surprised me. Sadness. By the time I finished with the telling, Issa, her commander boyfriend from Tolo, and Nino had joined us, and Rooslin had promised to look out for Giorgi's twin sisters.

After we'd discussed the incident with Kazimir ten different ways and there seemed no more to say, I retired to my room but the sadness stuck with me. What sort of boy had Kazimir been? Had he been cute as a child? Probably. Had his family loved him? Of course they had. Had he done good things in his life? He must have.

I took a candle from my drawer and held it up to the lamp to light it.

"For you, Kazimir. I wish I'd had a better choice than to do what I did."

I sat and stared into Kazimir's flame, then I opened my drawer. Two more candles remained. Of course they did. I lit a second candle.

"For you, man in Tolo, who once held a torch to kindling and might have killed a family tied to a pole for no reason I understand. I wish I knew your name. Your story. How you came to be part of something so cruel. I wish I knew of something kind you did as well."

I lit the third.

"For you, man in Tolo with the sword, man who taunted me. I don't know why I cannot see your death in my mind but …"

As I said it, I knew why. I'd been afraid, still was afraid, that the vision of my sword piercing his chest would haunt my dreams and thoughts for the rest of my life. I didn't want to see it once, because I didn't want to see it a thousand times. Better to never see it at all.

I closed my eyes and willed the image into my head. It was there. My leap off my horse, my sword piercing the man, my knowing how my actions drew the life out of him. The horror I'd felt, and later not remembered.

"Yes. It was horrible," I told the candle. "I wish there had been …I wish I could have found another way."

I heard the curtain across my door rustle and turned around in irritation. I didn't need an interruption now.

Rooslin and Tamara stood in the doorway together, taking in the scene.

"Three," he said. "Three now." His gaze moved from the desk to my face.

"Candles are good," Tamara added and they both turned and left me to my private ceremony.

I thanked the spirits and all my ancestors for giving me the skills and the courage to do the things I'd done, the things that needed doing. But then I asked them to guide me to better solutions than death whenever possible. I rarely engaged in conversations with those other than the living, but tonight, well, such activity seemed right.

Before I blew the candles out, I took the time to thank them all for one more thing, for the blessing of at least two people in this world who understood me. Plenty had far less to be thankful for.

~ 28 ~

The Stupidest Thing
You Could Do

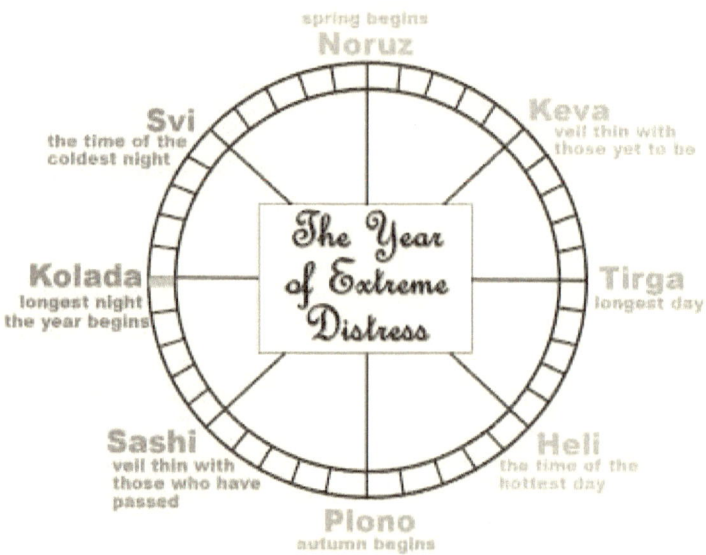

The next morning I met with Irakli, the man who now commanded our army. He and I had some issues to resolve.

"Your sponsor continues to recover under the care of our medical experts," he said by way of greeting. I nodded. I'd already ridden over there and seen Davor sleeping. Healthy color had returned to his face and I'd heard his even, relaxed breathing. He'd likely heal if they kept infections away.

"You've found another to lead the troops into the field in four days?"

"Yes. Our commander from Tolo asked for the assignment. He feels …" Irakli hesitated. "I believe he regrets his part in sending you and Tamara into that skirmish a year ago, her with so many novices." He lowered his voice. "The one that resulted in all the trouble for Tamara."

"Yes. I remember the skirmish. What does it have to do with now?"

Irakli shrugged. "Who understands what's in a man's heart. He said he wanted the chance to do something right."

"Well if he wants to do that, I hope he keeps himself alive and marries Issa when the battle is over."

"As do I." Irakli gave a nervous little nod. "Their marriage should pose no problems. Now."

We both knew he referred to Kazimir, the one subject neither of us wanted to talk about.

"And the remaining commander?" I asked. I knew the fourth one was from Pilk, was younger than Irakli and Kazimir, and up to now had generally followed both of their leads.

"He poses no problem. I think he's somewhat of a fan of your sister, or at least he admires her cleverness. The plan will proceed as discussed at the meeting two anks ago."

"Including the proposed negotiations, if possible?"

"Better than that. Our goal will be to bring the Mongols to the table, and reach an agreement to keep us safe for a long while. Believe me, no one in Ilari wants to go through another year like the one we just had."

"Well said. Today I leave to coordinate the many cow herders who've agreed to aid us. Issa will join me tomorrow."

"And the others?"

"Rooslin and the officer from Scrud are coordinating the fighting farmers in Vinx." Irakli raised an eyebrow when I said "fighting farmers" but he didn't comment. "Tamara and the remaining female officer agreed to provide military support for the floating Faroojers working with the reczavy."

"Floating Faroojers?" Irakli shook his head. "The less I know the better."

A noisy formation of birds flew over us, cawing to each other as they headed south. "Even the birds have the sense to flee," he said. We looked at each other, a helpless expression on both of our faces. We knew someone had to bring it up.

"About yesterday …" I said. "When this is over, I'll accept whatever punishment you deem appropriate for my actions."

"Punishment??" He laughed. "I came here hoping to persuade you not to capitalize on your heroics yesterday at the expense of Kazimir's reputation."

"Heroics?"

"I know Kazimir wasn't a popular man," Irakli said. "He could be …. stern, and at times he came across as cruel. Many in the Svadlu will be glad to see him gone. But he wasn't always like that, and he did much good. Please don't drag his reputation through the mud for your own gain."

It appeared we'd been avoiding the topic of Kazimir for quite different reasons.

"You needn't fear that. We have an understanding."

As I rode away, I wondered if Irakli realized he'd make a far better chief commander than his predecessor.

****

I rode straight to Bisu, not delaying by stopping in Vinx. Several in Bisu had offered us lodging. Joli, our Velka coordinator, suggested she, Issa, and I stay together the few nights before Kolada and use the time to share information.

The day was sunny and cool, with no wind, a pleasant day for riding. My horse needed little attention from me. However, the extra time to think while I rode didn't serve me well. Back when Ryalgar had formulated these plans, she focused on the tricks and magic that would reduce the number of fighters coming at us. The capture of the horseless ones lost along the way seemed an afterthought to her. *Oh yes, why not round them up and hold them prisoner?*

Sure. Why not?

Because they were deadly warriors, that's why. Because a six to one ratio might not be near enough. Because the high number of captors needed for this to have a hope of working required us to hide hundreds, yes hundreds of untrained and scared people. Did Ryalgar have the faintest idea how difficult it would be to pull off that last part? I didn't think she did.

I suppose if we failed miserably and most of the twelve hundred Bisuite cow herders died we would still have delivered two hundred fewer Mongol warriors to our troops to fight. Twelve hundred civilians seemed to me to be a terribly high price to pay for that. Yet, I had to marvel at how many Ilarians had signed on to pay it.

By the time I arrived at the large home of one of the wealthier Bisuites, my mood was foul. Joli met me as I dismounted.

"I thought you were going to arrive here yesterday?"

"I did too. I had some unexpected business in Pilk I had to return for."

"Everything okay?"

"There? Better than you'd think. Here? I'm not so sure."

She helped me with my saddlebags and led me inside.

"The residents have given us the house. Very gracious of them. What, beyond the obvious, has you so troubled?"

"No!" It came out as more of a bark than I meant it to. "It *is* the obvious that is bothering me, Joli. Practicing throwing rocks was fine but there's a lot more involved here. How the Heli is this going to really work?"

"Be more specific."

To the woman's credit, she sat me down, handed me an ale, and then let me list every objection I had. She only interrupted to give me facts I hadn't been made aware of. No, I didn't know the Velka had assigned all their second tier oomrushers to fill Bisu with fog the day before Kolada. What a great idea. Fog would help keep everyone hidden, at least until the following morning.

No, I didn't know someone had designed a complex communication system of flags to let us know when scouts sighted the horde on the horizon. Yes, knowing they rode towards us would help. No, I didn't know these scouts included extra long eyes watching from up on the cliffs of Vinx. Why hadn't all this information been given to the Svadlu?

"It was," she said. "Of course it was. We sent messengers to your commander Kazimir to apprise him of every modification we came up with. Did he not communicate this on to you?"

"No. And about that: Kazimir is no longer involved."

"Why not?"

"Because he's dead."

Joli looked at me with eyes full of questions but when I said no more she responded with, "I never thought he was much of a fan of our plan."

"That would be an understatement."

"So is Davor in charge now?"

"I wish. He's been seriously injured but is recovering."

"I'm sorry to hear it. Injured how?"

"Injured trying to kill Kazimir."

This time she laughed. "Possum scump. And I thought we had a lot of intrigue in the Velka."

"A bunch of caring women like the Velka have intrigue?" We stared at each other.

"Heli, you are naïve." Her face softened. "When this is all over, there will be stories to tell."

I agreed.

By the time Joli filled me in on the extra Bisu riders with ropes standing by to help, and the more adept fighters armed with maces and chains who would step in where rock throwers failed, I felt better. I learned my idea from eighths ago had gotten traction, too, and now all the long eyes and archers would stay put to shoot lightly-poisoned arrows at any Mongol fighters not subdued by other means. She reminded me that Issa and I would also be there to deal with the most vicious of our foes, and that neither of us was a force to be ignored. Maybe we did have a chance.

The next day Issa joined us in the house and most of our oomrushers and long eyes arrived. Our civilian conscripts had been gathering outside for days, camping and awaiting news.

The day after that was two days before Kolada and early in the morning a red square flag went up signaling that the horde had been sighted on the horizon. I suppose it was fortunate our calendar remained in sync with theirs. I can only imagine how restless we'd all have become if we'd had to wait for days more.

We called everyone together soon after the flag went up, and Joli, Issa, and I addressed them using one of Ryalgar's wooden cones to make our voices louder. We took turns reviewing what they'd heard a hundred times already, but we kept it short. We were all too nervous to concentrate.

Joli and I had exchanged more information by then about how our own past few days had gone. I'd been shocked to learn Ryalgar wouldn't even be part of this operation but had been sent off to Eds along with my grandmother to deal with other matters. It seemed a waste of her much-needed talents to me, but when I questioned Joli, she became evasive. I left well enough alone.

She told me more about the infighting between Ryalgar and other Velka and her stories bothered me. As did the problems we'd had with the Svadlu leadership. So as we finished talking to the cow herders, I shouted out to the group.

"What is the stupidest thing any one of you could do?"

They shouted tens of answers back at me, some of them quite imaginative, but if anyone said what I was looking for, I didn't hear it.

"Fight with each other," I yelled back. "I don't care how scared you are, or how *right* you are. Just for today, do not fight with your neighbor about anything. At all. If you want to live, you must hide, keep quiet for longer than you have in your life, and then do something incredibly brave. It's hard. So, that is *all* you do. Think of nothing else. Two days from now, you'll have the luxury of caring about something other than your immediate survival. Do? You? Understand?"

I got a chorus of 'yeses' and could only hope my words might have stopped a few of them from doing something stupid.

As I walked away, a slight woman in a green cloak waved at me in the distance.

"Olivine!" I shouted. I'd been hoping to see her, and I knew Joli was becoming concerned. Olivine and Joli were paired to work together as long eye and oomrusher. Tomorrow morning they would get into position. Olivine was supposed to have arrived by yesterday.

"Where've you been?"

"Long story but I'm fine and here."

"You and Joli are going to do this thing?"

"We are." She threw her arms around me. "Good luck, Sulphur."

I hugged my sister back. "Yeah. See you when this is over?"

"Right. We'll drink some wine together then."

As she walked away, I marveled at how this quiet, even meek woman obsessed with art had become an archer to save her realm. If she could make such a transformation, surely the rest of us could do our part, too.

****

The house we stayed in was far into Bisu, half a morning's ride from the border where the Mongols would arrive and expect to find our tribute. The watch house up on the cliffs sent a messenger down to tell us they expected the horde to arrive at the border in the morning. The Velka-induced fog would begin at dawn and get heavier as the day went on. Everyone needed to get in position first thing tomorrow.

No one slept well that night. Issa was more distressed than I'd ever seen her, having learned that her lover of many years had chosen to lead the Svadlu into the field. I could tell she was proud, but scared. The rest of us were simply scared.

We woke to a cold day and a heavier mist than I expected but I was thankful for it. Not only did it reduce visibility, but it countered the Mongols well-known penchant for setting fire to everything when they were displeased. Joli and Olivine prepared to move into their hiding position back against the cliffs while Issa and I worked to get the cow herders in place. To make it easier, we divided them into two groups and we each took half.

"You have water, right? Food?" It took longer than I expected, but eventually all my groups of six hid where I'd designed them to be. Issa took her position with her half of the people. I'd be the last one to take cover.

By late morning we could hear the Mongols. At first the hooves of so many horses made the ground tremble; not long after their voices carried across the open grassland. Their horses moved less and they talked more as the fog grew thicker. Their tones betrayed increasing confusion and even anger. No, they weren't happy about how this invasion had started. Yet, slowly, they grew closer.

We could tell when they reached the first clumps of the lush grass our Velka had cultivated. Much of the noise of hoofs stopped. The men's voices divided. Some had the sound of urging. Coaxing on the horses? Urging on their fellow fighters? I replaced the strange-sounding words with my own tongue. *We must keep moving... This was supposed to be easy ...*

Others began to argue. Funny how the cadence of "Why don't we do this" and "No we couldn't possibly" felt the same despite the strangeness of the words. The argument intensified, went on for a while, then it stopped.

Someone important had decided. Decided what?

Next we heard the clanking of metal. I feared they'd drawn their swords, but the tone was wrong for weapons. I smiled when I recognized it. Pots clanged. They set up camp.

Tones turned more jovial. I imagined a jug or two opening as they discussed how tomorrow this horrible fog would dissipate and it would be a better day to deal with these troublesome Ilarians.

Did some of them sit on the rocks and dead trees I'd scattered around? I dared not get close enough to see, but surely they'd made good use of any they'd found in the fog. I stood still and listened until the darkness began to edge out the light. I recognized the occasional slur of words and drunken laughter. Yes, our Svadlu would have had a few who overindulged, too, had the roles been reversed.

I tried to use the sounds to figure out how far the various camps set from each other and how far away they kept their horses. I lacked any way to get this information to the archers, but perhaps I'd be of more use in the morning knowing it.

As they quieted down, I crawled into my own sleeping space, a shallow trench lined with damp hay over which I'd lain a wool blanket. I pulled two more blankets over the top of my body and tried to find a comfortable position as I closed my eyes, determined to get what little rest I could.

I must have fallen asleep for stars sparkled in a black sky when my eyes opened. The mist was gone. I sat up. Perhaps the faintest bit of light shown in the southeast.

We'd hidden the four teams of archers and oomrushers back against the cliffs of Vinx, mostly west of their targets to take advantage of the emerging light. I knew long eyes possessed a cat-like ability to use a tiny bit of illumination. We'd planned for their work to be done well before the sun rose.

I listened but picked up no sound other than distant snoring. Then I heard them. Wind chimes jingled in the breeze. The tiny bits of glass tinkled so softly I knew the sound came from far away, carried by an erratic wind.

I squirmed in my damp trench, thinking of my teacher and the many odd things he'd said. I wished I could tell him he'd been right. One should head towards where they want to go. I'd done so and arrived here, exactly where I wanted to be. But perhaps he already knew.

Another sound, a nearby thud, pulled my thoughts away. I knew what that thump meant. I waited, imaging the lifting of an arrow from a quiver, the handing off of an arrow, the nocking of an arrow, and then the aim. Then the flight. Then, yes, there it was. Another thud.

The snakes of the Chimera had struck twice and the battle for Ilari had begun.

Thank you for reading my story of how I saved my entire world from oblivion
-- Sulphur Renata Glonti

What's Next?

The War Stories of the Seven Troublesome Sisters consists of seven short companion novels. Each tells the personal story and perspective of one of seven radically different sisters in the 1200s as they prepare for an invasion of their realm.

Which sister do you think saves Ilari? That will depend on whose story you are reading. For while each of these historical fantasy/alternate history books can be enjoyed as stand-alone novels, together they tell the full story of how Ilari survived. The last four books also describe the battle and its outcome.

Want to make sure you don't miss a release? Go to my landing page at https://mailchi.mp/11db23804c68/tell-me-about-new-books to be notified when each book is ready for purchase. I promise you'll only get notifications about the release of these books.

If you enjoyed this story, please leave a review somewhere. If you enjoyed it a lot, please leave a review in several places.

Sulphur's Older Sisters

She's the One Who Thinks Too Much

Ryalgar, a spinster farm girl and the oldest of seven sisters, has always preferred her studies to flirtation. Yet even she finally meets her prince. Or so she thinks. She's devastated to discover he's already betrothed and only wanted a little fun. Embarrassed, she flees her family's farm to join the Velka, the mysterious women of the forest known for their magical powers and for living apart from men.

As a Velka, she develops her special brand of telekinesis and learns she has a talent for analyzing and organizing information. Both are going to come in handy.

When this prince keeps meeting her at the forest's edge for more good times, she wonders if being his mistress isn't such a bad deal after all. Then she learns more about his princely assignment.

He's tasked with training the army of Ilari to repel the feared Mongol horsemen who have been moving westward, killing all in their path. And, her prince is willing to sacrifice the outer farmlands where she grew up to these invaders if he must. Ryalgar isn't about to let that happen.

She's got the Velka behind her, as well as a multitude of university intellectuals, a family of tough farmers, and six sisters each with her unique personality and talents.

Can Ryalgar organize all that into a resistance that will stop the invasion?

She's the One Who Thinks Too Much has been available in eBook and paperback since November 2020.

She's the One Who Cares Too Much

Coral, the second of the sisters, has been hiding her affair with the perfect man until Ryalgar can get her life together. But the perfect man is getting impatient, and now she's gotten pregnant. Coral decides it's time to consider her own happiness.

But what does she want? The perfect husband turns out to be less than ideal. She adores the small children she teaches but the idea of being a mother fills her with joy. Meanwhile, her homeland is gripped by fear of a Mongol invasion, and she can't stop crying about everything now that she's with child.

Then a friend suggests the ever-caring Coral has a power well beyond what she or anyone else imagines. Does she? And why is the idea so appealing?

When Ryalgar loses faith in the army and decides to craft a way to use magic to save Ilari, she decides Coral's formidable talent is what the realm needs. Can Coral raise a baby, placate an absent military husband who thinks he's stopping the invasion, and help her sister save her homeland?

She's the One Who Cares Too Much has been available in eBook and paperback since February 2021.

Sulphur's Younger Sisters

She's the One Who Doesn't Say Much

Olivine, one of the twins, has been hiding a secret as she travels to K'ba to meet her artist friends. Others assume she has fallen in love with another artist, and it's not a match Mother would consider suitable. But it's much worse. For on the way to K'ba is the dirt poor nichna of Scrud, a place scorned by other Ilarians. And in Scrud is the only man who has ever understood her.

However, Bohdan also recognizes the dangers posed by an impending invasion. When he learns of Olivine's unusual visual powers, he convinces her to pick up her bow and start practicing.

She does, though she'd rather be producing enough art to raise the funds to run away from home and live in K'ba, where she can paint all day and sneak off to see Bohdan as often as she wants. If only her sister Ryalgar hadn't learned of what she can do and decided Olivine and her fellow long eyes held one of the keys to defending the realm.

Then, as if life wasn't complicated enough, Olivine learns the artist community she yearns to be part of has developed a different take on the invasion. They feel certain the only way to survive is to capitulate completely to the Mongols' demands. Artists who feel otherwise are no longer welcome.

Where does her future lie? In Scrud, with the only man she's ever loved? In K'ba, where her talents can shine? Or with her family, who needs her help to stop a threat far worse than anything her people have ever encountered?

The invasion is coming soon and Olivine doesn't have much time to decide.

She's the One Who Doesn't Say Much will be available in eBook and paperback August 2021. It can be preordered until then.

She's the One Who Can't Keep Quiet

Celestine, the other twin, is the most social daughter in the family. She loves her music and pretty clothes and the crowds in the taverns who adore her and her singing. Yet, she's been hiding a secret all her life.

As a beauty with a lyrical voice, she's always been Mother's best hope for getting a prince as a son-in-law. When a liaison with a prince never happens, everyone assumes Celestine is being so picky because she can be.

But even in somewhat tolerant Ilari, a daughter hates to disappoint those she loves. How can she tell her family she's fallen in love with a princess instead?

Lucky for Celestine, all six of her sisters and her parents appear to be obsessed with an invading army headed to their realm. Celestine would rather ignore the threat, and enjoy the freedom their lack of attention gives her. Then she discovers her voice can unlock a power that may help save the realm and that the woman she adores wants to join the fight against the invaders.

Celestine knows she can inspire the citizens of Ilari to defend themselves, while her family, for all their talents, seem clueless about how to motivate the masses.

Is it time to put her inhibitions aside and use her voice to save those she cares about? Can she do it and still be true to who she is? And to who she loves?

She's the One Who Can't Keep Quiet will be available in eBook and paperback January 2022.

What About the Youngest Two Sisters?

Look for more information about Gypsum and Iolite in the next book.

About the Author

Sherrie Cronin is the author of a collection of six speculative fiction novels known as 46. Ascending and is now publishing a historical fantasy series called The War Stories of the Seven Troublesome Sisters. A quick look at the synopses of her books makes it obvious she is fascinated by people achieving the astonishing by developing abilities they barely knew they had.

She's made a lot of stops along the way to writing these novels. She's lived in seven cities, visited forty-six countries, and worked as a waitress, technical writer, and geophysicist. Now she answers a hot-line. Along the way, she's lost several cats but acquired a husband who still loves her and three kids who've grown up fine, both despite how eccentric she is.

All her life she has wanted to either tell these kinds of stories or be Chief Science Officer on the Starship Enterprise. She now lives and writes in the mountains of Western North Carolina, where she admits to occasionally checking her phone for a message from Captain Picard, just in case.

Find her at:
Facebook: facebook.com/46Ascending
Goodreads: goodreads.com/author/show/5805814.Sherrie_Cronin
Amazon: amazon.com/Sherrie-Cronin/e/B007FRMO9Q
Twitter: twitter.com/cinnabar01
Author Blog: sherriecronin.xyz/
Book Series Blog: troublesome7sisters.xyz/

Information About Ilari

Words Used by Ilarians

Ank: Nine days. Business is conducted during the first six days while the last three are intended for family life and leisure.

Heli: The hottest time of the year, but sometimes used as a cussword.

Luski: A feared, possibly imaginary creature who can control others with her voice.

Mozdol: A member of the Svadlu who has been made into an honorary prince due to brave actions defending the realm.

Nichna: One of the twelve principalities of Ilari. Each has its own royal family and is ruled by a prince. All twelve coordinate as regards the Svadlu and other matters of the common good. There is no king, therefore Ilari is not a kingdom.

Oomrush: telekinesis.

Pruck: An extremely rude word sometimes referring to copulation and other times merely expressing disgust or dismay.

Pruska: An extremely rude word referring to a female having any number of undesirable qualities.

Rantallion: A man who is being disagreeable, dishonest, or disgusting.

Reczavy: a group of free-spirited people living in the open forest who choose to continue and extend the sexual freedom allowed to tidzys.

Scump: a rude word referring to excrement.

Svadlu: The Ilarian army and police force. A member of the Svadlu is called a Svadlu.

Tidzy: A young adult who is searching for a mate and is allowed a great deal of sexual freedom around holidays.

Velka: A group of women who live in the open forest, possibly performing magic. A member of the Velka is called a Velka.

The Ilarian Calendar

A year in Ilari is divided into eight parts based on the seasons. Each eighth lasts for 45 days and is named for the holiday at its start.

Each eighth is subdivided into five anks. An ank is nine days long. Businesses and schools are open during the first six days of an ank while the last three, called the ank-break, are intended for family life and relaxation.

Every year astronomers consult the stars to decide which of the holidays will be inside their eighth and which will be treated as extra days. Most years, five or six are ruled to be extra days.

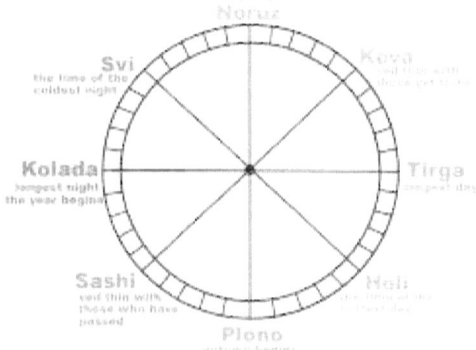

Holidays Marking the Beginning of Each Eighth

Kolada: The winter solstice, the shortest day of the year, and the start of a new year.

Svi: The coldest time of the year, halfway between the winter solstice and the spring equinox.

Noruz: The spring equinox, the start of spring.

Keva: A celebration of those yet to be, held halfway between the spring equinox and the summer solstice. More babies are conceived at Keva than at any other time of the year.

Tirga: The summer solstice, the longest day of the year, the halfway point of a year.

Heli: The hottest time of the year, halfway between the summer solstice and the autumn equinox. Ilarians are not fond of the heat and sometimes use "Heli" as a cussword.

Plono: The autumn equinox, the start of autumn.

Sashi: A celebration of those who have passed, held halfway between the fall equinox and the winter solstice.

The Twelve Nichnas

Bisu: These low grasslands at the eastern entrance to Ilari supply coveted beef and cows' milk to Ilarians.

Eds: These dry hills leading up to the mountains are sparsely populated with independent-minded goat herders.

Gruen: The fertile soil along the river makes for easy farming of fruits and vegetables and makes Gruen home to one of the two more densely populated areas outside of Pilk.

Faroo: This flood-prone nichna in the rivers bend struggles during heavy rains, but is known for fishing and the boating prowess of its residents.

K'ba: This drought-stricken nichna has survived by becoming home to artists, entertainers, and those seeking more freedom of choice. It is also a playground for the richest Ilarians and boasts a densely populated area known for its spectacular food and lodging.

Kir: Ilari's oldest farming region nestles between Pilk and Lev and grows specialty items for the connoisseurs in both of its neighboring nichnas.

Lev: This nichna is home to the realm's famed vineyards and supplies Ilarians with wine, their most important beverage. It also leads the fashion scene and sparks trends within the realm.

Pilk: As the informal capital of Ilari, Pilk is home to the Svadlu headquarters, most of the institutes of higher learning, and much of the commerce in the realm. The ruling prince of Pilk coordinates cooperation among the twelve ruling princes. The Pilk Palace outshines any other building in Ilari.

Scrud: Rain-deprived Scrud is the poorest and least populated of the nichnas and the most lacking in natural resources. Most Scrudites survive by taking menial jobs in adjoining Bisu or K'ba.

Tolo: Home to the highest mountains in Ilari, independent Tolovians mine for ore, produce lumber, and serve as a gateway to the even higher mountains to the north.

Vinx: With incredibly flat land sitting above cliffs, the high plains of Vinx provide the wheat, oats, rye, and barley that are the staples of an Ilarian's diet.

Zur: As the only nichna inside of Ilari's large central forest, Zur shares the woods with occupants of the Open Forest including the Velka, the reczavy, and scrounger Scrudites.

Map of Ilari

Meet the Ilarians in this Book

Aliz: Sulphur's grandmother
Celestine: Sulphur's younger sister, Olivine's twin
Coral: Sulphur's older sister
Davor: Sulphur's eventual sponsor and Coral's husband
Giorgi: new young ruler of Vinx
Gypsum: Sulphur's younger sister
Irakli: Mozdol who is second in command of the Svadlu
Issa: an officer who should have been a Mozdol
Iolite: Sulphur's youngest sister, a frundle
Joli: a Velka oomrusher, Sulphur's friend
Kazimir: chief commander of the Svadlu
Markita: Sulphur's mother
Nino: Sulphur's housekeeper
Nevik: A Prince of Pilk, the Royals' voice in battle preparation
Olivine: Sulphur's younger sister, Celestine's twin
Patela: Lady Patela, Prince Giorgi's mother
Rooslin: Sulphur's friend from Bisu
Ryalgar: Sulphur's oldest sister
Sulphur: Third child of Markita and Yasen, the one who gets in fights
Tamara: Sulphur's commander from Tolo and eventual friend
Yasen: Sulphur's father